w3/15

VEILED
THREAT

ALSO BY ALICE LOWEECEY

Force of Habit

Back in the Habit

ALICE LOWEECEY

A FALCONE & DRISCOLL INVESTIGATION

VEILED
THREAT

MIDNIGHT INK
WOODBURY, MINNESOTA

FIRST EDITION
First Printing, 2013

Book design and format by Donna Burch
Cover art: Candles: iStockphoto.com/John Philip Young
Cover design by Ellen Lawson

Midnight Ink, an imprint of Llewellyn Worldwide Ltd.

This is a work of fiction. Names, characters, places, and incidents are either the product of the author's imagination or are used fictitiously, and any resemblance to actual persons, living or dead, business establishments, events, or locales is entirely coincidental.

Library of Congress Cataloging-in-Publication Data
Loweecey, Alice.
  Veiled threat : a Falcone & Driscoll investigation / Alice Loweecey.
    p. cm. — (A Falcone & Driscoll investigation ; 3)
  ISBN 978-0-7387-2640-3
1. Ex-nuns—Fiction. 2. Ex-police officers—Fiction. 3. Private investigators—Fiction. I. Title.
  PS3612.O8865V45 2013
  813'.6—dc23
                              2012028505

Midnight Ink
Llewellyn Worldwide Ltd.
2143 Wooddale Drive
Woodbury, MN 55125-2989
www.midnightinkbooks.com

Printed in the United States of America

For Kent
(It was your idea, after all.)

ONE

G IULIA F ALCONE—D RISCOLL I NVESTIGATIONS' partner-in-training—hustled her friend up the narrow wooden stairs to the office door. Even after four months, the sight of her name on the frosted glass still gave her a shiver of pride.

"The hall isn't heated. If we walk, we'll have eyebrow icicles before we reach the landing."

Laurel Drury, owner-operator of Stage Door Soup Kitchen, reached the landing before Giulia. She didn't smile as she tapped snow from her red suede, spike-heeled boots onto the mat.

Giulia stomped snow from her low-heeled, practical ones and switched them for her flats. "Don't worry. Frank will help."

Laurel nodded, pulling a wadded tissue from her pocket. Giulia gave her a quick squeeze before she opened the door.

Their admin started and hid the window on her monitor. "Hi, Giulia—oh, you have a client?"

"Hey, Sidney. Is Frank in?" Giulia hung their coats on the rack behind the door.

"He's eating lunch."

"Great. C'mon. We have a captive audience." She tossed her purse on her own desk, kitty-corner to Sidney's. "Here's a fresh tissue."

Laurel honked into it. Giulia knocked once on the door separating Frank's office from theirs and opened it without waiting for an answer.

"Frank, we need to talk."

The head of Driscoll Investigations choked on a bite of pastrami sub.

"Giulia, those four words strike fear into the heart of the strongest man." He swallowed several gulps of Coke.

"Don't be a wuss. And it's nothing like that. This is my friend Laurel—you know, she runs the soup kitchen in the theater district. Laurel Drury, Frank Driscoll. Frank, Laurel."

Frank wiped his hands on a napkin. "Pleased to meet you."

Giulia dragged in her client chair while they shook hands. "Sidney, could you take messages while we're in here? Thanks." She closed the door and sat Laurel in Frank's client chair. "That one has better padding. Now tell him."

The tall, dark woman with circles under her eyes, wearing a wrinkled gray sweatshirt, shredded the tissue in her hands without speaking. Giulia put a hand over her restless ones, and her friend's mouth trembled.

Laurel inhaled a long, shaky breath. "They kidnapped our baby."

Frank's body language did a one-eighty. He sat straighter, pulled a covered notebook from the center drawer, and uncapped a pen. "Start at the beginning, please, Ms. Drury."

Laurel held onto Giulia's hands while she spoke. "Anya and I—she's my partner—we've been trying to adopt for three years.

We jumped through every legal hoop they threw at us. We've been background-checked, counseled, submitted our financial records, and got references from our families, friends, pastor, teachers, and co-workers. Giulia's appearance as a character witness tipped everything in our favor at the final hearing, because she taught the judge's grandkids back when she was a nun."

Giulia shrugged. "Anything I could do to help, you know that. You two were made to be parents."

Laurel swallowed. "We've only had Katie for a month. She's perfect. Big brown eyes, lots of curly hair. Her skin even looks like a cross between mine and Anya's because it's exactly the color of cappuccino." She freed her hands to wipe her eyes. "She was born with polydactyly." She looked at Frank's and Giulia's faces. "An extra pinky on each hand. The brand-new doctor at the hospital when she was born botched the removal and left stubs on both hands, but our pediatrician says he can snip them off and she won't have any scars by the time she's a year old." Her voice broke and she sobbed into the soaked tissue.

Frank cleared his throat. "Ms. Drury—please—"

Giulia waved a shushing hand at him. She moved to the arm of Laurel's chair and rested her friend's head on her shoulder. "Come on now. Come on. We can't help if we don't know the whole story. Come on, sweetie."

Napkins, she mouthed at Frank. He slid the remaining clean one across the desk. Giulia pushed it under Laurel's nose. She blew into it and wiped her eyes.

"I'm sorry. I'll try to stop. It's just that there's so little time."

Giulia returned to her chair. "That's why you're going to tell us what we need to know. Ready?"

Laurel dropped the crumpled napkin onto her lap and ran her hands over her short, ruffled hair. "Yes. You're right." She straightened and balled her fists on her thighs. "Anya's team played in the State Cup yesterday."

Frank, writing, said, "State Cup? You mean high-school soccer?"

"Yes. Anya's director of sports at Quaker Prep. Four of her seniors are going pro—they're an amazing team—and it's all because of Anya's coaching. My niece Erin is a Red Cross–trained babysitter. She's excellent with infants; she's sixteen-and-a-half."

Giulia said, "You're skipping around. Why did you attend the game without Katie?"

Laurel's voice hitched. "We didn't—didn't want her out in the cold for two hours. She's so little. I had to go, to support Anya and her girls. The pitch is only ten minutes from our condo. I had my cell phone. It was perfectly safe." Her voice wavered and threatened to break.

Giulia gripped her shoulder and shook her the tiniest bit.

Laurel took a deep breath. "They won, of course, and I congratulated them and came right home. Erin didn't answer my knock, but I figured she was in the bathroom or on the phone or changing Katie. My key turned too smoothly in the lock, but I didn't notice it till the police were asking me questions."

Frank finished writing a sentence. "What was the situation in your condo?"

"It was neat as a pin, just the way we left it. I went right into the nursery. Erin was tied up in the rocking chair and Katie was gone." She beat her fist on the arm of the chair.

"Was she injured?"

"Of course she was." Her fist increased its muffled staccato tempo. "They knocked her unconscious. Do you think she would've let them take Katie without a fight? They put a washcloth in her mouth and tied a long strip of sheeting around her head and her arms and legs. Bastards. They scared the life out of her."

Frank fidgeted. Giulia frowned at him.

"But she's okay now, right?"

Frank stepped on Giulia's last word. "Ms. Drury, you should be talking to the police, not me."

Laurel leaned forward. "We have talked to the protectors of society, if you can call them that. I don't understand how such do-nothing attitudes didn't get caught in psychological screening."

Frank dotted an *i*. "Ms. Drury, even an apathetic officer would still do his duty."

"I don't doubt that, Mr. Driscoll. What concerns me is the alacrity with which he might or might not perform those duties. We went to the station this morning to play the message the kidnappers left us, and he was less than sympathetic." She dug her fingernails into the arm of the chair. "His captain is nothing like him, fortunately."

"James Reilly?"

"Yes, Reilly is his name. Do you know him?"

"Quite well. I can assure you, Ms. Drury—"

"Play the message, Laurel." Giulia avoided Frank's eyes. It was unprofessional to cut him off like that, but saving Laurel's baby was worth the lecture he was no doubt already composing.

Laurel took out her cell phone and pressed several buttons. After the soothing instructions from the recorded voice, she pressed "4" and set the phone on the desk.

"You might have railroaded your agenda through the state legislature, but you don't deserve to have everything so easy." A man's voice, muffled and distorted by noise and other voices in the background. "You don't deserve to have anything easier than normal people, especially children. Get four hundred thousand dollars by seven thirty in the morning three days from today. We'll call with further instructions. Remember, don't be stupid. We'd better not hear an AMBER Alert or see anything that looks like the FBI. Get a Bible while you're at it and read. One Corinthians Seven. You know, about wives having sexual relations with their *husbands*."

Voicemail offered them a series of choices. Laurel stared at the phone as though she wanted to drag the kidnapper through it.

Frank spoke over the recorded instructions. "Play it again, please."

When the message finished, Frank nodded and Laurel ended the call.

"Ms. Drury, do you plan to pay the ransom?"

"We're trying. We've cashed in our IRAs; we've written checks on our credit cards and maxed them out; we've emptied our savings. It's still not enough. Anya's at the bank signing paperwork for a home equity loan on our condo. We'll need a miracle to get approval by the twenty-second. Banks can't even process some deposits in three days." She ran her hands through her hair, making it stick out every which way. "We're not rich. You don't get wealthy running a soup kitchen and coaching high-school sports. He asked for that much money because he knew we couldn't come up with it."

"How do you know that?" Frank's voice remained neutral.

"The kidnappers had a copy of our key. The police said there weren't any signs of a break-in. They knew we'd be out yesterday afternoon. Erin said they came in half an hour after we left. Who knows how long they've been watching us? Who knows how much of our lives they've invaded? They stole the most important part of our lives—our baby."

"Ms. Drury—"

"Don't take that condescending tone with me!" Laurel transformed from distraught, sobbing victim into a Valkyrie in rumpled clothes. "I had a bellyful of it yesterday from the detectives at our condo. They pretended they didn't know about the other kidnappings. They took notes and fingerprints and asked question after question and, no matter what they said, I saw the sneer in their eyes. The younger one took his cues from the older one, and the more they talked to us the less they cared. The younger one gave us that look—like we're some kind of porno sluts. We see it in guys all the time." She slammed her hands on the desk, making the phone jump.

Giulia stood. "There's always a few scumbags in any organization. You know Frank's not looking at you that way."

"I know. You told me. I trust you. It's the police—they're so slow." A wail crept into her voice, but she got hold of herself. "We played the message for them this morning. They wrote it down and said they'd get back to us." She stood and paced the small office. "Get back to us? This isn't a job interview. It's Katie's life! They'll kill her if we don't give them the money. They'll kill her!"

Giulia stepped in Laurel's path and put her hands on the taller woman's shoulders. "You don't know that for sure."

"They killed one of the other babies—they may have killed both of them. The mainstream media paid more attention to Iraq and Afghanistan and North Korea, but everyone in our network knew about the other two kidnappings."

Frank said, "These other two kidnappings. Did they occur here in Cottonwood?"

Laurel shook her head. "No. One happened in Erie and the other in Akron."

"Then I don't quite see how they are connected to your situation."

Giulia thought at Frank, *Stop being so cold. What are you trying to do?*

Laurel got an "I'm counting to ten" expression. "I don't expect you to be familiar with gay adoption, but there is an extensive network dedicated to helping each other through the legal and financial mazes. We share all the news, good and bad. The Akron kidnapping took place a year ago February. The Erie one took place last April. Both sets of parents are gay women. Both sets of parents received the exact same message we did. The first baby was never seen again. They left the body of the second baby at the same place as the ransom drop." She broke away from Giulia and braced herself on Frank's desk. "Do you see the connection now? We only have two more days to raise the money and, no matter what, we won't get Katie back unless we find out who's doing this. Giulia said you could help us." Her voice shook. "Please."

Frank stood. "Ms. Drury, I still think your best solution is to let the police do what they're trained to do. But," he overrode the beginning of her protest, "based on the information you've given me, I'll consider whether Driscoll Investigations can assist you."

He glanced at Giulia, then at the door.

Laurel's rigid posture sagged. "Thank you." Her voice sagged with it.

Giulia opened the door. "I'll walk you downstairs."

The phone rang as they entered the main office. Sidney's always perky voice made "Good afternoon, Driscoll Investigations," sound like an invitation to chat with one's best friend.

Laurel didn't speak till they were halfway down the stairs. "He's going to hand this off to the police."

Giulia wished for an injection of Sidney's eternal optimism. "He used to be a cop, I told you that. He still has something of a cop's mentality, but at the very least I'm sure I can convince him to work with them. No, to let both of us work with them."

"There are rules. Confidential information and all that. The police can't share everything they know." Laurel took her gloves out of her pockets.

"Well, you'll give us all your confidential information, so we'll have that as ammunition." Giulia squeezed her. "I'll work on him. Don't worry about that part. I'll call you as soon as we know something, but it might not be till tomorrow."

"Tomorrow?" Laurel's voice veered from defeat toward desperation.

Giulia put on her teacher face. "Some things take time, especially wheedling the police. I'll light a candle for you and Katie tonight. You try to get a little sleep. Give Anya a kiss for me."

Laurel nodded. "Call me anytime. My cell's always on now." She opened the door to the snow-covered street. "Thank you."

Giulia ran back upstairs, rubbing her arms to counteract the goosebumps. When she opened the door, Sidney's big brown eyes were stretched to their limit.

"Mr. D.'s banging drawers and talking to himself."

TWO

GIULIA STARTED TO FROWN but couldn't hold it in the face of Sidney's idea of speaking softly.

She glanced at Frank's door. "Sidney, you've got to work on your stage whisper."

"But I'm not an actor."

"I know, but your whisper could carry to the second balcony."

Frank's voice interrupted them. "Giulia, could you come in here, please?"

She pulled down her sweater and straightened her shoulders. Then she whispered to Sidney, "Better take messages again."

Without waiting for Frank to say it, she closed the door, shutting them in together.

Frank struggled with the side drawer that stuck unless he caught it on the rollers just right. "Piece of crap." Yank. *Bang.* "I'll turn you into firewood." Yank. "Giulia, what the hell do you think you're doing?"

"I'm trying to help a friend."

11

"No, you're trying to trespass on police territory."

"Frank, let me explain."

"Finally." He slid the drawer into place. "You'd better, because that meeting sounded to me like you've committed us to finding batshit religious kidnappers on an impossible timeline, despite the fact that Jimmy's already involved, as he should be and as we should not be."

Giulia plucked a shredded tissue and a sodden napkin from the client chair and tossed them in the trash before she sat.

Calm. Rational. You have to convince him.

"Some things are more important than the rules."

Frank, pacing like Laurel had, stopped at the window. "Did those words really just come out of your mouth?"

Giulia smiled even though his reaction triggered her guilt reflex. "*Cosmo* says a woman should always keep a man a little off-balance."

He laughed. "If I were to tell my basketball team that an ex-nun quotes *Cosmo* magazine to me, they'd make me take a breathalyzer test." He wiped the condensation from the glass. "Sorry I jumped down your throat."

"A good Confession should take care of it."

When his head whipped around, she smiled for real. "Catholic humor, Frank. That's all."

The phone rang twice, then Sidney's muffled voice came through the walls.

Giulia said, "Laurel kept me from losing my mind after I jumped the wall. I went through a bad stretch—I'd just been fired from that Mexican place on King Street. I had no money, and I was working myself up to pawn the wedding ring I received at final vows."

Frank retrieved his pen from under the desk and pulled up his chair. He doodled basketballs on his notepad and said in a casual voice, "You worked at her soup kitchen?"

"Not right away. At first I came there a few times to get a meal. Then when I landed the barista job in Common Grounds downstairs, I went back to help." She stared at his reddening ears. "Why are you upset?"

"Nothing. Just tell the story."

She schooled her face into a neutral expression. There was no time to get into a futile discussion—again—about Frank's chivalrous streak and how she was a self-sufficient adult.

"You didn't know me then. I was a cross between an experienced twenty-something teacher and a clueless eighteen-year-old, since the last time I was a regular person I was a senior in high school. Model Sister Mary Regina Coelis versus gauche Giulia Falcone." A crooked smile twisted her lips. "It's a good thing I didn't have any friends who liked to post videos to YouTube. I could've starred in a whole series of 'How Not To' clips. Anyway. I asked Laurel what nights she needed help, and I became the Tuesday cook."

"In a soup kitchen."

"Now who's distracted? Yes, in a soup kitchen. Frank, I seriously wonder what kind of mental image you have of me. When did I ever give you the impression of a sheltered flower? Remind me to tell you more of my inner-city high school stories."

His lips compressed, but he stayed silent.

"Thank you. To continue. Laurel and Anya were the first real friends I made out here in the world. We would have dinner at each other's apartment every month. I helped them with the adoption paperwork when I could, and they taught me how to dress in regular clothes again."

Frank stopped clicking the pen. "That's heartwarming, but it's not a sufficient explanation."

She almost gave voice to her thought: *When did you replace your heart with an ice cube tray?* Instead, she said, "Laurel and Anya told me a lot more than what Laurel said to you in here. Their kidnapping is a clone of the other two. The messages, the ransom demands, everything. They're clinging to hope right now, but they really don't believe anyone can help them. That's why they called me—it's a nun thing." She shrugged. "I know. It's been a year and a half, but sometimes I might as well still be in habit. People talk to me."

"Giulia, look—"

"We can help them. We have to help them. Please. This is right up my alley, just like Sandra the crazed stalker was."

"You mean her psycho biblical ransom messages?"

"Exactly. This guy has an average voice, like someone you'd meet at the grocery store or the gym. But anyone who quotes that part of Paul and complains about some states' new marriage legislation sounds exactly like one of those TV preachers who rail against homosexuality while they cheat on their wives. I have the expertise for this. You don't—no offense. I bet Captain Teddy Bear doesn't either, and it's obvious the officers who responded to Laurel's call yesterday don't."

"Giulia, you're not the only detective with a knowledge of obscure parts of the Bible." He stood.

Giulia remained seated. He was not going to truncate this discussion before she got her way. "No, but you have to admit I'm one of the few detectives in Cottonwood who knows Christianity inside and out. I can get into this guy's head. I can give the police an edge that the kidnapper isn't going to expect." She leaned forward on the desk. "As a favor to me—not Laurel or Anya or their innocent four-week-old daughter—to me, would you just call Captain Jimmy and ask if we can talk to him?"

Her conscience jeered at her. *Since when did you become so manipulative? You're playing on his emotions to get what you want. You're a weasel.*

Giulia admitted it all, but Laurel's baby was more important than moral platforms. She kept her eyes on Frank.

He drummed his fingers on the desk, ignoring the *bing* of incoming email, staring at the series of basketballs he'd drawn.

"Fine."

"Thank you."

"Don't thank me. The most likely outcome is Jimmy telling me to stay out of his business."

His posture screamed reluctance. Giulia wasn't dense—she'd pushed him to this. It should've been against her better judgment, but every time she'd thought that from lunch till now, the knowledge that Laurel's tiny new baby was in mortal danger overrode any scruples. Because she knew it was mortal danger the same way she knew—despite how hokey it sounded—that she was called to help them.

Better not say that to Frank. We haven't argued about faith yet and I don't want to start over this.

Now Giulia stood. "I'll get this out of your way." She picked up her own client chair and closed the door behind her. Only when she'd returned the chair to its proper place did she allow herself a deep breath.

THREE

"GIULIA," SIDNEY ALMOST WHISPERED. "C'mere."

Giulia rolled her mouse first and cringed at the stack of emails waiting for her.

"Since this is the day I break all my usual habits ..." She walked over to Sidney. "Conversation before email sorting."

Sidney giggled. "You're so funny. Mr. D. won't care. He knows you'll always get your work done."

"Of course." Giulia looked down, puzzled. "And so will you."

"Well, duh." She beckoned Giulia down by her. "You know Olivier and I decided to give bags of my family's alpaca fertilizer as wedding favors, right?"

Giulia raised her eyebrows. "No. Last time you talked about favors it was between pine tree seedlings and heirloom seed packets."

"Oh, I forgot to tell you. The tree place made a huge stink about not giving them enough time to package a measly eighty-five seedlings. Olivier actually lost his temper." She lowered her voice further.

"It was kinda epic. He didn't yell or anything, but I swear the A/C kicked on in the greenhouse. So, no trees at the wedding."

"And the seed packets?" Giulia didn't trust herself yet to comment on the image of ribbon-tied bags of alpaca poop at every place setting.

"They lied." She typed an address in her browser window. "Look at this: They claim they're all-natural. See? This page even has photographs of the owner's grandmother harvesting seeds from her tomatoes and peppers. But"—she clicked on a tiny link in the lower right-hand corner—"here's the truth. They sold out to one of the megacorporations that genetically alter the seeds. Our wedding is not going to be remembered for depleting the monarch butterfly population. And what about the honeybee die-off?"

Giulia schooled her face into a neutral expression. "I'm sure none of your guests would ever think you'd condone either of those events."

"But we'd know! It's a good thing we hadn't printed out the paper sleeves we designed to fit over the packets. Anyway, here's what I wanted to show you." She brought up a Word document divided into quarters. A smiling pair of alpacas, one in a bridal veil, the other in a top hat, filled the two left-hand quarters. "My brother drew them. He wanted to dress them up more, but I told him it'd just look silly."

"They're cute." *And silly. Bad Giulia. Don't let Sidney see that thought in your face.*

Sidney grinned. "They are, aren't they? He's getting his degree in cartooning next year. He wanted to put them on the programs for the church, but Mr. D.'s brother said it wasn't appropriate." She scrolled to the next page. "Catholics are sure into rules. I'd go bonkers trying to learn all the RCIA stuff without you and Mr. D.'s brother. We're going to send the cards to one of those bookmark-postcard printers tonight. You know, so they're shiny and sturdy and will last."

Giulia looked from the screen to Sidney. "It's Monday of Christmas week. Your wedding is this Saturday. Will they deliver on Christmas Eve?"

"Oh, no, we're not having them delivered the morning of the wedding! I'd go bonkers. They guarantee everything will arrive on Thursday. And they use only recycled paper. They're perfect." She looked up, giving Giulia the full force of her sweet, eager eyes. "Can you read the back of the card for me? I've reread it so many times I couldn't see a typo if my life depended on it."

"Of course." She crouched next to Sidney. "'The Earth Loves Us Just Like We Love Each Other—Pay It Forward.'"

Sidney grinned. "Catchy, huh? We want to let everybody know the reason behind the foods we chose and all the recycling—I'm wearing my grandmother's wedding gown, and Olivier's renting his tux, of course. We also wanted to sneak in a little how-to information. So maybe they'll want to make little changes to start with. You know, natural foods, like the way you grow tomatoes and herbs in your apartment. But we didn't want to hit them over the head with it, so we started with humor."

"Humor is always a good way to start." Giulia bit the inside of her cheek this time and read to herself. The card listed the local food sources; the local low-sulfite, fresh-grape winery; and a lecture (there really was no other word for it) about the carbon footprint of trucked- and flown-in food.

"There aren't any errors in this."

19

Sidney exhaled. "Oh, good. Do you think we should add that the flowers are local?"

"Flowers from here? In December?"

"Holly and mistletoe and pine branches." Her hands formed an invisible ball about nine inches in diameter. "We grow all those on our farm. Mom and I designed bouquets for me and my sisters and the boutonnieres will be mistletoe sprigs, because holly would keep poking them every time they moved. But do you think we should add something about composting, since we're all composting the flowers and the boutonnieres after the reception?"

"In the winter?"

Sidney did a perfect "take." "We add to our compost pile all year-round."

Giulia held up her hands. "I've always lived in apartments."

"That's no fun." Sidney pointed to the screen. "Do you think adding flower-origin and composting instructions is too much? We have some of this on our wedding website, but I've been too busy to get all of it on there."

Giulia stopped herself from saying, *Your wedding guests want to party, not go to school.* "The card is easy to read as is. You'll be putting up wedding pictures on your website, won't you? Why don't you add in the composting ideas next to a photo of all of you with the flowers?"

"That's perfect!" She opened a new email window and typed it all in. "I knew you'd have the right answer. So," she hit *Send*, "are you and Mr. D. going to make it a real date?"

Giulia twitched.

Sidney looked at her from the corners of her eyes, a sly and nervous smile on her lips.

"Since when did you become a professional matchmaker?" Giulia said at last.

"Uh-uh. Don't change the subject." She lowered her voice even further. "Olivier and I met at his sister's wedding. He is such a great dancer."

Giulia smiled. "He's perfect for you, isn't he?"

"Well, he would be if he'd quit eating carnivore food. But I'll work on him. I figure me becoming Catholic gives me leverage. You know, I compromised on this, so he can compromise on that."

"Sidney, the faith is not meant to be used as matrimonial blackmail."

She giggled. "You sound just like a teacher when you talk like that. Don't worry; I won't really. I just need to get my head around all the rules, 'cause I think Catholicism is kinda cool. Besides, I'll be making all our baby food from homegrown, raw foods, so Olivier's bound to agree that it'll be easier for me to cook one dinner for all of us."

Giulia raised her eyebrows in a parody of surprise. "Are you trying to tell me something?"

"Oh, no, no." Sidney looked properly shocked. "We always use two forms of protection. No babies till Olivier's practice gets going."

"Smart." *Sidney and Olivier will make adorable parents … just like Laurel and Anya are.*

"What's the matter?"

Giulia shook it off. "I'm worried for my friends and their baby. She's been kidnapped."

"A baby? Those scumbags. You're going to include me, right? Anyone who kidnaps babies should be turned into compost."

"It's up to Frank. That is, it will be if he can convince Captain Jimmy to let us get involved."

Sidney waved that away. "Piece of cake. Captain Jimmy'd do anything to make you happy."

Giulia laughed. "Frank doesn't like that. Every time we share information with him he tries to hire me away."

"I've heard him. It's funny. You're not going to leave, are you?"

"No, don't worry. I know when I've got it good."

"Damn right you do."

Giulia and Sidney jumped. Frank stood in his doorway frowning like Moses watching the Israelites dance around the golden calf.

"Jimmy says ten o'clock tomorrow, and the only reason he's doing it is because he wants to show you firsthand how much you'd rather work for him than me."

Giulia got to her feet, hoping her irrational guilt over helping Sidney with wedding details during work hours didn't show in her face. "Thank you."

"I'm assuming that you'd never consider for even half a minute going to work with that pack of baboons." The frown faded. "You wouldn't, right?"

"I wouldn't."

Sidney's latest family-commercial jingle came from her desk drawer. When she opened the drawer, the bouncy trumpet melody tripled in volume. She read the text and clapped.

"Mom says using two zippered plastic bags blocks every bit of odor."

Frank looked from Sidney to Giulia. "From?"

"Sidney and Olivier and giving away baggies of their alpaca fertilizer as wedding favors." Giulia averted her eyes from Frank's face before she lost control.

Silence from Frank. Then, "Are you sure that the guests will be okay with a baggie of fertilizer next to their food?"

Sidney laughed. "Mr. D., you are so funny. We're not going to put the favors at the place settings. They're going to be on a table in the front hallway with everyone's names on them. We don't want the health department raiding our reception."

"Ah. Good." He eyed the calendar on the wall above the printer. "Are you taking just Friday off or do you need Thursday, too?"

"Nope. Friday's fine. Everything's pretty much done except for the place cards and bagging up the favors." She scowled at the clouds out the window. "Now if it'd just stop snowing. You hear that, winter? We've got people driving in from Ohio and Virginia."

The phone rang. Sidney took a deep breath, her nostrils flared; she picked up the receiver and said in her usual perky voice, "Driscoll Investigations. May I help you?"

FOUR

AT QUARTER TO FIVE that afternoon, Giulia stepped off the bus into a mound of slush. She didn't care. The cold, clean air—emphasis on clean—more than made up for wet boots. After the doors squealed together behind her, she shouted into the sky, "Doesn't anyone use deodorant in the winter?"

She stomped her boots on the sidewalk. The streetlights turned the grimy slush pus-yellow. Diesel fumes stank up the air as the bus pulled away.

Everyone she passed on the sidewalk was bundled up the same as she was, so she got a little silly behind her scarf.

"O city bus, O city bus,
How filthy are your windows.
O city bus, O city bus,
How cracked and ripped your seats.
You stink in spring, winter, and fall,
Your pick-up times don't work at all.

O city bus, O city bus,
Soon I'll be done for good with you!"

She reached her apartment house's front stoop as she sang the last line. With the skill of the cold and tired, she keyed herself in, stuck a hand in her—empty—mail slot, and quick-stepped the length of the hall to her door.

Giulia's small apartment had one big advantage: it heated up quickly. Her teeth stopped chattering after only two minutes crouched over the forced-air vent.

New super-bright mini lights (fifty cents at last year's end-of-season sale) glowed all over the two-foot artificial Christmas tree on the end table, lighting the corner of the living room. The miniature glass ornaments threw pinpricks of colors onto the walls. Starry silver garland, a matching star on top (two dollars), and artificial snow all around it (also fifty cents) made the apartment as festive as she could afford last year, her first year back in the world.

"I can splurge on a bigger tree at the after-Christmas sales this year. The World Market might still have those hand-beaded ornaments I drooled over. I'm not living on ramen and peanut butter anymore. I have to remember that."

The microwave beeped. She changed into sweats and her fuzzy Godzilla slippers, flipping on the TV as she passed it. The newspaper ad of the used Saturn Ion stuck dead-center on the fridge rippled as she passed it. "Soon you'll be mine, and my days of riding the bus will be relegated to memory."

Leftover chicken parmigiana steamed up the microwave, releasing mouthwatering aromas as soon as she opened the small door. Armed with a hot pad so she wouldn't scorch her hand and drop dinner and her glass of red wine on the carpet, she sat at the coffee table and hit the mute button.

"No news. Not tonight. What about movies?" She'd splurged on basic cable last month but still only used the TV late at night or on Saturday mornings.

Click. "No reality shows, either." Click. ESPN. Click. Sitcom reruns. Click. More reruns. Click. C-SPAN. Several more clicks. Jimmy Stewart and Donna Reed singing "Buffalo Gals."

She hit the off switch and pushed away the remote. "I don't care how much I love *It's a Wonderful Life*. I am not going to end the day crying into the couch cushions."

Instead, she powered up her antiquated boom box and put in Denver and the Mile High Orchestra's *Timeless Christmas*. Sunday's crossword puzzle sat unfinished on the other end of the table. She cut her first piece of chicken and studied the clues while chewing. The energetic, happy music made her smile, finally.

"That's more like it." She tapped her foot to "Sleigh Ride" as she filled in another clue.

The meager scattering of gifts under the little tree tried to depress her. *What good is Christmas without family?* it whispered in her ear. *Dozens of your relatives are stuffing presents under their trees and planning the huge Christmas Day dinner and gift frenzy. Too bad those relatives don't talk to you now that you ditched the convent. Enjoy your second Christmas alone.*

She finished the last forkful of chicken. Very good, even if it was bad manners to compliment one's own cooking. Despite her shrewish conscience, she knew she wasn't alone. She'd spend Christmas Day at the soup kitchen again, adding homemade jam to the adults' trays and dollar-store toys to the kids' trays as she dished up their food. In other words, Giulia Falcone seriously needed to get over herself.

The presents under the tree—no matter how few—proved she had friends, if not family. More homemade jams for Laurel and Anya; chandelier earrings for Mingmei, the barista downstairs from Driscoll Investigations; and her own sauce for Sidney, since the jams used sugar. The sauce was 100 percent natural. She'd already mailed Sister Bart's gift: the same CD she was listening to right now. Sister Bart needed some fun in her life after surviving Father Ray and Sister Fabian.

Giulia dithered for a moment about giving Frank a gift, like she dithered at least once a day. Employees don't give gifts to the boss. But they were more than employee and boss. But she shouldn't initiate gift-giving—it wasn't proper.

"Lord above, Falcone, what a flake you are. Grow a spine and give him a Christmas present. You know you want to."

The perfect idea came to her while she washed the dishes: coupons for home-cooked meals. Frank ate at burger joints or chain restaurants and refused to go back to his parents' even for Sunday dinner. All part of his youngest-child, "I can make it on my own" quest.

She'd have to create the coupons on her work computer since she didn't own a PC. Frank would laugh at that—another instance of out-of-touch Giulia. *Cosmo* might not approve of her gift. Too domestic. Unless she found a Little French Maid outfit to cook in.

She snorted into the dishwater. *Not likely.*

FIVE

AT NINE FIFTY TUESDAY morning the Cottonwood Police Station looked more like an empty stage setting than an overworked, understaffed division of town law enforcement. Frank and Giulia hung their coats in the entrance-hall closet as the phone rang at the receptionist's desk. A Bond Girl wannabe picked it up on the second ring. Her strobe-light smile blinded Giulia as her manicured hand waved both of them back into the central office.

Six desks practically on top of each other. Computer screens all in password-protected lock mode—most obscured by coffee mugs and stacks of file folders. Scuffed linoleum flooring, well-used rolling chairs, and not a human in sight.

They wove between the desks toward the glass-paneled door marked *James Reilly, Captain*, next to the kitchen. Frank turned the handle. As though he'd tripped a switch, three telephones began to ring and officers piled into the room. Two headed for the kitchen.

"Hey, Driscoll." The taller one paused on the threshold. "Basketball's canceled this week."

"I know," Frank said. "Next week's still on, right?"

"Yeah. Joe, pour me one, willya?"

"Make your own," the detective already in the kitchen said. "I've got the last of this pot."

"Asshole," the tall detective said without heat. "I hope the next old lady runs over your Harley."

"Up yours," Joe said with a smile. He made a show of sipping his coffee. "Perfect."

Frank ushered Giulia into the office and closed the door. "Charming, aren't they?"

The door opened again. "They just need a woman they can respect to keep them in line. Good morning, Giulia. Sorry I wasn't here to greet you. Emergency meeting."

"Good morning, former boss," Frank said.

"Since when do I need to be polite to you, former subordinate?" Jimmy winked at Giulia. "Good morning, Frank. Be grateful you're no longer a member of this department. We're getting flak from all sides over all these idiots driving their cars into storefronts."

"If you'd arrest more of these delinquents, it might deter the others."

"Do grandparents qualify as delinquents? I never thought the geriatric crowd would give me more grief than teenagers who text while driving. If the state would make yearly eye tests mandatory for drivers over sixty-five, my job would be a helluva lot easier." He pulled a chair away from his desk. "Coffee, Giulia?"

"Thank you, no." She sat. "I saw the latest accident on the news. At least this time no one was hurt."

"Frank, you want coffee?"

"I'll get it for myself. Behave."

Giulia smiled up at Jimmy. "This is where you tell me how much better I'll have it if I come work for you."

"Well…"

"And this is where I tell you, as politely as possible, that I'm happy where I am."

Frank's wide shoulders filled the doorway. "And this is where I'm glad that I don't mind black coffee when the need arises. Didn't waste any time, did you?"

Jimmy grinned. "Doggedness. It got me where I am today."

Giulia seized the opening. "I'm just as persistent. Thank you for letting us come talk to you this morning."

His grin flattened. "I'm not happy about this, but you both know that. Frank, close the door."

When the escalating chaos in the outer room dimmed, he sat at his desk. "I don't have to tell you that in an ordinary situation I'd rip Frank a new one rather than let you in on a police case." He cleared his throat. "My apologies. But you have to realize, Giulia, that this is our job. The police have a handle on this situation, especially since the parents refuse to contact the FBI."

Giulia sat as though she was interviewing for the job he was always after her to take. "With respect, Captain, I think there are important ancillary facts that require more emphasis placed on them. The other kidnappings, first of all."

"The other—wait a minute." He clicked his mouse several times. "There's a footnote in the report, but …" He picked up his phone and punched two numbers. "Poole, my office."

A beardless Abraham Lincoln entered a minute later.

Jimmy looked up from his screen. "Poole, the Drury-Sandov kidnapping. What's this about copycats?"

Poole shrugged. "The women yammered about dead babies up in Ohio and Erie somewhere. Months ago. Didn't mean a thing." His deep voice sounded like a classic Lincoln portrayal, but its scorn belonged to a TV political talking head. "Davis and I are thorough. It's in the report."

Giulia dug her fingernails into her palms. "Excuse me. This kidnapping isn't a copycat. It's the third in a series."

His expression dismissed her. "Anything else, Cap?"

Jimmy's gaze took in all three of them. "Yes. Unless you want six weeks of retraining, work on your definition of 'thorough.' I know Davis thinks you're God's gift to rookies, but if I catch him copying your attitude, I'll reassign both of you."

Poole glared at Giulia and Frank. "You're telling me that you think those—women know more about investigations than me?"

Frank gave him a cold smile. "Nothing changes around here, does it?"

Poole sneered. "That's why you're here, Driscoll? Cap still thinks you got some magic insight spell that'll solve the case and get your picture in the paper?"

"Enough." Jimmy slammed his hand on a stack of manila folders. "Poole, I'll talk to you and Davis later. Close the door behind you."

Jimmy dropped his head into his hands. "Asshole. So much for the speech I had all planned out for this meeting." He sat up and turned his monitor toward the end of the desk. "I will now do something officially stupid but morally correct. Come around here, you two."

Giulia clamped down hard on her own speech. *Unproductive. Katie's important. Not that idiot. Take it out at the gym tonight.*

The small office appeared to shrink further as the three of them crowded into the corner. The monitor was not quite large enough to show two documents side-by-side at a legible size.

"Frank, I was all set to tell you to quit straddling the fence. You're not a cop anymore and all that. But I didn't realize Poole was still butthurt over always being in your shadow."

"What about his partner?" Frank said.

Jimmy shook his head. "I won't get anything useful from Davis. He thinks Poole's the Ultimate Cop, no matter what. Rookies." He eyed Frank. "I remember getting saddled with a wide-eyed rookie once. Giulia, did he ever tell you about the drunk nursing mother who squirted us with breast milk when we tried to give her a sobriety test?"

Giulia choked with laughter. It felt good.

Frank aimed a punch at Jimmy's shoulder. "Are you through? I've got six separate cases waiting for me. Rent's due next week."

"Right. I'm going to spend my morning on this report. Poole and Davis can take over the Senior Citizen Weeklong Car Crash Flash Mob." He opened a blank document. "Giulia, let's have what you know, and we'll compare it with what I've got here."

Giulia opened her purse. "I don't have all the details, but I know Laurel has pages of them. Can she email everything to you?"

"Sure." He spelled out his email address.

Giulia opened her cell. "This'll only take a second ... Laurel? It's me. Write down this email address." She waited while Laurel repeated it. "Yes. Email everything you have on the other two kidnappings to Captain Reilly ... I know it's already ten thirty ... I know it's Tuesday ... I'll call you in a little while, sweetie."

Jimmy waited till Giulia returned the phone to her purse. "Giulia, briefly. I see that the ransom deadline is Thursday. Does your friend think there is an underlying deadline as well?"

"Yes, based on the other two kidnappings. Neither infant was returned alive." She clenched her hands together. "I wish you could know how hard it is for me to pretend I'm calm and detached about this."

Jimmy gave her a brief smile. "Your hand-wringing and non-verbal cues are telling me everything I need to know."

She didn't return it. "Are they telling you how much I want to vent my anger on your homophobic detective out there?"

He closed his eyes. "I swear that idiot expects me to screen crime victims so every case he's assigned to gets him adulation or a raise. I don't make enough money for this."

"If his omissions cause harm to the baby, I will show him the other side of polite, inoffensive Giulia Falcone."

Frank coughed. Giulia started. She'd almost forgotten he was in the room.

Jimmy clicked his mouse. "I'd pay money to see that. The documents just hit my in-box. Frank, I'll call you. Giulia, if you accidentally spill hot coffee in Poole's lap, I promise not to see it."

"You shouldn't tempt people to be naughty so close to Christmas. Santa may be listening."

This time they smiled at each other.

"You sound like my kids," Jimmy said. "You'll hear from me this afternoon at the latest."

In the outer room, Poole was saying to the other policemen in a voice pitched to carry, "How many ex-cops does it take to screw in a light bulb?"

SIX

Giulia didn't speak until Frank's car was stuck in a long line at a red light.

"That miserable, self-centered—"

"Asshole." He reached over and squeezed her gloved hand. "Any other words you want me to use so you don't have to?"

She bit her lips. "A few."

"Consider them said. The ironic thing is, you should thank Poole."

"What?"

Frank laughed. "Your voice cracks when you're angry." Their turn at the light came, and he continued onto the freshly salted street. "Think about it: Jimmy was going to freeze us out of his office. I knew it even though he agreed to talk to us. This is police territory, period."

"But—"

"But nothing. Jimmy's people have the case. If he asks us to help, then we have an opening. You've seen enough movies where the police hate the PI. Constantly threaten to take away his license, won't share information. That's not my style. I've still got a great working relationship with Jimmy. I'm not jeopardizing that."

Giulia's arguments withered on her lips.

Frank glanced at her and nodded. "But then Poole-the-Asshole screwed up the report. Jimmy knows he's lost a day on a time-sensitive case. The responsibility is his; he's in charge. He knows we won't make a public stink about it, but your friends might."

"What would you do it if were your baby?"

"Exactly. So we're his early Christmas present. We want to help, we're skilled, we're his friends. Bam. We're now officially assisting the police investigation and my excellent working relationship remains intact." He flipped off a minivan as it ran the light. "I hope you skid into a telephone pole, asshole."

"Frank."

"Yeah, yeah, I should be more charitable. Tell the idiots who forget how to drive in this weather to stay off the road, and maybe that'll happen."

"At least you have a choice. Dealing with drivers who text and eat while steering with their knees is better than another winter taking the bus."

Frank parked behind their building but didn't shut off the ignition. "That's the voice of someone who's been reading *Auto Trader* magazine. You're finally joining the ranks of the self-mobile?"

"I should be, but my allergy to debt is paralyzing me. My savings account has a few hundred dollars more than I need for the down payment on a certain used Saturn. Six years old, tan inside, copper outside."

"You have car lust." He laughed. "I wouldn't have thought you had it in you."

She rubbed her gloved hands together. "When did you last ride the bus in winter? The closed windows give free rein to the body odor."

"Ouch."

"Deodorant is cheap. Certain items should never be cut out of one's budget." She pinched her nostrils to clear out the phantom odor. "Since we're still in the car, you must want to talk about something that can't be discussed around Sidney."

"Who said anything about talk?" He leaned across the seats and kissed her.

She responded like it hadn't been two weeks since he'd said anything to her that wasn't work-related. Then her brain rebooted. She pulled her lips away from his.

"It's cold out here."

"That's why I left the heater on." He reached for her again.

I'm going to regret this. "We're supposed to be working."

He grinned. "I'm the boss. I can change work rules if I want."

No, I'm not going to regret this. "This is why office romances are a bad idea. We're not on equal footing." She unbuckled her seat belt to alleviate the trapped sensation. "Snogging belongs on dates, in private, not at eleven a.m. in a public parking lot."

She stifled a smile at his baffled expression. *Did the man think his considerable charm offset everything else?*

"But … we've been busy. When else are we supposed to have some private time?"

"People make time for what's important."

He leaned away. "I see you finally learned how to play hard-to-get. Tell *Cosmo* they can bite me."

"I am not playing at anything. I'm tired of getting treated as your girlfriend when it's convenient and your employee when it isn't." Her heart rate increased like she was at the end of a five-mile run. "Right now what's important is getting Katie back."

Frank popped his seat belt. "Fine. Glad to see I can always count on you to earn your pay."

As they walked upstairs, Giulia imagined Frank taping a sign to her back: *Ice Queen*. For a moment she wanted to curse herself, until her *Cosmo*-studying kicked in. Instead, she patted herself on the back for not being a doormat to his erratic face-sucking moods. The convent had been hard. In a karmic-payback sense, dating should be easy. *Thanks for nothing, Universe.* She toed off her boots and opened the office door.

"You piece of crap!" Sidney was pulling at the file-cabinet lock.

"Sidney?" Giulia said.

Sidney jumped. "Giulia. Mr. D. Um … I pushed in the lock and it won't pull out and I can't find the key."

Frank huffed. "There is no key. That's why I got it so cheap at the used office supply place." He scanned Sidney's desk and picked up a large paper clip. "All right, ladies. Time for your first lesson in breaking and entering."

"What?" Giulia and Sidney said in unison.

"Lock-picking. All good investigators know how to do this—unofficially, of course. First, open the paper clip so you have a bigger half-loop and a smaller half-loop. Break it in the middle." He snapped the thin metal in two. "Now open each loop into an L."

Sidney reached for the pink phone-message pad, but Frank stopped her. "If you stop watching to write it down, you'll miss the technique. Okay, see this little hook at the end where I broke the clip in half? You stick that end into the bottom of the lock so the L points up."

He pushed the smaller half of the paper clip into the jagged opening using his left hand, working it till it stopped. "See how I've placed it below the section that holds the wafers?"

"Wafers?" Sidney said.

"The pins, in some locks. The pieces of metal that the key fits into. Now you bend the pick down. If I did this right, I'll get torque." He applied pressure to the paper clip, and it popped out of the lock. "Good. That's what happens when you do it wrong." He reinserted it and pushed down. This time the metal stayed in place. "Good. See how I turned the L out of the way of the lock? Now take the other half." He manipulated it in his right hand until the straight end pointed toward the file cabinet. "Slide this end— not the broken end with the hook—under the wafers."

Giulia stood on tiptoe to see over his shoulder. "How do you tell when it's in the right place?"

"You can feel the wafers. Here, take it."

Giulia grasped the second half of the clip. "I don't feel anything."

"Move it in and out. Yes, like that. Can you feel the pins shift slightly?"

"Yes. Okay, now I get it. Here, Sidney."

When Sidney had mimicked Giulia's and Frank's motion with the straight paper clip, Frank took it back.

"Here's the tricky part. You're going to want to practice this at home. A bike lock or a plain old padlock is fine. What you have to do with the bottom piece is turn the keyway clockwise, but without interfering with the pins—wafers. The pick does that." He glanced over his shoulder. "You both watching? Okay. Keep your left index finger on the torque half and hold the pick half at the rounded bend. Now you jog the pick up and down, fast but not rushed; you want to feel the wafers move. At the same time, you put clockwise pressure on the torque half. It's like driving a stick." After a few more wrist movements, the lock clicked and the cylinder popped out of the top corner of the file cabinet.

"There." He removed the paper-clip pieces.

"Mr. D., that was awesome." Sidney took the broken metal from him and turned the pieces over in her hands.

Giulia applauded. "I am officially impressed. However, I do not know how to drive a standard transmission."

"I do," Sidney said. "Dad taught me on the roads in the cemetery near our farm. It's super-easy, Giulia. I could teach you in like half an hour." She handed her a large paper clip and dropped one in her knapsack-sized purse. "Does that mean you're getting a car?"

Giulia tucked the paper clip in the inner pocket of her much smaller purse. "Soon, I hope. Much sooner than I'll need to break into a house or steal a bicycle with this new skill."

"Always be prepared. You never know when you might encounter a stray file cabinet in need of help." Frank peered into his part of the office. "That's right. I didn't bring coffee because we went to Jimmy's."

Giulia opened her mouth to offer to run downstairs to Common Grounds, but the *Cosmo* fairy sitting on her shoulder shut it for her.

"Eh, I drink too much caffeine anyway. Sidney, any messages?"

"Oh, yes. Sorry. I forgot when I tried to find the key to that stupid lock." She picked up two bright-pink message slips. "Monsignor Harvey's assistant said he really wants you to call before noon, and your mom called right after you left."

Frank's shoulders slumped. "Is there anything less professional than having your admin tell you to call Mom?"

Giulia laughed. "Real men call their mothers regularly. This lets them cut the line into heaven."

"I'll remember that." He closed the door of his half of the office behind him.

Giulia pulled out her cell and redialed Laurel. "It's me again, sweetie. Can you email me everything you just sent to the police station? Here's my address." She waited while Laurel clicked her mouse. "I'm going to take a look at it on my lunch hour … yes, of course I'll call you if I have any ideas … I know … I have to get back to work now."

Sidney plopped a stack of documents on the edge of her desk and opened the top file cabinet drawer.

"I told you we're going to have food stations at the reception, didn't I?"

Giulia discarded three emails. "You did. What did Olivier decide to have on his side?"

Sidney jogged papers into one of the hanging folders. "Teriyaki pork kebabs at one, little corned beef sandwiches with Swiss cheese and sauerkraut at another, chicken wings at the third one."

Giulia looked up. "Reubens?"

"Yeah, that was it. He went into rhapsodies over sauerkraut and Russian dressing and rye bread—which I could eat if I liked sauerkraut—but corned beef? Ew. I can just picture his poker gang glomming onto that preservative-filled heart-attack fodder." More papers disappeared into the file drawer.

"Maybe their wives will encourage them to try your stations." Giulia opened an unfinished spreadsheet and her Day-Timer and started typing in her handwritten information.

"Puh-lease. Olivier says they might try the free-range chicken dumplings if we don't tell them they're healthy. But he says they'll run away from the mushroom pâté and the corn-and-pumpkin stew. It's all grown locally—even the wheat used to make the bread for the bruschettas."

"As long as everyone has a good time …" Giulia's voice trailed off as she deciphered her own writing.

"That's what Mom says. You're right. I'm just nervous."

Giulia hit *Save*. "Why?"

Sidney closed one drawer. "Not about marrying Olivier. He's wonderful and I love him and I love his family too. About everything being perfect. I worry that I'll turn into one of those Bridezillas or that we'll get to the church and the Pope will burst open the doors and tell everyone that the wedding is canceled because I failed that test on church history."

"You failed that test?" Giulia fought—and conquered—her desire to smile at the picture of the Pope and two dozen attendant Cardinals invading quiet little Our Lady of Perpetual Help. "Did you freeze?"

"I overloaded. I was okay with the real early stuff, but when the test got to the Borgias and all those corrupt popes, everything scrambled in my brain like eggs. Plus I hadn't eaten that morning and I thought of eggs and—*poof.* There went half my studying. All I could think about was a mushroom omelet."

"You can retake it."

"Not till after the honeymoon. It wouldn't have changed the wedding plans even if I did pass, because I've got a bunch of steps to go before I become 100 percent Catholic and can join in Communion and everything. Father Pat's got our whole liturgy set up, and says that everyone'll be going to church the next day for Christmas anyway because it's Sunday, so it's not like they'll be missing their Communion for the week."

Frank opened his door. "Seven."

"Seven what?" Giulia said.

"Seven separate commissions from the Diocesan Office. Did you have any idea the Church had so many projects they didn't want to handle themselves?"

"That wasn't my area, but I'm not surprised. Look at the scope of their works and the number of parishes."

"Plus all the nuns are jumping ship."

She stuck out the tip of her tongue. "Wall. Jumping the wall."

"You are such an English teacher."

"Besides, what makes you think that any Community would handle these commissions? Nuns aren't private investigators."

Frank's expression was the picture of ingenuous. "Come on. Nuns are all-powerful and all-knowing. Like all the nuns who taught me in high school."

The phone rang. Sidney ducked under the open file-cabinet drawer to answer it.

"Perhaps I should've kept one of the habits from the Mother-house undercover job. It seems to be the only symbol you respect."

"Not true." Frank ticked points off on his fingers. "I respect the Steelers' defensive line, the power of Jameson, Manchester United's keeper, and the prompt person who cuts the checks for the Church. DI's account balance is a joy to behold."

"Sidney and I will expect fat Christmas bonuses, then." As Sidney hung up the phone, Giulia added, "Right, Sidney?"

"What?"

"Just say yes."

"Um, yes?"

Frank made head-clawing motions. "You two will bankrupt me."

"If you want to retain good employees, you have to give them proper incentive."

Sidney looked from Giulia to Frank, worry lines forming between her eyes. "Um, Mr. D., that was Captain Reilly."

"Sidney, don't listen to Giulia, she's just trying to apply that famous Catholic guilt. What's the message?"

"He says please come back to his office. He'll buy lunch."

"Crap."

Giulia said," What's wrong with that?"

"He wants to soften me up. Lunch is his favorite weapon."

"Maybe he's going to give me another opportunity to pour hot coffee on Poole." Giulia stood and headed for the coat rack. "It's Tuesday. It's nearly noon. The window for getting Katie back is closing fast. I'm willing to discuss anything that may help."

SEVEN

"I went with the safe choice," Jimmy said as he ripped open a large white paper bag. "Isaly's chipped ham, lettuce, tomato, brown mustard, no pickles."

"God be praised," Frank said, unwrapping a foot-long sub.

"What do you have against pickles?" Giulia folded her sub wrapper into a neat rectangular placemat without disturbing the actual sandwich.

"How do you do that?" Frank studied Giulia's paper and shook his head, unscrewing the top of his Coke bottle. "Pickles are zombie cucumbers: green, droopy, and excreting unspecified innards. I only eat clean kills."

Giulia laughed. "Next Halloween I may dress up as a zombie pickle, just to see the look on your face." She smiled at Jimmy. "Thank you for lunch. This smells heavenly."

"Nothing says brain food like a hot chipped-ham sub. We're gonna need it." He clicked his mouse with his right hand and took a bite from the sandwich in his left. "I got Davis away from

Poole, and we combed through their report and the documents your friend sent me. Assuming that the three kidnappings are connected, we're looking at the same person—or people—running a kidnapping ring. If not, we're looking at a mighty long coincidence."

Giulia set down her own Coke. "Of course they have to be the same person."

"Not necessarily. Black-market baby rings are more prevalent than you want to know."

She shuddered. "But isn't it obvious that in these three cases the kidnappers deliberately targeted adoptees of gays?"

Frank said in between bites, "Where's conclusive proof that gay couples are the only target?"

Jimmy set down his sub and wiped his hands. "The information your friend has focuses only on two kidnappings, which, granted, have a very similar pattern."

"Show me, please. She sent everything to me, but I haven't been able to study them yet."

He handed them a set of printouts and reentered his password to unlock his screen. "The top pages are about the first couple in Akron. Young woman with middle-aged partner. One hundred percent honest on their application, as you can see."

Giulia snickered. "I don't suppose I'd have the nerve to ask a male friend to ejaculate into a turkey baster, either."

"The things I see in this job." Jimmy clicked his mouse. "They had contacts at several local hospitals. A mother gave birth, stayed overnight, and walked out."

Frank stopped in the act of taking a bite. "She left her newborn? Every time I think I've seen too much, people surprise me."

"Fifteen-year-old black mother, forty-year-old Asian father. Neither family wanted the baby. The father had already skipped town; the teenager boarded a bus and hasn't been seen since."

Frank swallowed. "I take it back."

Giulia pointed to the bottom of her page. "The adoption laws are less strict in Ohio."

Jimmy said, "Yes and no. This couple had all their paperwork and background checks in place. They also had connections and money. Bribes are effective grease. Three months later, the baby was theirs."

"Two months after that," Giulia said, still reading, "the young woman took the baby for an evening walk. It was a beautiful April night. Someone clocked her on the head and took the baby. The same phone-call pattern."

"Untraceable because the kidnappers used burn phones, no doubt," Jimmy said.

"I'm sorry?" Giulia said.

"Prepaid disposable phones. Untraceable because the most the recipient's carrier can do is use the nearest cell towers to triangulate the signal. All the kidnappers had to do was call from a densely populated area. A train station at rush hour, or a sports stadium during a game. By the time the police get there, even if it's only a few minutes, the caller's thrown away the phone and melted into the crowd."

"Oh. I see. After that call, this couple paid the ransom, but they never saw the baby again." She swallowed, picturing Laurel's face as she told her story in the office.

"They got a follow-up phone call the next day," Jimmy said, pointing to the corresponding places on his screen and the print-out. "Said the baby was safe and in a God-fearing home."

Giulia hit her hands on the desk. "I am sick of people using God to suit their own purposes."

"I'll keep you away from Poole when you leave." Jimmy smiled at Giulia.

Frank turned the page as Giulia took a drink. "Here's one similarity: birth defects. The abandoned baby had a cleft palate. The next one was born deaf."

"Katie was born with an extra pinky finger on each hand." Giulia snatched the paper from Frank. "Laurel said that nontraditional couples fared better adopting hard-to-place babies."

Jimmy typed the birth defects into an open Word doc. "Good. The second kidnapping happened in Erie. Older women, already had one child from a failed marriage, wanted a second. Heard of a deaf-mute one-year-old that had already been in three foster homes. Long story short, they were approved after the child's second birthday."

"They snatched this baby like they did Katie," Giulia said. "The couple paid the ransom, but this is why Laurel and Anya are so frantic."

Frank read on, setting down his sub. "Son of a bitch."

Jimmy said, "The little girl's lungs were filled with water. A bathtub accident was the obvious conclusion, but there was no soap mixed with the water. It wasn't chlorinated, either, so probably not an indoor pool."

"Why not outdoor?" Frank said. "Right, February."

"Here's how she was left." Jimmy turned his screen. A snow-covered bicycle path shelter held a tiny, blanket-wrapped bundle. Off to one side, two women in long coats clung to each other. A piece of paper pinned to the front of the blanket, its sunny yellow color garish against the bright pink blanket.

Giulia kept her voice steady as she traced her finger down her page. "What does the note say?"

"That the child is in the arms of her Heavenly Father." Jimmy tossed his wrapper into the trash.

Frank put a hand on Giulia's arm. "I'll say it. Bastards."

EIGHT

GIULIA GAVE FRANK A tight smile. "I notice that the kidnappers kept the money both times."

"Of course," Frank said. "It's all about the money."

She gripped her Coke till the plastic buckled. "Captain, may I have a pen?"

When she uncapped the ballpoint, she turned over the first printout. "Similarity number one: all three babies had a medical issue. The kidnappers could be working at hospitals. No. The victims lived too far apart. They could have hacked into hospital databases."

"Across three states?" Frank said. "Keep in mind that I'm playing Devil's Advocate in this scenario."

"Drag yourself into the twenty-first century, Driscoll," Jimmy said. "My neighbor's kid hacked into the school district's database to change his girlfriend's GPA."

"I'll give you that. But this could also mean we're dealing with three different kidnappers. A small ring, but still a ring."

Giulia finished her sub. "That's possible. Laurel and Anya's contacts don't think the police in Erie or Akron tried to connect the crimes."

Jimmy looked at her over the monitor. "There wouldn't be an obvious reason to. Of course, if either set of parents had disobeyed the phoned instructions and called in the FBI, their resources might have found a connection where local authorities couldn't. And I say that as a local authority."

"I know. The adoption assistance group did insist there was a pattern." She folded her wrapper into a small square.

A quick knock on the door and a detective poked his head in. "I kid you not, Cap, a geezer just rammed his '55 T-Bird into a 7-Eleven."

"Is he hurt?" Giulia said.

"Is the T-Bird hurt?" Frank said.

"He's okay enough to be cursing in German and kicking pieces of his bumper. The two clerks and a guy who was getting a Slurpee are trying to salvage the front displays. The T-Bird sustained minor front-end damage."

Frank and Jimmy groaned.

"You two," Giulia glared at each of them in turn, "need to rethink your priorities. Cars can be replaced. People can't."

"Vintage T-Birds cannot be replaced." Jimmy waved the detective out. "Get the uniforms' report and plug it into your metrics. Close the door."

"Men." Giulia said. She spread out the papers. "Look. All three couples use the same bank chain."

Frank and Jimmy followed her pen as she circled the bank name three times.

"I know it's possible to hack a bank, but it's not easy." Giulia tapped the pen next to one of the circles. "Laurel said that they used credit cards for most of the expenses and left their bank accounts intact. This way, when the agencies ran credit checks, they always had enough money to pay the bills."

"Yes," Frank said. "Meaning I agree with you and we should discount that as a possible connection."

"You're quick to shoot down an idea, but slow to help us look for possibilities."

Frank raised his eyebrows. "You're channeling Sister Mary Regina … don't tell me …"

"Mary Regina Coelis." Giulia bit off each word. "But you remember who won the FA Cup the past five years."

Jimmy said, "God help us, don't get him started on soccer. Frank, I don't know what's up your ass about this case, but can you get with the program here?"

"Fine." He pulled over two printouts. All three of them studied the papers onscreen or on the desk for a few minutes.

"Hey." Frank scooped up the rest of the printouts. "Here," he set one aside, "here," another, "and … yes, here it is again." He set those three pages on top of the rest. "They all went to someplace called the Wildflower."

"They did?" Giulia ran her index finger between the documents on the screen. "You're right."

"Isn't that a resort on Raccoon Lake?" Jimmy said.

"Yes," Giulia said. "Even though it's less than half an hour from here, it's very private. It's hidden away on a cove, doesn't advertise or anything. If you have to ask, then it's not for you, you know?"

Frank and Jimmy looked at her.

She huffed. "It's for gay people only. Technically for lesbians only."

Frank whistled. "They must get lots of rubberneckers during trout season."

"Will you be serious? I said it was secluded. Captain Reilly, may I use your computer?"

Jimmy traded chairs with her and she typed the name in a search window, then clicked on the correct link. "See? Ten-foot-high privacy fences all around, private beach, private everything."

"People from Akron would come all this way just to stay on Raccoon Lake for a week?" Frank shook his head. "There've got to be resorts closer to home."

"Not single-sex resorts. Don't you get it? Didn't your family ever go to a favorite vacation spot, no matter how far it was?"

Jimmy said, "My parents drove us to Hershey Park every year when we were in grade school. That was the car ride from hell. We loved the park, though."

"Exactly. Trust me, same-sex resorts are rare enough for people to make Odyssean journeys to reach them." Giulia shuffled the printouts. "The Akron couple was at the Wildflower six months before they got their baby in April of last year. The Erie couple went the week between Christmas and New Year's last year, and got their daughter this past February." She reread Laurel's information. "Laurel and Anya went for Thanksgiving week, but that wasn't their original plan."

Jimmy had pulled the keyboard in front of himself and was typing almost as fast as Giulia talked. "Why did they change?"

"The baby's mother had complications from high blood pressure, and they scheduled a C-section two weeks before her due date. Laurel and Anya had already paid for their week and wanted one last romantic getaway, just the two of them, before they became parents. The resort wasn't full and switched their reservation. I remember, because Laurel had to scramble for coverage at the soup kitchen—it's always packed on Thanksgiving."

"That's why you turned down my invite for dinner at Mom and Dad's," Frank said.

She nodded. "I worked Wednesday, Thursday, and Saturday that week."

Jimmy said, still typing, "It has possibilities." He saved his document and scrolled to the pages on all three reports that mentioned the resort. "Someone could've traced their credit card history and pinpointed that as a good place to get to know the three couples."

"Wait." Giulia sagged. "A Bible-spouter isn't going to stay at a gay resort."

Jimmy frowned, forehead wrinkling. "It's unlikely, I admit. However, if these kidnappers are all about getting the kids, then they might be willing to suck it up and pretend to be a couple."

"I don't want to sound like Frank, but not any extremist I've ever met."

"Thanks," Frank said.

Jimmy grinned. "I like you. You keep his ego in check. About—shut up, Frank—the amusing image of a Bible-thumper in a gay resort: I've seen them crash a Gay Pride parade in full Jesus regalia."

Frank leaned forward. "Remember the crazy lady who broke up a PFLAG meeting screaming about defending traditional marriage?"

"The one who'd been divorced four times? She was a prize. Tried to bite me when I cuffed her, if I remember right."

"Didn't you dress up like her for Halloween that year?"

Frank laughed. "Your face was priceless. Anyway, we're off track. Why do you think there are two?"

"Come on," Jimmy said. "You've worked kidnapping cases. Have you ever seen a kidnapper go solo?"

"I'll give you that one."

Giulia poked her pen through the top paper. "That must be the connection. Should we look for religious actors? The kind that do religious plays for Advent and Easter Week?"

Frank gave her a blank look. "Why?"

"Because actors would be able to hide their feelings. Regular extremists might not."

Jimmy tapped a finger on his mouse. "I wasn't thinking along those lines. It's a little far-fetched."

Frank shook his head. "We'd better hope it's not actors, because it'll take forever to track down the ones who specialize in Passion Plays and the like. Let alone getting them to give us their church affiliation. I can hear complaints about Big Brother already."

"Wait a minute." Giulia navigated the resort's website with the mouse. "I thought I remembered Laurel telling me something about entertainment … Here. On Friday nights after dinner, the employees put on a lip-sync and funny skit show for the guests. Laurel said it was hokey and silly, but most people got into the spirit of things." When Frank and Jimmy stared at her, she said, "Everyone they hire must be required to have some kind of acting talent."

They blinked, practically in unison.

"What?" Giulia gestured at the screen. "Memorizing. Practicing. Becoming someone else, even if only for three minutes at a time. In other words, pretending to be someone they're not."

Jimmy opened his mouth, then closed it. "All right. I'll talk to the owner about even letting us see parts of her employee files. Subpoenaing their guest records of the resort is going to take a couple of days as it is."

"Oh no—we don't have a couple of days." Giulia's voice almost squeaked. "Where's the timeline for the other kidnappings? Here. Day One: they take the baby and call the parents. That was two days ago. Days Two through Four: gather the ransom money. Day Five: the kidnappers call with the location for the parents to leave the ransom. Day Six: the ransom is dropped off. Day Seven is when the dead two-year-old was left, and when the call saying the first baby was with a new family." She fixed her gaze on Jimmy. "This is already Day Three. If they decide Katie isn't worth saving, they'll do it in less than three days."

NINE

Frank and Jimmy looked at Giulia. Jimmy turned back to his monitor a moment later.

"You may be right. I spent more time on the police reports." He clicked page after page, reading pieces of each.

Giulia drummed her fingers on her lap. Frank finished his Coke. Giulia restrained her desire to kick his shins. She still couldn't fathom Frank's less-than-urgent attitude.

Jimmy leaned back. "All right, I concede your timeline. This puts us in a miserable position. We don't have time to run down the other possibilities: the bank accounts, the hospital databases. The resort fits the potential timeline of targeting the first two victims and learning their movements. The time elapsed between your friends' vacation and their kidnapping is short by comparison, but"—he forestalled Giulia's protest—"that could have been triggered by them changing their vacation dates."

Giulia didn't care if her face showed her relief. "How can we help?"

Frank made a restless movement next to her.

Jimmy said, "This is actually the point where the police take over again. Please don't think I'm dismissing you, Giulia. Without your insistence, Poole's negligence would have relegated this investigation to his back burner. Now we'll be able to do our job."

"Then I'm glad you invited us here," Frank said. "Thanks for lunch, Jimmy. Call me or Giulia if you get any more news?"

"Of course." Jimmy stood, holding out his hand to Giulia. "Thank you again, Giulia. This case is mine personally now. I'll do everything I can to get your friends' baby back safely."

Giulia shook his hand. *What's happening? Why is Frank hustling us out of here and why is Captain Teddy Bear acquiescing? What am I going to do? I can't lock the door and refuse to leave till they make me part of this investigation.*

Frank opened the door for her and she went through the crowded detectives' room ahead of him. Poole, thank goodness, wasn't in sight. The pseudo–Bond Girl nodded at them as they buttoned their coats.

Giulia chose silence on the ride back; lunch traffic and winter roads didn't lend themselves to conversation. Frank didn't curse any drivers, not even the city bus that fishtailed when a light turned green and sent the Camry's anti-lock brakes into overdrive.

You're railroading me, Frank. Captain Teddy Bear's okay with us helping—or he was. Why are you dead against it? She stared at the dashboard, mentally pasting Frank's and Jimmy's faces onto it. *Did Frank send him some kind of signal left over from their partner days? The Captain was willing to let us help until I pointed out the resort link. It can't be professional jealousy. I'm a detective—almost. I've trained myself to spot connections. The police have multiple cases and emergencies pulling them every which way all the time. I'm focused on Laurel's baby. It only makes sense that I'd see some details before they would.*

It wasn't till they got trapped behind a whale-sized SUV apparently driven by someone's grandmother that Giulia realized her teeth were chattering.

"Frank, heat?"

"Sorry." He diverted part of the blower from the windshield to their feet. He visibly shivered even after the switch, and cranked the heat all the way. "Perfect time for the heater to go on the fritz."

Silence filled the car again. The air blowing on Giulia's toes never climbed above "tepid." She thought about calling Laurel, but what was the point? They had nothing useful to report. Telling Laurel about the resort connection would only give her and Anya another obsessive hamster wheel to run in.

Giulia and Frank climbed the back stairs to the office several minutes later, still in silence. She toed off her boots as Frank opened the door. Sidney had her coat on before Giulia reached her own desk.

"This is perfect timing because my mom's picking me up so we can try on my dress. Did I tell you I'm wearing my grandmother's wedding gown? I know I did. The seamstress messed up the alterations the first time, but she called just now and we want to see it ASAP in case something else has to be fixed because it's Tuesday already and I think my head's going to explode." She inhaled like a vacuum cleaner. "It'll only take an hour, I'm sure. Nobody called when you were gone. See you!" The door closed behind her.

Frank and Giulia grinned at each other.

"She is the best hiring decision you ever made," Giulia said.

"No. You are." Frank crossed the room and embraced her. "I know I'm being an ass—sorry—a jerk. I know I've been treating you like you're a computer program I can open and close at will. Let me explain, okay?"

He turned Giulia's client chair around and leaned on the back. Giulia sat in her own chair and waited.

"It's a lost cause, *muirnín*."

Giulia didn't say anything.

"I know you don't want to think that, but I know what I'm talking about. I worked on four kidnapping cases while I was still a cop, three with Jimmy."

Giulia pinched her lips together.

Frank's mouth worked but the smile still showed. "You look like Sister Regina, um, Coelis when you do that. Don't get mad."

"Francis Xavier Driscoll, I am not Sister Mary Regina Coelis anymore. I have not been her for twenty whole months. I curse the day we decided that me going undercover in the convent two months ago was a good idea. I could swear you still see an invisible veil on my head." She ruffled her frizzy brown curls. "See? Hair. And what does any of that have to do with your sudden desire to let me down easy?"

"I know you want to keep your friend's spirits up. I know you're always optimistic, but the plain fact is that kidnappings don't end well."

"Statistics?" Giulia let disdain creep into her voice.

"Yeah, yeah, I know. The general statistic for kidnappings by strangers is 57 percent are returned unharmed and 43 percent aren't. We both know what happens to the 43 percent."

Giulia set her jaw. "You are deliberately applying the worst possible outcome. How many of the 43 percent are infants?"

"I'd have to look it up. That doesn't mean—"

"It does mean that there is a chance for Katie to come home. A good chance."

"No. Listen to me. You can discount teenagers running off together and non-custodial parents never returning the kid from their weekend visit." He gripped the top of the chair. "I don't care if the guy who took your friend's baby quotes half the Bible over the phone while he implies they'll get the baby back if they come up with the ransom. The most likely outcome is he's already sold the baby to a hetero couple, if he's serious about the biblical trash-talk."

"So what? You're a detective. We're detectives. We can find out who has Katie now and get her back."

"It's not impossible. Whatever we can do on top of what Jimmy's doing, we'll jump on it." He put a hand over hers. "But I want you to face this fact: the statistics are skewed. This is a non-parental kidnapping by perps with a two-part agenda: God and money. It will not end well."

"How can you think that?"

"Real-world experience. Not just mine. Talk to experienced cops. They'll tell you the same thing—that your friends need to prepare for failure. I know this. Jimmy knows this. It's not pessimism. It's realism. We'll put everything into finding the baby because we're professionals, but that timeline you worked out? It doesn't exist. No amount of hopeful prayers will change that."

A piece of Giulia that had been twisting into knots all through Frank's stories finally snapped. *He's right*, an evil voice whispered in her ear. *Facts can be one-sided*, a calmer voice whispered in her other ear. She sat quite still in her chair, imagining angels and demons from old *Tom and Jerry* cartoons, her hands still under Frank's.

"So what exactly have you been doing since I brought Laurel in here on Monday?" she said at last. "Humoring me?"

"No, no, nothing like that. I'm just trying to let you down easy."

"I am not a sixteen-year-old whose boyfriend is dumping her for a cheerleader."

Frank said, after a second, "What?"

"I am not fragile. I don't know where you got that idea." She moved her hands.

Frank tightened his grip. "That's not what I mean. I don't think you're a sheltered kitten who doesn't know enough to come in out of the rain."

She gave him the "Precious Moments" eyes again.

"Stop that. You're doing it on purpose now. I don't want you to break your heart over this. It's doomed to fail."

Her eyes crinkled in the beginnings of a smile. "I don't believe you."

His mouth hung open a moment. "Why the hell not?"

TEN

GIULIA LET THE CURSE slide. The Tom-and-Jerry imps on her shoulder popped into nonexistence. She wasn't fighting a pile of statistics; she was fighting Frank's pessimism sinkhole. The way he skewed to the worst possible conclusion no matter what. This was a familiar adversary.

"Remember how you reacted to those vile Photoshopped pictures Don Falke created of Blake and me?"

"Huh? What does that have to do with kidnapping stats?"

"Not with kidnapping statistics, with you. Remember how a character in old cartoons would get a tiny angel on one shoulder and a tiny devil on the other, giving advice? If you were in a cartoon, you'd always be listening to the devil. I'd find pricks from the pitchfork tines in your neck if I looked."

Frank leaned back in the chair. "Is this code? Should I have a translation key?"

"Only if you need to translate the way your own mind works."

His cynical detective face morphed into something plain and simple. Giulia loved that face. It was the face of the Frank Driscoll who first said hello to her when she was a barista in Common Grounds downstairs. The face disappeared when he learned she'd been a Sister of Saint Francis, but as they got to know each other, the face had become the familiar one she saw every day.

"I wish I had a mirror for you to see yourself. Frank, the difference between you and me is which side of a problem we choose to see."

"Don't get all sappy greeting card on me. The world is a darker place than you want it to be."

"It's also a brighter place than you want it to be." She scrunched up her face. "You're right. That belongs on a sappy card. Not my style." Her hands slipped out from under Frank's. "I don't agree that because the statistics about kidnappings skew negative, it automatically means this kidnapping will fall into the negative side."

"Christ help us, things will not come up sunshine and roses just because you want it to happen."

"Of course they won't. That's not what I'm saying. And please stop cursing."

"Sorry. You've got to be realistic about this. Jimmy might not call us in to help. Don't pretend you aren't hoping he will—I saw it in your face when he shook your hand. He likes you and he wants you to replace that manicured piece of fluff who answers the phones, but he's not getting you."

"You don't own me, Frank Driscoll."

"I know. It's a figure of speech. I mean that even though he wants to hire you out from under me, he's not going to do anything underhanded like bring you in on this case and feed you information to keep your hopes up."

"Do you expect me to lie to Laurel for the next three days?"

"No, because I know you won't. But you might want to hedge. Tell her that the police have all the information and that they're keeping things to themselves. That's how they usually work, so it's not lying."

Giulia stood. "Sin of omission, Mr. Driscoll. No thanks."

Frank dropped his head into his right hand. "How do you manage to do this job so well without compromising your Franciscan-ness?"

"I don't think that's a word." She laughed, but it faded with her next breath. "Stop looking at me like I'm a plaster saint, because I'm not. I'm angry at Captain Jimmy and worried about Katie and disappointed in you. I'm going to prove you wrong. Before the timeline is up I'm going to hand Katie to Laurel and Anya and make you eat your words." She made shooing motions at him. "Get out of my client chair. I have work to do. I wish I knew how I could want to yell at you one minute and kiss you the next."

He stood up and the next moment he was kissing her. Thoroughly. Angry Giulia flounced to the curb. The Giulia in Frank's arms returned the kiss with all the frustrated passion of the last several barren weeks.

When Frank broke the kiss, he said, "This is one of the times I don't think you're a plaster saint."

"About time," Giulia said, and kissed him again. The empty office, the wind rattling the windows, the hum of the computer fans didn't make a dent in the very pleasant shivers running through her body. Frank knew how to kiss. It more than made up for her inexperience.

A door slammed downstairs and they jumped apart. No footsteps ascended the stairs, but Giulia didn't return to Frank's arms.

"I need to fix my face," she said, going into the bathroom behind her desk. The light makeup she used was intact; she hadn't worn lipstick because of the weather. *My hair's mussed. So is my sweater. That man is dangerously charming. No, more than charming. He's captivating. I need to be careful.*

The imp on her shoulder whispered, "Careful is for old maids. You've got years of celibacy to make up for."

The angel on her other shoulder didn't reply. Giulia almost looked for it. She shook her head. *My brain hates me. Both sides of it want me to give in to Frank.*

"You almost done?" Frank's voice, right outside the door.

She opened it. "Polite humans give each other privacy in the bathroom."

"I wanted to apologize for not coming clean to you about the realities of kidnappings."

"Accepted. I will expect another apology when Katie gets home."

Frank made a frustrated noise, but cut it off. "If it happens, I'll apologize. Look, will you come to my folks' for dinner tonight?"

"I—uh—I'll have to make sure there's coverage at the soup kitchen."

Frank made that same noise.

"I'm not going to leave them hanging so I can go out to dinner. Let me call someone."

"Fine." He loomed over her. "You're right about one thing: I've been treating you like furniture. I'm ... well ... an *amadán*. Sorry. That means 'idiot.' I'll work on it. Deal?"

"Deal. Let me fix your tie. We don't want to scandalize Sidney."

He raised his chin. "When she's on her honeymoon we should do this more often."

She smiled. "What will the boss say?"

"I'll keep him out of the way."

Sidney returned half an hour later.

"It's perfect! Wait till you see it. Mom says I look just like my grandmother in it—and my grandmother was so beautiful and happy in her wedding pictures." She tossed her coat at the coat rack and unlocked her screen. "I'm starving. Everyone talks about brides dieting for the wedding, but that's nuts. Sure, I'm in shape, but the stress'll make you lose three or four pounds at least. I can't wait till it's all over."

"I'm sure you'll have a wonderful day," Giulia said, not smiling even though she wanted to.

"Oh, I guess, if I can remember to enjoy it instead of worrying that I'll drop the flowers or trip over my shoes—if it were summer I swear I'd wear white flip-flops." She unwrapped a wheat bagel and nibbled the scrambled egg and tomato sticking out of the front. "Mingmei downstairs says she has a Christmas present for you, and when can you get together?"

"I'll stop by tomorrow morning." Giulia dialed another phone number and held up a "wait a sec" finger toward Sidney when it rang. "Audrey? It's Giulia. I have a huge favor. Can you take my turn tonight? ... You're the best ... Let me know when you want me to fill in ... New Year's Day? Of course I'll take it for you ... He is? That's great ... He is? Are you sure? ... I'll stop by the day after to admire the ring. Congratulations in advance ... Bye. Thanks again."

Sidney gave Giulia a "dish it" look.

"Frank asked me to dinner at his parents' house tonight. I work at the Stage Door Kitchen on Tuesdays, so I had to get a sub."

Sidney shook a finger at her. "Dinner with the folks is one of the Three Big Signs, you know."

Giulia's cheeks heated up. "I don't know."

"Trust me. My aunt is like the world's biggest matchmaker. She's always giving us tips and rules and signs." She drank from her spring-water bottle. "It's about time, too. You've been sort of dating for what? Four months?"

"Stop it."

"You're blushing. I can see it. Hah! You think it's about time too. Maybe Mr. D. will propose to you for Christmas."

"What?" Giulia stopped halfway to Frank's door. "We aren't anywhere near that stage, if we'll ever be."

"Uh-huh." Sidney turned her concentration to her lunch.

Giulia knocked on Frank's door.

"Yeah?"

She went in, leaving the door open. "I switched nights, so I'll be happy to come to your parents' house for dinner."

Frank grinned. "Great. I'll pick you up at seven."

"Good. I'll have time to take out all of today's frustrations at the gym."

The phone rang.

Frank said in a low voice, "So why'd you leave the door open?"

Giulia stuck out the tip of her tongue.

Sidney rolled into the doorway. "Captain Reilly on line one, Mr. D."

ELEVEN

"Yeah, Jimmy? … What? … Uh, no … I'm sure, but … Yes, but … Giulia, wait."

Giulia was already on the other side of the door, even as she was dying to eavesdrop.

"Come in and close it, please. Jimmy wants me to put him on speaker."

She sat in the client chair and had to pretend to adjust her socks to paste a neutral yet interested expression on her face.

Jimmy's voice on speaker was clear and cheerful. Giulia heard "I'm going to ask you a favor" undertones in it.

Yes. He found out something.

"We got a break, Giulia. The owner of the resort knows about that adoption assistance group. She did a one-eighty from guarded hostility to all cooperation when I explained why I wanted to see her records."

"Good," Frank said. "Digital?"

"No. They had a fire last month. Destroyed the back office, phones, computers, but not the hard copies of the records. Get this—she keeps physical copies in a fireproof safe because she's a pyrophobic."

Afraid of fire, Giulia mouthed at Frank.

I figured that, he mouthed back.

"So they're still re-keying all the records and she doesn't want to let them leave the premises," Jimmy said.

"Are you sending Poole out there?" Frank said.

Jimmy's snort came through with perfect clarity too. "Only if I could send the camera crew for *America's Funniest Home Videos* along with him. I had a different idea."

Frank fidgeted. "Jimmy, I object to this."

Giulia sat forward in Frank's client chair. *You were wrong, you were wrong, you were wrong, Frank,* she chanted to herself.

Jimmy's voice continued, "Objection noted. The resort has a small staff during fall and winter: cross-country ski instructor, masseuse, two child-care people, and the usual chefs, wait staff, and cleaning people. Here's the thing—" Another line rang on his end, loud enough for Giulia and Frank to jump back. "Just a sec."

"He wants me to go out there and ask them questions," Giulia said to Frank.

"Sort of."

"Sort of? Let me in on the rest, please."

Click. "Sorry about that. So here's my idea. We need the records examined, and I'd like to know if you're willing to talk to the staff. It's a female-only resort, and the only female I have here is Carlson—you remember her, Frank?"

"The bulldozer?"

70

"Yeah. Can you picture her trying to ease into someone's confidence to get information?"

"Hell, no. The woman makes a pile driver look gentle. What about Zimmerman or Janus?"

"Zimm's on maternity leave, and Janus left last year for Orlando." He paused. "So I was wondering if we could borrow you, Giulia?"

Giulia glanced at Frank. *He's too upset for this to be a plain old interview request. Too bad. This is about Katie.* She chose a disingenuous reply for Jimmy. "To talk to the resort employees? How big a staff is there?"

"I'm hoping you'll agree to work undercover there for a few days. They can use the help so it won't be an obvious plant. You're so nondescript, you'll fit in without a problem."

Giulia aimed a crooked smile at Frank. "That is probably the most backhanded compliment I've ever received."

"You're not nondescript. Jimmy, you know what I'm going to say." Frank glared at the phone. "You seem to forget that Giulia's an employee of Driscoll Investigations, not a public servant."

"I know she doesn't work for me, Driscoll. You were the one who called me about this yesterday, remember? Said you wanted to help. What with Poole and the department's scarcity of females, it turns out I could use the help."

"You know I called you under pressure from Giulia. And let me remind you this business has casework to complete and my employees have their salaries to earn—"

Giulia cut off his last word. "I know you called him to get me to shut up. That doesn't bother me. You are welcome to dock my pay for the rest of the week. Captain Reilly, I'll be happy to go undercover at the resort." *I'll put off buying that used Saturn for a couple of weeks, but that's fine. Cars are replaceable. People aren't.*

"Terrific," Jimmy said. "The resort owner will send a courier over this afternoon—wait, what time is it? One forty already. Damn. Giulia, can you get there by three? I'll call and have her cancel the courier. She was going to photocopy the relevant information and get you everything you need to know, but she can hand you the packet in person now. She's mostly in our corner on this. I know you'll win her over completely. Frank, I owe you one." His phone rang again. "Dammit, I forgot to make up a name for you. Sorry. I'll call you if there's anything else. Thanks again."

Giulia jumped out of her chair and opened the door.

"Sidney, could you do me a huge favor and call Rent-A-Wreck? I need something small. An Escort or a Cavalier, maybe, and I'll need it through the end of the week."

"I'm on it." Sidney was already typing into a search window.

Giulia closed herself in with Frank again. They stared at each other across the desk.

"What the hell, Giulia?"

"I told you why I needed to help Laurel and Anya. Like I said to Captain Jimmy, I know you agreed to call him just so I'd stop bugging you." She leaned back against the door, trying to look like she didn't want to shake him. "I know Sidney's kind of useless this week because of the wedding, but I also know that none of our current projects are rush jobs."

"That doesn't give you the right to bail on me." His voice was dead level.

Giulia didn't like that voice. "I am not bailing on you. What are you afraid of—that I'm going to choose to answer phones and paint my nails all day? Or go back to cleaning toilets for a living?" When the corner of his mouth twitched, she pressed her point. "Didn't you wonder why I insisted we hire a cleaning service for the office? We have a toilet out there, you know." She relaxed a fraction. "You agreed to help."

"I did not agree to split this company in half."

"You agreed to the possibility that Driscoll Investigations resources could be used to help find Katie. This is an assignment for Driscoll Investigations. In which I am your partner." She kept her voice quiet, persuasive—a counterweight to Frank's.

He banged his fist against the desk, the staccato thumps falling dead on her ears. *Don't think of dead. Katie's not dead. We are going to bring her back.*

Wait.

She wrenched her attention away from her "rescue Katie" obsession and onto Frank's body language.

"Hey." She pushed away from the door. "What's really the problem?"

His jaw clenched. She walked around the desk until she was staring down at the top of his head.

"Look at me. Stop pretending you're angry about me going undercover." She covered his hand and the noise stopped. She waited.

"You'll laugh," he said.

"Excuse me?"

He looked up at that. "You're right. I'm talking to the born listener." He nudged her hand off and planted his elbows on the desk, leaning his forehead on his hands. "I'm a victim of youngest-child syndrome."

Giulia blinked. "What?"

"You're the oldest. You wouldn't understand, but I've got the sick feeling that I'm about to snatch defeat from the jaws of victory."

She sat on the corner of the desk. "May I have that in words of one syllable, please?"

He grimaced. "Fine. Here goes any kind of respect you've gained for me. Driscoll Investigations is finally legit. We've got almost too much work to handle. We're gaining a positive reputation. Word of mouth is bringing in new clients."

Giulia tilted her head. "And?"

"You're leaving. Sidney's leaving. I'm screwed. Who am I going to get on this kind of notice? I'll have to back out of commissions and trash my company's reputation with my own hands."

"But Sidney's only gone for seven working days. I'll come in here in the mornings and go out to the resort in the afternoons."

"It's going to crash and burn. Just like when Sean got promoted and Michael picked up a fat Christmas bonus for being top salesman." He slumped in his chair, flopping his head backward off the top.

Giulia stared at his upside-down face. "Those are your brothers, right? Where did all this come from?"

"From two family phone calls and Jimmy's eagerness to snatch you away." His frown had the opposite effect with his head in that position. "Could you be any more eager to work for him? Why don't you just hand in your resignation now? I'm going to have to go live in my parents' basement again. If you'd bothered to get your gun license I'd ask you to shoot me now and put me out of my misery."

The laugh burst through Giulia's mouth despite herself. "That's why you've been giving me grief? What a stereotype you are." She put her hands on his shoulders. "Listen very carefully because there'll be a test later. The work will continue to get done. I will pull ridiculous hours at both venues for the duration. I have already lined up a temporary receptionist, remember? He starts Friday morning."

"Yes, but—"

"Don't interrupt. We will find Katie; Captain Jimmy will pat us on the back; and come Monday morning I will not, repeat, not be handing in my resignation."

His inverted face was such a muddle of hope and forlornness that she bent down and kissed him.

"I prefer kissing you right side up. Now sit up, remember what I said, and set an example for your employees. Come drive me to the car rental place, please."

She escaped to the outer office to regain her composure, rather than react with all-too-typical embarrassment at kissing him in the office.

"Sidney, did you have any luck with the car place?"

"Oh, yes, no problem. They've got a 2007 Escort waiting for you."

"You're a gem. Thank you." She stared at Sidney's ruler-straight brown hair.

"Um, Giulia?" Sidney reached up and patted her hair straighter —an unnecessary movement.

Giulia pulled back her own curly mop into a tight ponytail. "Does this make me look nondescript-er? I mean, unobtrusive?"

This time Sidney blinked. "Um, I guess. Oh, wait. You're going undercover again. Cool!" She pushed back her chair and stood up in one fluid motion. "Try braiding it. Here, let me." Sidney's long fingers separated Giulia's thick hair into three sections.

"Ouch. You're yanking it out of my head."

"Am not. I'm pulling it into a super-tight braid." She tugged right, then left, then right. "Your hair's always loose and bouncy. If we plaster it real close to your head, you're going to look …"

Giulia's hair flopped against her back as Sidney came around front. "Yes … you look just different enough on real short notice. Ask Mr. D." She raised her voice. "Mr. D., can you come out and see this?"

Frank's door opened. "What?"

"Well?" Sidney said.

He looked around. "Well, what?"

Giulia and Sidney rolled their eyes at each other.

"Giulia's hair, Mr. D. Doesn't it make her look different?"

Frank's face blanked. "I guess so. You pulled it back, right?"

Sidney shook her head. "Never mind, Mr. D. Giulia, you look different."

"Thanks, Sidney. It'll help me get into character." She looked down at her blue sweater and jeans. "The clothes are all right, but my shoes aren't." She grabbed her gym bag from behind her desk and pulled out her beat-up Reeboks. "Perfect."

Sidney said, "Perfect for what?"

"Housekeeping."

"Ew. Cleaning other people's toilets and getting ignored like you're part of the furniture. I did it one summer for a hotel chain that I refuse to name. Never again."

"I could use the time off of my sentence in Purgatory."

Sidney made a face. "I've gotta ask you about that when I come back. Father Pat and I keep butting heads over it."

"My brain is yours to pick, but right now I really have to go. Frank?"

"I live to serve. Sidney, back in a few."

Giulia waited till they were in the car to say it.

"Are you reconciled to treating this as a case yet? Are you taking it seriously?"

"Why do you ask?"

"Experience. You have years more of it than I do. You see—frankly—the evil in people first, and that includes potential evil."

He remained silent until they were almost on top of the car rental place. "Don't get mad. Sometimes being with you is like waiting in the Confessional."

Giulia flung herself against the headrest. "You are going to drive me to violence."

"I know it sounds awful, but what I mean is sometimes what you say reaches inside me like a fishing hook and snags the one thing I'm trying to hide."

"Great. Thanks. How many other oppressive descriptions of my effect on you can you think up between here and an open parking space?" She slumped in the seat.

"I knew that would come out wrong." He steered into the nearest available space. "What I mean is you have this thing you do without any warning. It's like supercharged insight and I saw it when you'd only been working for me a month. It's one of the reasons I wanted you as my assistant."

She scooted sideways to see his face better. "That's complimentary ... I think."

He nodded. "It is. In this particular case what you've hooked is the cynical cop part of me." He turned off the car. "You're right. In my head I've dumped this into your lap. I've—to be biblical— washed my hands of it." His eyebrows met. "That's from the Bible, right?"

He must know how charming that look is. "I think you should attend RCIA classes with Sidney. You could stand a refresher."

"You're a much more pleasant teacher. Pat and I would just argue in public like we do when we get together at home. That'd be bad for his priestly image."

"I've been called many things as a teacher. 'Pleasant' was never one of them." She checked the dashboard clock. "I've got to go."

"All right." He pulled her over the gap between seats. "Be careful. Keep it all in your head. Don't take any notes somebody could find." He kissed her. "Your hair looks okay. Plain Jane stuff. Jimmy had the right idea."

The warmth from his kiss evaporated. "Thanks. Really."

"What?"

"Go ask your brothers. Even Pat could clue you in on this one."

TWELVE

THE BABY-BLUE ESCORT HATCHBACK drove like only its rust held it together. The last rental Giulia drove—a tiny Kia Soul—was solid as a tank compared to this car. *Stop complaining. This rust-bucket is exactly what your new persona would drive.*

At least the snow had held off for an entire day. Interstate 376 was clear and slush-free. She fiddled with the radio and found an all-Christmas station. "God Rest Ye Merry, Gentlemen," "Frosty the Snowman," and a series of alternating carols and Santa songs took her down the interstate. The Boston Pops' nine-minute medley got her to the park entrance. She let "Silver Bells" play until she saw the sign for the resort.

This story is simple. Early-morning barista who took this extra job because Christmas bills will be coming in. I wouldn't mind if the job became permanent. Simple.

She drove through a tunnel of pine trees at least eighty feet tall. They made the driveway so dark that the old-fashioned streetlamps lining its sides only created a parade of light-puddles.

At its terminus the trees ended as though someone had guillotined them smooth. Snow glare slammed Giulia in the eyes. She braked while her vision adjusted. A group of three small buildings clustered directly in front of her across the parking lot. A white-sided two-story hotel stretched along the left side of the lot. The sidewalk next to it led to an even longer white-sided building with a painted wrought-iron sign that read, *The Wildflower—Est. 2007.*

The half-filled guest part of the lot had room for about a hundred cars altogether. Piles of plowed snow blocked several spots. Snowed-in tennis courts and stables ranged away to her left. The long, gray lake lapped at the snow-covered bank a few feet from the right-hand hotel. Fifty feet behind it, a boathouse with frosty windows sat dark and silent amidst snowdrifts.

She drove to the cluster of buildings and fit the Escort in a narrow slot next to an older pickup truck by the back wall of the building labeled *Laundry.* Steam belched from its chimney. At first Giulia thought that was the only sign of life, but a moment later four cross-country skiers appeared from behind a maintenance shed and passed the stables.

Get to work, Falcone. No, no, no. I need a name. Um…Regina. Something I'm used to answering to. Last name…What's the love interest in the book I'm reading right now?…Ryan. That'll work. Regina Ryan.

Horses whinnied when she slammed the car door. Wind whipped off the lake. Her long, violet wool coat was almost not enough for the end of December. She slung her purse over her shoulder and locked the door with her right hand, her sneakers dangling from her left. Her boots gave excellent traction on the salted parking lot, despite a few stubborn patches of black ice. If it had been a different season, she would've looked for the employee entrance. Today she went right to the main doors.

A fireplace. Wonderful.

It was meant for paying guests to bask at, so she reluctantly walked past it to the front counter, which stretched across the entire east wall. Giulia heard the desk clerk before she saw her. A high, thin voice, but sweet nonetheless. As Giulia got closer, the desk clerk stood up from where she'd been seated behind a large computer monitor.

"May I help you?" Her smile matched the voice—thin and sweet.

"Good afternoon. I'm the new part-time person in housekeeping."

The smile became admonitory. "Use the side entrance from now on, through the kitchen storage area."

"Sorry. I didn't know where the employee entrance was."

"Everyone gets a mulligan the first time." She pointed to her right. "Go right through the gift shop. There's a door next to the DVD shelf. I'll unlock it for you."

Giulia walked to the end of the counter and entered the shop. She caught a glimpse of sweatshirts and T-shirts among other things she couldn't place. A narrow door opened and she slipped through.

"Come this way. I hope you're ready to get dirty. I'll show you where to hang your coat. There's a boot rack next to the proper entrance. Barbara is expecting you. She has paperwork for you to fill out."

Giulia took off her coat and hat, set her sneakers on the floor, and removed her boots. The desk clerk waited for her while she laced her sneakers. Her braid flopped over her shoulder, and one of her Santa Claus earrings caught in it. She untangled the earring and flipped the braid back into place before standing.

"Did you overspend on Christmas this year?"

How rude. Giulia took in the other woman's inquisitive expression. *Get over it. She probably just wants harmless gossip, like the hostess in that Mexican restaurant where I used to work.*

She nodded. "Impulse buys. No one to blame but myself." *Shut up, conscience. You know Father Carlos will absolve you from lies told for the greater good.*

"Then I'm glad we had an opening. Barbara's office is this way."

Mustering every ounce of "nondescript," Giulia followed. The desk clerk was several inches taller than Giulia's five-five, but she stooped. Not in the way people who worked all day at a computer did; more like she'd spent her life perfecting what Giulia was trying for: to be unobtrusive. *Odd for a woman in the hospitality industry. Maybe she was the tallest girl in school and couldn't get a date unless she made herself look shorter than the guys.*

The clerk knocked on a white door stenciled around the edges with violets and buttercups.

"Yes?" A brisk voice from the other side.

"The new housekeeper is here."

"Oh, good. Have her come in."

The desk clerk opened the door and Giulia stepped into a small, crowded office. Two desks sat against the east and north walls, one covered with stacks of paper, the other with a multi-slot organizer. A computer monitor rose above the papers like a ship above whitecapped water. The woman sitting at the monitor turned toward them.

"Good afternoon. Maryjane, would you let Monica know that we'll be finished in about fifteen minutes?"

"Of course." The desk clerk closed the door.

"Please sit down. I'm Barbara Smith, really and truly. Did you like how I avoided calling you by name just then? I never got a chance to ask that police captain what name you'd be using." The resort owner's pixie-style haircut fit her round, smiling face.

"Regina Ryan."

"Okay. Let me type that in." She swiveled back around to her keyboard. "I'll make up an address for you, just in case someone tries to get at my files." Her fingers paused, then continued typing. "This is killing me. I would've sworn on a stack of Bibles that the worst thing any employee of mine would get into is weed. We hire college kids in the summer, you know?"

Giulia put a hand on her shoulder. "Someone who can orchestrate stealing babies from their parents would have no problem acting like a model employee."

Barbara's shoulder tensed. "That's just it. I feel like I have to be suspicious of everyone I've hired."

"Not at all. Evil people depend on the trust of good people. We'll take care of this and the Wildflower will be fine."

The shoulder relaxed. "You're not at all what I expected. I'm so glad. All night I worried that they'd send someone whose every move telegraphed 'plant.'"

Giulia smiled but it wasn't sincere. *Nondescript. Captain Jimmy was right.* "I'll do my best to fit in. Point me in the right direction to get suited up."

Barbara finished typing and closed the file. "Right. Maryjane will take care of you. She was here when the original owners ran the place as a family vacation spot. She can tell you anything you want to know. Come see me before you leave today and I'll give you all the papers I was going to courier to the police station earlier." She opened the door, which gave them a clear view of the front counter. "Good. No one's needing help right now. Maryjane? Regina's all set. Could you take her to the staff lockers?"

Giulia followed the desk clerk through an open office of four desks and the biggest magnetic In/Out board she'd ever seen.

Maryjane stopped next to it. "Everything is alphabetical. Your name will be on a gray magnetic strip like the other indoor staff. Move it to 'Out' when you leave for the night and note the time with one of the markers. I'll show you the timesheet program tomorrow." She opened another door that led into a staff break room. "I pulled three uniforms for you, sizes ten, twelve, and fourteen. Monica will be thrilled to see you." Lockers are through that swinging door to your left. Yours is the last one in the row against the wall." She looked Giulia up and down. "The twelve should fit you. Go ahead and change. Monica will be down in a few minutes."

"Thank you."

"You're welcome." Maryjane walked out, sensible shoes making no sound, tailored khaki slacks blending with the orchid resort-logo shirt.

Giulia took another look at the desk clerk's retreating figure. *She made those slacks. Impressive.*

The lockers were alphabetical too, except for the row of blank ones against the wall. She tried on the size-twelve beige uniform dress trimmed with white collar and cuffs. *Of course she knew it would fit me. She's a seamstress.*

She hung up her sweater and pants and stashed her purse in the top compartment. *Good thing I remembered to bring the combination lock from my gym bag. Also that I'm not too uptight to change in an open locker room. Which reminds me, I need to locate the bathroom.*

"Regina? Oh, good, the uniform fits. And you wore sneakers. And you brought your own lock? You're my favorite employee already." Monica, the head of housekeeping, appeared at Giulia's side. "We've got one checkout and one weeklong to clean. I'll work the first one with you. You've done this kind of work before, I understand?"

Monica walked them through another door that led into a break room with two round tables, a counter with sink and dish drainer, and a small refrigerator. Her beige uniform clung to her ample figure, unlike Giulia's, which had room to move in. Her black-as-ink bobbed hair swung side to side with every step.

"The rooms are in Snapdragon—that's the hotel alongside the parking lot."

They walked to the end of a short hall, wallpapered in retro-Victorian floral. Bathrooms on one side, doors marked *Maintenance* and *Electrical* on the other. Monica opened a third door after those, labeled *Utility.*

"There's a covered walkway between here and every building on the property: both hotels, the pool, the rec area, the auditorium, and the stable. The guests think we built it for them." She gave Giulia an elaborate wink. "But it's really for us. It's a lifesaver in bad weather. Here's the cart you'll be using."

She put a hand on one of two wheeled carts twice the size of the grocery store kind. "Towels in these drawers on the side, washcloths on top, hand towels in the middle, bath towels on the bottom." She opened each drawer. "Only emergency replacements, of course. The laundry staff stacks them on these shelves for us to take when we ready a room for a new guest."

Giulia put her hands on the other side of the cart, touching each item in the top compartments so she'd remember them. "Soap, miniature shampoo, conditioner, lotion. Stationery, pens, tea lights, matches, coffee, tea, sugar packets, powdered creamer, plastic stirrers." She met Monica's appraising gaze. "Where are the cleaning supplies?"

"Opposite side from the towels."

Giulia opened a deep drawer. "Oh good. Rubber gloves. The mild version of Lime-Away, too. Yay. I've used the industrial-strength version. It's nasty."

"Ready? Let's go." Monica backed out of the room, towing the cart. Giulia closed the door after them, wheeling an upright vacuum cleaner.

They wheeled the cart back down the hall and took a right at the bathrooms. This led them into a chilly glassed-in walkway. Snow covered the arched roof and drifted up the sides. Giulia shivered.

"I saw that." Monica smiled at her. "It's mostly psychological. The temp in here is about sixty-two."

Two women holding hands walked toward them. They smiled and said, "Merry Christmas." Monica responded.

When the women were out of earshot, Giulia said, "The owner doesn't mind if the staff talk to the guests?"

"Where have you worked before? Prison? Barbara likes it when the guests realize that the staff are people too." The hall opened into a standard hotel hall lined with doors. Monica opened room 133, and Giulia wheeled in the cart.

"You take the bathroom and I'll strip the beds. Supervisor privilege." She lowered her voice. "There's one unbreakable rule here. No casual sex between staff and guests at the Wildflower."

THIRTEEN

GIULIA KEPT HER FACE neutral. "I assure you that won't be a problem." *Don't laugh, Falcone. Don't even think about smiling.*

Monica patted her on the shoulder. "Good. Barbara doesn't mind if we hang out for a bit after our shift is over or even if we share a drink with the guests. Just remember that as far as bed-hopping is concerned, the staff are as celibate as nuns."

Giulia went into the bathroom and stuck her head into the shower, camouflaging herself by gathering up the used soap and shampoo bottles. *Don't have casual sex with the guests? Pretend I'm as celibate as a nun? Good Heavens. Frank is going to laugh till he chokes when I tell him that one.* Several deep breaths later, she had herself under control.

When she got a good look at the bathroom, the overpowering desire to transport it all to her apartment took over. Ivory-tile floor and walls, both with a wandering periwinkle pattern. Shell-shaped sink in the center of a five-foot-long vanity. Matching shower curtains and periwinkle-colored towels.

Work, Falcone. Don't lust after the interior decorating. You're supposed to be making a good impression your first day on the job.

She scrubbed the toilet, sink, and shower; wiped down the floor, set out new soaps, and replaced the miniature shampoo bottles. Monica inspected while Giulia hung fresh towels.

"Very nice. Good job on the floor. Don't forget to clean the mirror."

"Sorry." She sprayed it with cleaner and wiped it with the correct cloth.

"Let me show you the way we do sheets."

Together they made up the king-sized bed with standard hospital corners to the sheets and a lavender-scented blanket. Four pillows plumped into two duvets and a quilted bedspread with similar pattern to the bathroom tiles finished the bed. Giulia vacuumed; Monica straightened the couch cushions and opened the sliding door to the small balcony. The snow on it was trampled in an oval, just far enough for an arm to flick ashes into an ashtray on the small wrought-iron table out there. Giulia emptied the ashtray.

"Smoking is allowed only on these outside balconies." Monica closed the door on the weather. "No place else on the grounds, especially not near the childcare area."

"Childcare?" Giulia busied herself with the used sheets and towels.

"Did you know this used to be a family resort?" When Giulia nodded, Monica said, "When Barbara and her partner bought it, they wanted to keep that family-friendly atmosphere. So while they renamed the place and redecorated the hotels, they kept the childcare section as it was."

"Do they get a lot of couples with children?"

Monica rolled the sheets tighter while Giulia wrapped the cord around the vacuum. "In the summer, yes. The kids love the lake and camping out and all that back-to-nature stuff. Hardly any in the winter. They get antsy. Most families do, well, family stuff for the holidays. We run a wild Valentine's Day week, too—we discourage kids for that week." She gave the room a last check and closed the door. "Very good. It makes my job so much easier to have someone hit the ground running. I'm going to let you handle 137 on your own. If you run into anything you can't handle, call the front desk for help. Leave the sheets in the hall. I'll be back to check in twenty minutes."

Giulia set the rolled sheets on the floor outside 133's door, pushed the cart down the hall, and went back for the vacuum. Room 137's occupants hadn't been quite as neat. Wet, crumpled towels littered the bathroom floor. Makeup and lipstick smeared the buttercup-yellow hand towels and washcloths.

She scrubbed out the toilet with cleanser and tried to flush it. The handle fell off the tank into her hand.

"Fancy plumbing shouldn't break." She scowled at it, then set it on the top of the tank and headed for the phone on the nightstand.

The desk clerk answered on the second ring. "Maryjane, it's Regina in Snapdragon room 137. The toilet handle broke."

Maryjane huffed. "Again? Give me strength. I'll send my Phineas over to fix it."

Giulia stripped and remade the bed in the meantime, tossing used tissues and an empty tube of—she read it twice to make sure—arousal lubricant into the trash. *I guess I missed that issue of* Cosmo.

"Maintenance." A man's voice followed by heavy boots clomping into the bathroom.

Giulia followed. "Good afternoon. You're Maryjane's Phineas?"

"Yep. Married twenty years last June. Wasn't surprised when she called. This cursed handle breaks every other week." He worked a wrench with one hand and a pliers with the other. "I know I put in a requisition for a new fixture—" his wrench slipped.

Giulia waited for him to say something unprintable.

His nostrils flared, but he said nothing. He gripped the nut and turned the wrench. The handle followed the wrench, rotating till it was parallel to the floor. He jiggled it, then flushed. The toilet made all the correct sounds. He wiped a spot of oil on the tank with a rag. "No machine's ever beaten a McFarland. Not in the Navy, not at home, not on the job."

The wrench and pliers clanked into the toolbox. He looked up at Giulia. "You the new housekeeper?"

"Yes. Thanks for fixing the toilet."

"I could make it a recurring appointment on my calendar." He stood and spoke over his shoulder as he walked out. "Have to get back to the light display in the gazebo. Got an angel without wings."

Giulia scrubbed his bootprints off the floor before cleaning the sink. She slid him into a niche in her mental filing system as she wiped down the mirror. *Handy. Middle-aged. Gruff but friendly. Makes sense—resorts wouldn't hire curmudgeons.*

Monica reappeared as Giulia wound up the vacuum cord. "Let's see." She counted the towels, checked the soap and lotion, straightened the duvet, and checked the balcony. "You're hired forever. I see these two use that new lotion. You're lucky. The couple in the room I just cleaned had the most interesting trash. And by 'interesting' I mean I'm going to check my kids' Internet usage when I get home. There are websites for everything nowadays."

"I don't think I want to know." Giulia rolled up the sheets.

"Do you have kids? No? That's why there's no gray in your hair."

Two women wearing fluffy blue bathrobes stopped at the doorway and kissed. Then they walked into the room and kissed again.

"Hi."

"Excuse us."

"Are you done with the room? We just got out of the spa and need to shower."

"We didn't think we were messy enough to need two people to clean up after us."

Giulia had to smile at their giddy happiness. Monica explained about training the new staff.

"Oh, thanks."

"We really love it here. Everyone is so friendly."

"We sound silly, don't we? We have a reason, honest."

They kissed again.

"We're on our honeymoon."

"Congratulations," Giulia said.

"Thank you so much." The honeymooners hugged Giulia, then Monica, then each other again.

Monica said, "Did you tell Maryjane when you registered that this is your honeymoon? We provide a bottle of champagne for newlyweds."

The one on the left squealed. "This is the best vacation ever."

The one on the right hugged Monica. "We didn't know. You are all so awesome."

Monica imitated Giulia's grin. "I'll let the bartender know. He'll send it up after supper."

She took the vacuum, Giulia the cart. As Giulia closed the door, the newlyweds were kissing again.

"Someday I'd like to be that happy."

"You just gotta find the right man." Monica stopped dead. "I'm sorry. I mean, if you're into men."

Giulia grinned wider. "No worries. I'm into men."

Monica relaxed. "Every so often someone gets all self-righteous about presuming someone's sexuality. It's like saying 'Merry Christmas' and getting a lecture about how the whole country isn't Christo-centric."

"Or the other way around."

"Yeah. Spare me the crusading self-righteous. Okay. I'll take the sheets and you head upstairs. And 212 and 229 just need cleaning too. After that, bring the cart back to the closet and take a break. Fifteen minutes."

FOURTEEN

GOOD HEAVENS, THIS COFFEE is terrible. Giulia sipped it again. *More sugar won't help. I refuse to touch that powdered chemical pretending to be creamer. A good Catholic would offer it up.* She set down the cup and put a hand on the small of her back. *Working for Frank has made me soft. Cleaning out three rooms wouldn't have made me this sore in my convent days.*

"I know, I know, we have to be at your mother's by nine a.m. Christmas morning." A tall man in an open puffy ski jacket came in from the hallway. His boots clomped on the floor.

"She's not that bad. Come on. You got through it last year." A woman in yoga pants and a loose Wildflower logo sweatshirt followed on his heels.

"Look, I like your mother. She's a nice person." He held his hands over the steam from the coffeepot.

"But?" the woman said in a dangerous voice.

He rubbed his hands together. "This sludge is finally good for something. But I swear to you, babe, that if she nags us during another holiday dinner about having children, I will shove every dish off the table, throw you on it, and tell her we're going to try making one right now."

The woman laughed. "You are such an idiot. Mom would die of embarrassment. So would Aunt Louise."

"They'd get off our backs then. Christ, my hands are still freezing. I've got one last cross-country run to lead today, too."

"If my brother hadn't plowed into a telephone pole blind drunk on his graduation night at ninety miles an hour, they'd have another target to aim their guilt at." She took his hands between hers and rubbed them. "Stupid kid."

"Stop it." He kissed her forehead. "You know it makes you miserable. It's five years since he did that. And especially don't bring it up on Christmas."

"God, no. You want some of this swamp water before you head out?"

"Nope. Cleaned the skis already today." He let her zip up his jacket. "Early night tonight?"

"Yes, because I'm in at eight tomorrow to get ready for the wedding."

"Someday we'll open up our own wedding business with ski lessons and massages on the side."

Giulia snickered under her breath. She took a quick sip of coffee to cover it.

The ski instructor pulled on fleece-lined gloves. "Right. See you after the lesson." He went through the door to the outside.

"Up."

Giulia jumped and twisted around in her plastic chair. Now that she didn't have to pretend not to look, she saw that the masseuse was a taller, darker version of Sidney. Giulia envied the beautiful drape of her white yoga pants and sweatshirt.

"I'm sorry?"

"Up. Your back is a disgrace."

The woman tapped her foot, waiting. Giulia, bemused, stood and the woman's fingers worked her upper back like a piano.

"*Tsk*. You're carrying way too much tension in your shoulders." She ran her hands along Giulia's shoulder blades. "How often do you get headaches? Didn't anyone ever tell you about the connection between spine alignment and lower back tension and headaches?"

"No."

"My mother used to lecture me all the time about the evils of salt and sugar and red meat." She pressed her thumbs at several points on Giulia's spine. "I used to say I'd never turn into her. But I didn't have my masseuse license two months before I started lecturing people on proper alignment." She chuckled deep in her throat. "We all turn into our mothers, don't we?"

"We do."

The masseuse wrapped her arm around Giulia's collarbone and pushed. Giulia's back went *pop*. She stiffened. The masseuse tapped her shoulder. "Stop that. Relax." She repeated the hold-and-push four more times down Giulia's spine, generating four more *pop*s. She slid her hand down Giulia's spine one last time.

"Much better." She released her.

Giulia stretched, her back opening and relaxing in a way she'd never experienced. "I didn't know anything was wrong till you fixed it."

"I popped your adjustment cherry? Love it." She bent down toward Giulia's face. "Are you blushing?"

Giulia rubbed her cheeks.

The masseuse grinned. "You're in the wrong resort if you get embarrassed easily. Wait till a few of them get drunk and go skinny-dipping, then call the front desk because they forgot their towels."

"Nakedness doesn't bother me." *Shut up, conscience. That's not really a lie.*

"That's good." She went to the refrigerator and took out a Vita-min Water. "You're actually drinking that coffee? Brave woman."

"I'm headed to a Christmas dinner after this and I need the energy. It's not that bad ... for certain definitions of bad."

"I think it's fine, with sugar and creamer." Maryjane appeared, took a Nativity scene mug from the dish drainer, and poured coffee.

The masseuse's smile was less than genuine. "Happy Solstice, Maryjane. May the Goddess look with favor on your petitions."

Maryjane gave her a raised-eyebrow primmed-mouth smile. "May the Good News take hold of your heart and bring it to glory."

The masseuse winked at Giulia behind the desk clerk's back. "I'm always at a disadvantage in these fencing matches because my faith doesn't have a quotable holy book."

Maryjane stirred powdered creamer into her coffee. "Come to our church on Christmas, Penny. I promise you'll enjoy it."

"Only if you can convince my mother that Christmas is about church and not about family dinner, a boatload of presents, and nagging me to give her grandchildren before she's too old to appreciate them." She turned back to Giulia. "I ought to know the name of my conquest. I'm Penny."

Giulia laughed. "Regina. When I woke up today, I never thought I'd check another milestone off my life list."

"I'll tell my husband. He thinks the only people who need my magic are the ones who throw out their backs playing naked Twister." She capped the Vitamin Water and returned it to the fridge. "Nice to meet you. My hands are at your service whenever hauling that cleaning cart gets to you. Have a nice day, Maryjane."

When the masseuse left, the desk clerk sat at the table facing Giulia. "How are you holding up?"

"I'm getting back into the swing of it."

"You've done this kind of work before?" She sipped the thin, bitter coffee without a grimace.

"A few years ago. Laundry and all-around cleaning. My muscles got lazy in the interim." Giulia looked at the half-cup of coffee in front of her and decided against it.

"Well, Monica stopped by the desk a few minutes ago to say that you're perfect, so I think you'll fit in just fine."

"Thank you. I suppose my only disappointment is this beige uniform. I like bright colors."

"Neutrals are always a good choice. They match multiple skin tones and blend well. Look how well the lavender resort shirts go with my beige pants." Maryjane stood and gestured to her outfit.

Giulia shrugged. "Not my style. You made those pants, didn't you?"

Maryjane looked pleased. "I make all my clothes. Trousers today are cut much too low to look professional or modest."

Giulia thought of her low-rider jeans and how well they fit her gym-toned hips. *Shut up, Falcone. Don't offend people you're scop-*

ing out. She looked at the clock over the sink. "Yikes. Break's over. I have to get back to work now."

"Did Barbara tell you there's a wedding here tomorrow?" Maryjane followed her to the sink. "She'll be sure to ask you to put in extra hours."

"I just heard Penny talking about it. I have an early-morning job, too, but it shouldn't interfere." She set her cup in the drainer. "Sleep is for the weak, right?"

FIFTEEN

THE ENTRANCE LIGHT ON Giulia's apartment building's front stoop flickered and snapped. *Again? Come on, landlord. I know you've got three bucks for a new bulb. This neighborhood's not as bad as the last place I lived, but only an idiot would think it's safe to walk here unprepared.* She kept her gym bag on her shoulder as she climbed the five steps, looking on all sides to confirm she was alone. *It's a good thing my gym bag is a decent weapon on its own post-workout. The sneakers and combination lock give it some heft.*

She unlocked the door and right away pushed it closed, listening for the *click* as the lock re-engaged. Her mailbox opened with its usual nails-on-chalkboard screech. Since it was empty again, the screech echoed good and loud in the shoebox-sized vestibule.

Sometimes I feel like Charlie Brown, opening the mailbox on Christmas and Valentine's Day with irrepressible hope, and always disappointed. She closed the mailbox. *At least there are still a few days left before Christmas.*

Her phone played the first bars of *Eine Kleine Nachtmusik*. She pulled off her gloves to answer it, her hands registering an instant protest to the unheated vestibule.

"Yes, Frank?"

"You're not dressed yet, are you? I forgot to ask if you have something Christmassy to wear."

She opened the inner door and shivered in the sudden warmth. "Yes, I think so …" She mentally paged through her closet and drawers. "Yes, I do."

"Great. Can you wear it?"

She walked down the hall through aromas from different dinners seeping from under various doors. "Sure. I didn't realize your family was that fancy."

"No, no, you don't have to be intimidated. Mom's really into Christmas, that's all."

She dropped her gym bag and fit her key into the lock. "I'm just walking into my apartment now. Are you picking me up early or something?"

"No, still seven o'clock."

She got an eyeful of the kitchen clock. "That's only half an hour. Bye." Her hip bumped the door closed and she threw the deadbolt home. She set the phone on the kitchen table and slid the gym bag into the bathroom. Her snow-damp hair raised goosebumps on her neck as she tossed her coat next to the phone.

"Heat for fifteen minutes, so I don't catch pneumonia." She turned the thermostat dial to sixty-five. A minute later, dust-flavored air pushed into the rooms.

Clothes first. She pushed her work clothes to one side of the closet and pulled out her prized consignment shop discovery: a

crimson velvet skirt and faux-silk ivory blouse. Last year the only Christmas activity she'd participated in was the soup kitchen after-hours cake feast, and her party clothes had gathered dust.

Not this year. She ran into the living room to punch up the soundtrack to *A Charlie Brown Christmas*. She stripped off her sweater as she ran back; her black trousers followed it onto the bed. Her one pair of not-too-high heels came out of their box still polished—hooray.

Makeup. She headed for the bathroom, singing along with the CD. Dinner with Frank's parents required the whole shebang. Before she opened the plastic shoebox that held her going-out makeup, she shook out her gym towel and hung it over the shower curtain rod.

"Nothing sultry, not to meet Frank's parents. No eye shadow at all, I think. I'm still not an expert at too much versus not enough."

She applied the basics, then added mascara. While that settled, she returned to the less-chilled bedroom and stared at herself in her everyday underwear.

"Nondescript. That's what Captain Jimmy said." The word made her think of gray days, flat landscapes, cafeteria food. But she didn't want to switch to one of her lacy silk sets to counter the image. Like the eye shadow, they weren't what to wear to dinner with the parents.

Frank's Irish Catholic *parents. What if they're horrified because I'm no longer a nun?*

The digital clock on the nightstand read 6:46.

"Stop thinking about what you can't change and get dressed, dummy." She worked into pantyhose—*ridiculous things*—and but-

toned the blouse. The skirt came with a lining, and a moment later she was 95 percent ready.

"Lipstick." She borrowed a trick from the actors at Cottonwood's Marquee Theater and dusted her lips with powder when she dusted the rest of her makeup. "There. Not too nondescript."

Between the bathroom and the bedroom it came to her: *If relative strangers think I blend in, I can keep using this unwelcome attribute plus that lovely beige uniform to my advantage at the resort.* The vague sadness that had glued itself to her shoulders slid off. Katie mattered. Whatever it took to get Katie back, and Giulia Falcone's self-image would be sacrificed gladly on the altar of Whatever It Took.

She knotted a glittery silver lace scarf just below her left shoulder and chose crystal angel earrings because they were too short to catch on the scarf.

"Gotta change my purse. Argh—no time—at least it's black. Where's a shoe bag for these heels—"

The doorbell rang.

"Forget it. I'll carry them." She turned off the bedroom lights, yelled "Coming," grabbed her phone, and skated on the linoleum to the door.

"Hey, Frank. Come in for a second. I just have to shut off the CD."

He took her by the waist and pulled her close. "You look beautiful."

She let herself become still in his arms, the warmth of his compliment spreading through her. Her eyes closed when he kissed her—that is, until Old Man Krieger wolf-whistled from across the hall.

Giulia jumped backward. Krieger's shaggy-bearded head appeared leaning against his own apartment door, eternal bottle of St. Pauli Girl in hand.

"Good evening, Mr. Krieger." Giulia closed the door.

Frank was laughing. "You get stuck with the nosiest neighbors."

She stuck out the tip of her tongue. "He'll lurk for the next week hoping to see something else."

"I volunteer to kiss you with the door open every night."

What switch did you flip to go from all-work to all-boyfriend, Frank? "Thank you, no. I'm not Krieger's personal entertainment. Or yours."

"Spoilsport. Come on, before the car gets cold."

Giulia turned off the CD and got into her coat. *I do prefer this Frank, although I'm not sure how we'd conduct business Monday through Friday.* "All set." She picked up her purse and shoes.

"It's only ten minutes to my folks' house." Frank talked faster than usual as they walked down the hall. "Mom and Dad are really Catholic, but they won't badger you about the convent. Grandma's the one who'll ask you for insider stories."

"Shall we tell her about my old nemesis, Sister Mary Stephen, fondling my lacy underthings on my October trip in the Wayback Machine?"

He held open the vestibule door, then the outside door before he answered. "Grandma would love it. My brother Pat would, too."

"He's been the soul of patience with Sidney's RCIA classes." She got into the passenger side of Frank's Camry. When Frank had buckled himself in, she added, "I plan to thank him profusely at Sidney's wedding. He must have the gift of making the Catechism interesting, because Sidney has learned heaps of it in record time."

"He uses that gift against me when we argue dogma." Frank pulled into traffic.

"Wait. You said, 'Grandma.' I thought you said this was dinner with your parents."

He turned onto Oak. "My grandparents live there, too. Mom's father and Dad's mother. Sorry. I'm so used to them being there that I automatically include them in 'dinner with the folks.' It's a big house."

Giulia tapped her feet on the car mat. *Okay. Parents and grandparents. I can handle this. Grandparents are usually indulgent, and Frank's the youngest. In a perfect world, the indulgence will extend to the youngest's date … um … girlfriend … um …*

"Am I being introduced as your partner or as your date?"

The light changed. The car was halfway down Walnut before he answered. "I've told them about you. They know you used to be my admin and now you're my partner-in-training."

That answered that. "Fine. Just want to know where I stand."

They turned onto Crabapple. Houses lined both sides of the street: multi-storied, graceful, and all at least a hundred years old. Christmas lights glowed on most of them, perfect outlines of ice-white or many colors, smaller trees blending in with every sign of excellent decorating taste. As they drove past, Giulia saw huge Christmas trees in many windows, lights on their branches appearing just as symmetrical as the ones outlining the houses.

"I'm not dressed up enough."

"Of course you are." His voice sounded distracted as his head turned from one side of the street to the other. "That spot's too small. There's one—damn. A fire hydrant."

"Someone's hosting their annual Christmas party." Giulia pointed two spots up and left. "There?"

"Excellent." He parallel parked in three efficient moves.

"That was impressive."

He shrugged. "Years of city driving."

They walked back toward a wide, two-story brick Colonial with three cars in its narrow driveway. An ornament-studded wreath took up half the front door; a Father Christmas with a sack over his shoulder smiled at them from the front porch.

Frank rang the doorbell. It was flung open by a broad-shouldered silhouette as soon as his finger left it.

"Frank! It's about time."

"Nobody left me a spot, as usual, Sean. Let us in."

"Ma! Frank's here." Sean stepped aside. "Everyone's been dying to meet your partner."

Giulia looked up from the boot mat, one boot still on. An older man and woman who looked enough like Frank to be his parents waited in the room beyond. Behind them, at least a dozen more people talked or sipped drinks. Two grade-school-sized children chased each other up garlanded stairs. One of the Mannheim Steamroller Christmas CDs played loud enough to mask the conversations.

The woman stepped forward. "Sean, let the poor girl get her shoes on. Welcome to the Annual Driscoll Christmas Chaos Party, my dear."

SIXTEEN

Giulia shot her Teacher's Glare of Death at Frank. "I'm going to kill you," she whispered.

His grin became a fraction less cocky, but only for a moment. "Would you have come if I'd told you the truth?"

"Of course not. It'd be like I'm on display. I hate that." She slipped on her right shoe. "Oh, yeah—just like I am now."

Frank took her coat. "Stop whining. Take it like a man."

"The hearts of men are deceitful above all things, and desperately wicked. As illustrated by the man standing in front of me this moment."

Sean yelled into the room, "Frank's girl just quoted the Bible to trash-talk him."

Several voices laughed, "Woot!" "Serves you right, Frank!" "You tell him!"

The older woman gave Sean a gentle push. "Get out of the way, firstborn, or I shall dote on my youngest in front of your face all evening."

"Aw. Ma." Sean retreated to the living room.

"I'm Fiona, and you're Giulia. We've heard so much about you from Frank. Frank, why haven't you taken Giulia's coat and purse?"

"I'm on it, Ma, soon as I get out of my overshoes." Frank helped Giulia off with her coat and took her purse. "Master bedroom?"

"Yes, dear. Come in and meet everyone, Giulia."

Frank deserted her and Giulia went into the gauntlet with a smile. Fiona—tall, graceful, silver bob framing a still-freckled face—smiled back at Giulia.

My mother used to smile at me like that right before grade-school dance recitals. Half of the massive weight of intimidation fell away from Giulia.

"Did Frank ambush you into coming to this party?" Fiona sent a formidable glare upstairs in Frank's direction.

"He said it was dinner with his parents."

"Brat. I will chastise him for you. Don't worry; no one bites, except my youngest grandchild, but we have teething rings at the ready." She took Giulia's arm and led her around the crowded living room. "You've already met Sean, and this is his wife, Tina."

Sean resembled a blond linebacker whose name Giulia couldn't remember. His wife, a foot shorter, had skin the color of Sidney's, and she was quite pregnant.

"Pleased to meet you, and I hope you're not one of those people who touch pregnant women's bellies."

"Tina!" Sean poked her.

Tina's smile became forced. "Sorry. Sean's office party happened today, and only our need for health insurance kept me from stabbing half the women there."

Giulia infused extra warmth into her smile. "I could steal one of my old habits for you to wear. People would give a supposedly pregnant nun a wide berth."

Sean guffawed and Tina laughed. "God, that would be hysterical. I wish we'd met two days ago."

Fiona steered Giulia toward a group of four next to a mantelpiece supporting a miniature Irish village decorated for Christmas. "You're the first person to get her to smile tonight. She's had a dreadful pregnancy—twins, and she's borderline diabetic." She raised her voice over "God Rest Ye Merry, Gentlemen." "Patrick, Michael, Darlene, this is Giulia. The one who keeps trying to eat my ceramic village is Helen." She tickled the baby's tummy, causing a giggle eruption.

Giulia held out her hand to Father Patrick. "Finally."

He shook it. "Always happy to welcome a fellow Franciscan into the family."

Giulia lost her grip on Patrick's hand. *What? What has Frank led them to believe about us?*

"Pat, you're going to give her a heart attack." Frank appeared on Giulia's other side. "He's been trying to marry me off for years. Thinks it's a blot on his priestly reputation that he hasn't officiated at every Driscoll wedding."

Father Pat released Giulia's hand. "Sorry. I didn't mean anything more than friendship. Sidney raves about your clear way of explaining abstruse points in the Catechism for her."

Giulia's heart rate returned to near-normal. "She says the same thing about you."

He chuckled. "Between the two of us, we'll get her through the RCIA program by Easter."

Michael saluted Giulia with a glass half-full of amber liquid and ice. "Nice to meet you."

Red-headed Darlene carried herself like an athlete and could have been Michael's twin. She shifted the baby to her shoulder and hugged Giulia. "I remember my first Driscoll party. You'll stop feeling overwhelmed soon, I promise."

"Thanks." Giulia felt instant camaraderie with her. "It's kind of intimidating."

Fiona tickled the baby again. "There will be no quiz at the end of the evening; don't worry."

"Mom! Mom! Joey spit at me!" A miniature Darlene shoved into the circle, one finger locked onto a wet circle in her green velvet party dress.

"Tattletale!" A blond, freckled ten-year-old pushed in next to her. "Mom, Gwen said you were taking her ice skating tomorrow and I couldn't go! Then she said I was a brat and that's why you're not taking me!"

Darlene cuffed Gwen—lightly—on her curled updo. "Serves you right. You'll wash that dress by hand tomorrow morning, miss." She stared down at Joey. "And you know very well why you're not coming. Shiro's birthday party is tomorrow, remember?"

Joey's air of wounded innocence vanished. "Oh, yeah. Duh. We're playing laser tag tomorrow and you're not invited. Neener!" He ran away, grabbing the arm of a tall boy with Clark Kent glasses, and they both pelted upstairs.

"Our other offspring," Darlene said. "Christmas is such a calm season for kids, isn't it?"

Giulia smiled. "I used to be a teacher. The entire month of December was torture for them and us."

Michael said, "Excellent. Next time they misbehave, can we threaten them with quizzes in—what did you teach?"

"English, Religion, and Sex Ed."

His eyes widened. "That'd scare 'em straight. Dar, make sure we tell those two that Frank's girl is a teacher and she's got standing orders from Sister Maureen to quiz them whenever she wants."

Giulia grinned. "I'll be sure to look severe whenever you give me the signal. You can put a ruler by my place at the table if you'd like."

Darlene nuzzled the baby. "Perfect! I'll go find one. Fiona, where's Giulia sitting?"

"Four seats from the end nearest the credenza on the right."

"Got it." She headed into the hall.

Fiona looked around. "Where's Danny?"

"Eva dragged him into the kitchen to check the stuffed mushrooms, last I saw," Michael said.

"Ew, mushrooms."

Giulia looked down. A dark-haired boy built for football was appraising her and Frank. He stared at Giulia's midsection for a moment.

"Are you going to have a baby?"

Giulia's mouth fell open.

Fiona gasped. "Joshua Anselm Driscoll, you apologize this minute!"

Michael put his head on the mantelpiece and laughed so hard, the fake snow on it scattered all over the hearth.

Joshua looked genuinely puzzled. "But my friend's sister has a boyfriend and my friend said his sister's gonna have a baby." He put both hands on Giulia's stomach. "It must be a pretty small baby."

Fiona took him by one arm. "I beg your pardon, Giulia. Josh, we are going to find your father."

Frank didn't laugh until Fiona marched Josh out of the room. "Christ preserve us. If he's like this when he's nine, he'll be a terror when he hits puberty."

Michael's entire body still shook with laughter. Pat pounded his back till he slowed down. He un-propped himself from the mantel and turned, his face tomato-red. "That was even better than the first time Colin—he's our oldest, Giulia—met Tina. His first words to her were, 'It's about time we got some color in this pasty-white family.'"

Giulia tried to stifle her laughter, but it burst through her covering hands. "How old was he? Was he able to sit down for the rest of the day?"

"He was eleven and considered himself the family comedian. Tina thought he was cute, thank God."

"I thought Josh was funny, too. However, I guess I need to hit the gym more often," Giulia said.

A short, dark, plump woman stalked over to the group. "You do not. I'd kill for your figure. You have boobs that don't take a back seat to your butt." She shook her head, rattling her dangly snowman earrings. "I'd like to apologize for my son, who will be apologizing in person when his father finishes swatting his backside. I'm Eva."

Giulia hugged her. "Please don't worry about it. I used to be a teacher. I know the age where their mouths move faster than their brains."

"You are so sweet. Frank, keep this one, please." She turned her head toward the hall. "I believe I hear repentant footsteps."

Another Driscoll—Giulia could have picked them out anywhere now, despite slight differences in hair color and muscle mass—entered the room, leading a sniffling Josh toward the mantelpiece.

"I'm"—sniff—"sorry I was rude, Miss Falcone." He wiped the back of his hand under his nose.

"I accept your apology." Giulia held out her hand.

Josh looked at it, then up at her before he shook her hand in a half-child, half-adult way.

"All right, get out of here," his father said.

Josh dashed upstairs.

"So much for teaching them manners. I'm Danny. Nice to meet you, and sorry about the Blurter's mouth."

Giulia smiled. "Nice to meet you. Please don't worry. It's better than being called 'nondescript' by a well-meaning adult."

Eva boggled. "Don't tell me Frank said that?"

"No, someone else entirely."

"Good. Glad to see his eyes are working. You are the furthest thing from nondescript. Your hair, your smile, the way you carry yourself. I think you'd stand out in any crowd."

Danny patted Eva's rump. "Babe, Giulia's good-looking, but you are gorgeous. No offense, Giulia."

"None taken." Eva's compliments didn't reassure her. *If a complete stranger thinks my looks are easy to remember, then I can't stay undercover looking like this. What if the kidnappers saw me at the soup kitchen while they were tracking Laurel and Anya's movements?*

SEVENTEEN

An hour later, everyone was just about done with a dinner that would've made both of Giulia's grandmothers proud. Baby Helen chose that moment to make a six-month-old's version of the raspberry with her mouthful of mashed potatoes. Giulia helped Darlene clean it up.

Frank's family is almost as easy to fall in love with as Frank is. Oh, no, I just put together "love" and "Frank" in the same sentence. I have to be careful, or I'll let this warm, loving group of people seduce the sensible right out from under me.

Eva and Daniel started to gather plates. Giulia stacked the plates on her end of the table, glad when Fiona didn't protest at her helping with the work. *Then again, it's another symptom of how accepting they are—and how easily I'm fitting in here. Should I be worried?*

"Giulia, could you keep an eye on Helen while I help with clean-up?" Darlene wiped a stray dot of mashed potato from the baby's face.

"Sure."

Darlene lifted Helen out of the highchair and handed her over. "Here, use this napkin for a burp cloth. You never know. And watch out for your earrings. She's into shiny things."

Helen was warm and cuddly. She clung to Giulia's left arm and looked over her shoulder, cooing at everyone. Giulia stood to get them both out of the way of the cleaning crew. She walked her into the living room, singing to the carols playing from the iDock under the tree. Helen grabbed Giulia's nose, and Giulia laughed and kissed the plump little hand.

"Darlene soft-soap you into babysitting?" Frank tickled Helen's chin.

"She's adorable. I used to help my sister-in-law with her kids when I got vacation. They loved to pull off my veil at this age." *And the Pope will approve the Pill before my brother will let them see me again.*

"Why the frown?"

Giulia shook it off. "Sorry. Just thinking of my family. Holidays are the worst for that kind of memory."

"I forgot your family's got their collective heads up their asses." Giulia snorted.

"Ha. Made you laugh." He walked over to the iDock and scrolled through the songs. "You like Nat King Cole?"

"Of course." She blew a raspberry into Helen's belly button and Helen giggled. It sounded so good, Giulia did it again. More giggles.

"Caroling, Caroling" began. Giulia sang it to Helen, and Frank joined in from his spot by the tree. When she glanced over at him, he was still squatting next to the player, an odd look on his face as he watched her.

Sean entered the room. "For the love of God, Frank, stop singing. You'll make the baby cry."

"*Go n-ithe an cat thú, is go n-ithe an diabhal an cat,*" Frank said without heat.

A loud noise from Helen's diaper punctuated the Irish sentence. Frank laughed.

Sean turned on the old people still at the table. "Granddad, what did you teach Frank that you didn't teach the rest of us?"

The Driscolls' grandfather gave Frank a thumbs-up.

His mother-in-law poked him. "You're going to burn in Hell."

"That's where the party will be. Sean, that means 'May the cat eat you, and may the devil eat the cat.' Francis, your accent is slipping."

"I'll work on it, Granddad."

Darlene came three feet into the room and stopped dead. "Whoa! The little princess left me an early Christmas present." She scooped up the baby by her armpits. "That's one full diaper, there, missy. Let's go. Thanks for watching her."

"Caroling, Caroling" finished, and "The Christmas Waltz" began. Frank tapped Giulia on the shoulder and the next moment they were waltzing on the gold-and-white carpet.

"You're quite smooth, Mr. Astaire," Giulia said in Frank's ear.

"Taught by my grandmother over there, who won dance competitions in her wild youth." Frank pulled her closer. "You're about to drop a broad hint about babies and hope and how can I look at Helen and even think about giving up on finding Katie, aren't you?"

Giulia turned her face into his shoulder. "Curse you, Frank Driscoll. When did I become so easy to read?"

"Only on certain subjects. Now that that's out of the way, allow me to tell you again how beautiful you look tonight." He twirled her around the carpet exactly in time to the easy pulse of the song.

"Thank you. I'm glad your Grinch tie doesn't play music."

The song ended. Giulia felt a pang of disappointment—dancing with Frank was a pleasure she wanted to continue as long as possible. Until he kissed her.

His kiss was as slow and intimate as the dance. His arms wrapped around her waist and hers curled around his neck. Warmth filled her, making her knees just a little trembly.

Several loud whistles interrupted them. Together they looked in the direction of the noise. Every Driscoll adult stood in the doorway, applauding and whistling some more.

Giulia knew her face matched the red velvet of her skirt.

"Hide the kids, Eva," Tina said.

"No, no, bring 'em in here," Daniel said. "They can learn something."

"Pervert," Eva said.

Fiona pushed through the crowd. "Dad, what are you teaching Frank now?"

Sean said, "Don't blame Granddad for that kiss. Frank took the initiative for this display himself."

Frank got in Sean's face. "Don't embarrass Giulia."

"Hey, you were the—" He looked twice at Frank and raised his eyebrows. "No problem, little brother."

Fiona raised her voice. "Robert! Did you find the cards yet?"

"Coming." The Driscoll boys' father sounded like he was in a closet.

"Pat, would you see if anyone needs a drink?" Fiona came over to Giulia. "We play darts and Twenty-five before dessert."

Giulia's face returned to its normal color now that everyone wasn't staring at her. "I've played competitive darts, but not Twenty-five."

"I'll teach you Twenty-five before my children get too many whiskies in them. The play gets a little wild then."

"Ma! Ma! Uncle Pat says Gwen and me can play darts this year 'cause we're finally eleven years old!" Ben ran into the room behind Pat, Gwen on his heels.

"Thanks, Pat," Michael and Daniel said in unison. "You can repair Ma's wallpaper when these two miss the board."

Pat grinned. "I told Ma that any repairs were part of your Christmas present to her."

"You're a bad priest, Father Patrick, and you'll come to a nasty end."

"On the contrary, I'm dutiful to my mother and small children love me. That makes me quite Jesus-like."

Giulia and Fiona laughed. The kids looked puzzled.

Daniel said, "Ben, where are Colin and Josh?"

"Downstairs. Josh challenged Colin to a Guitar Hero battle. Colin says he's going to make Josh beg for mercy."

"Good. Less jockeying for position. Wait—" He looked around. "We're missing Joey."

Darlene returned with a much better-smelling Helen. "He's rehearsing his song for the school play tomorrow night. I promised to call him for dessert and carols."

The chaos in the room broke into smaller clumps.

"Ha! Ten points. You're gonna lose lose lose, Gwenny!"

"Let me cut those cards, Mike."

"Don't you trust me?"

"Double ten, hah to you!"

Frank resumed his seat next to Giulia. "All right, Falcone, prepare for a smackdown."

Giulia smiled sweetly at Frank. "Did you ever wonder what nuns do on long winter nights after prayers and before bed?"

"Uh…"

"Get your mind out of the gutter. We played cards." Giulia cracked her knuckles. "Ready?"

EIGHTEEN

"I LOVE YOUR FAMILY," Giulia said in the car on the way back to her apartment.

"Mom let me know that you have the Matriarch Seal of Approval."

She laughed. "Why?"

"Because you're charming and polite and good with kids and can beat me at cards." He paid attention to the road for a minute. "Also, let's just say the last two women I brought home were not exactly the right choices."

"I gathered that when your nieces and nephews interrogated me."

"Christ above, I wanted to strangle those brats."

She laughed again. It was past eleven and she was tired and comfortably full from dinner. She was glad the roads required attention; otherwise she'd have been tempted to snuggle against Frank. And after an evening of warmth and family, her common sense was snoring under a fluffy blanket of "belonging again." *I'm still not ready to make a commitment to Frank. Tonight would be a dangerous time to make such a decision. We're both all Christmased-up.* She snugged her alpaca-wool gloves—bought from Sidney's family store—tighter on her fingers. *I wonder if I'm technically on the rebound from my ten-year marriage—my divorce from Jesus came through less than two years ago.*

She snickered under her breath.

"What's so funny?"

Oops. "Nothing. It's silly."

He turned onto her street. "You are stuffy, spiritual, strict, and sometimes funny, but I can state with confidence that you are never silly."

"That's not a desirable catalogue of attractions."

"Depends on your point of view." He pulled into her parking lot and idled the car.

She gave him a sly smile. "That's a broad hint, Mr. Driscoll. Come see me safe inside, please."

"I'd be happy to." He turned off the ignition.

She didn't wait for him to open the door for her. Regardless of his chivalric training, she was too used to doing everything for herself. She did let him take her arm without even the excuse to herself that he was steadying her across the icy parking lot.

The thin hall carpet muffled their booted feet, giving Old Man Krieger across the hall no excuse to play voyeur. To add to the lovely feeling of privacy, Giulia knew how to open and close a door in near-silence.

"Why do you keep this place so cold?"

"It's set at sixty-five. If this were spring or fall, you'd call it balmy." She flicked on the light and turned the thermostat up to sixty-eight. "It'll warm up soon. Would you like coffee?"

He unbuttoned his coat. "No thanks. I'm stuffed to the gills."

"Me too. Come sit on the couch. I'll find you an afghan and light the tree."

Eine Kleine Nachtmusik, muffled, sounded from her purse.

"Who could be calling at this hour?" *And why are they interrupting potential snogging time?* "Hello?"

"Giulia, they called us. They're sick, twisted, evil people." Laurel's voice came thick and broken, the voice of someone after a long crying jag.

"What? Wait a sec. I'm going to put you on speaker." She beckoned Frank over and set the phone on the kitchen table. "All right, go ahead. Frank's here, too."

Anya this time, angry rather than weepy: "A woman called a few minutes ago. She whispered, so we didn't recognize her voice. We record everything now. Listen."

The sound of a tape recorder rewinding, and then an eerie, half-human voice: "She is so precious. We're going to name her Pearl, because she is our pearl of great price." The voice stopped and the sound of a kiss came through, and steady breathing. "She's asleep, the little angel. You'll never come up with the money. We know. We know everything about you. He's playing with you. He's good at that. He likes games."

Laurel's voice: "Don't hurt her. Please. We're getting the money. We promise. We'll have it all for you, if you can just give us a little more time."

A whispery laugh. "That's exactly what I expected to hear. Bargaining, like Judas bargained for the money to betray his Lord. I hope you writhe in agony every time you think of us with our precious Pearl. It's exactly what you deserve."

A door slammed on the tape, far away from the whispering female, and a distant male voice said, "It's me." Then tape hiss.

Anya said, "I'll kill her."

Giulia didn't try to sound soothing. "She's messing with your heads, that's all, trying to spook you."

"It worked. That bitch has our baby and we have no idea where or who or how to find her." Anya's voice rose at the end of each phrase. "You said you'd help us."

"I will. We will. How much have you raised?"

"Three hundred thousand and change. We have an appointment at our bank for nine tomorrow morning."

"Don't erase that tape. Captain Reilly will want to hear it on Thursday when we meet at your house for the ransom-instruction phone call."

"He can't trace the call though, can he? I checked our call history on the phone and then went online to see if I could find any more information. Nothing. The number wasn't local."

"It's most likely a disposable phone," Giulia said.

"God, I want to dismember these people like my father used to gut deer," Laurel said in the same stuffed-up voice. "You tell your Captain Reilly that I hope he treats this as though it were one of his own children in the hands of that psychotic bitch."

"Laurel, we're on it. I promise. Anya, did you hear that? I promise."

"I heard you. I'm sorry. I don't mean to take this out on you."

"Don't worry about it. Don't keep playing that tape. Just go to bed. Take a sleeping pill if you have to."

"I bought some today." Her voice was grudging. "It goes against everything I teach my students."

"Some situations call for exceptions to the rules." Giulia took a deep breath. "I'll call you if we learn something, but don't be surprised if you don't hear from me till I show up at your house on Thursday morning for the ransom call."

Anya laughed, a drained sound. "The only surprises I ever want in my life again are when Katie brings home a pet snake or something equally . . . Shit."

"I know," Giulia said. "Get some sleep, please."

"Better sleep through chemicals. Hooray."

Three *beep*s and silence. Giulia pressed the *End* button. "Games."

Frank looked at her. "What?"

"Games. She said, 'He likes games.' Resorts have people who organize games and activities."

"Sounds a little obvious."

"You never know. She also sounds like she was disobeying the mastermind with that phone call, since she hung up when we heard his voice. So she could've been so eager to gloat that she let her guard down."

Frank pinched the bridge of his nose. "We'll see what the papers from Jimmy have to say. Maybe it'll be obvious."

"No objection from me. I wish I was alert enough to analyze things tonight." A shiver fluttered along her spine. "You're having a deleterious effect on me. Now I think it's cold in here."

"Good. You mentioned something about an afghan?"

Five minutes later the tree was twinkling and Nat King Cole played softly through the speakers. They curled together on the couch under her yellow-and-white seashell afghan.

"Now this is a potentially compromising position," Giulia said, and yawned. "I can't even blame it on the booze. All I had was a glass of wine with dinner."

He kissed the back of her neck. "Thanks for inviting me in."

"Mmm." Too tired to open her mouth, she snuggled against Frank as his arm came around her waist.

Nat King Cole sang "The Christmas Song" as she drifted off to sleep.

∽

Beep-beep-beep-beep. Beep-beep-beep-beep. Beep-beep-beep-beep.

Giulia reached out to hit the alarm's *Off* button. *Why did I turn down the volume?* Her hand slapped the nightstand. The alarm kept beeping. She opened her eyes.

Coffee table. Not nightstand. *I'm staring at the coffee table.*

A loud snore tickled her ear. She jumped.

Party. Frank. Afghan. Couch.

She sat up. The apartment was freezing.

She clutched the afghan with one hand and shook Frank with the other.

"Frank! Wake up!"

"Mmm?"

She bent closer. "Frank, wake up."

He felt for the back of her head, pulled her on top of him again, and kissed her. "Morning." He waggled his eyebrows. "Nice skin."

She pulled away. "Frank. It's six thirty. We have to get to work."

His eyes roamed the room. "Did we sleep all night on the couch?"

"Yes. I have to catch the bus in forty minutes. How fast can you shower?"

"Not that fast. You don't have any clothes I can wear, anyway. Unless you have a secret lover I'm unaware of."

She scowled at him. "Hello? Still a virgin at thirty, remember?"

"Someday I hope to change that." He sat up. "Holy God, it's freezing. Forget the bus. You've got a rental car, remember? I'll make coffee if you turn up the heat."

"Your bargaining savvy has won me over. I'm going to turn off that alarm before I heave it through the window."

She padded to the thermostat. A shiver pattered down her spine. She ran into her bedroom and slapped the clock, cutting off that grating *beep-beep-beep-beep* in mid-beep.

Frank was right behind her when she turned around.

"Did you hear what I said just now? Damn, woman, you do crazy things to me." He wrapped his arms around her and kissed her neck. "This is what months of enforced celibacy will do to a healthy male."

"Who forced celibacy on you?"

"You did."

NINETEEN

GIULIA'S MOUTH DROPPED OPEN. "I—what?"

Frank looked "Wake up" at her. "After we took down the Falkes, remember? They tried to do some sick stuff to you and it freaked you out."

"I'm not likely to forget getting stripped naked and threatened with rape and murder."

He put a hand on her arm. "Stop. You know they're out of the way now. My point is that afterwards, in my car, you agreed that I might have a chance with you."

She pictured that June evening, staring at Frank's dashboard, trying to remember who she'd been before the psychotic Falkes had played their games with her and DI's client. And then Frank's odd, unexpected declaration that nothing the Falkes tried to do to her meant anything to him. And shouldn't mean anything to her.

Her voice softened. "I remember."

"So you're the reason I've been celibate. Not that I ever tom-catted around; don't worry. I've only slept with three women, and none of them were tomcatters either." He paused. "I don't think that word is appropriate for women."

"*Promiscuous* is a better choice." She turned around in his embrace, facing him. "Why are you telling me your sexual history?"

"Full disclosure. You're not shocked?"

She sighed. "I taught high-school sex ed. Not much shocks me. Did you forget that I read *Cosmo?* It leaves little to the imagination."

"I may revise my opinion of that magazine again." He stopped talking to the ceiling and looked right at her. "I don't date more than one woman at a time. When I said I wanted to pursue you, that meant you, exclusively." He looked over her shoulder. "It's twenty to seven. Tell me where the coffee is and I'll make some while you shower."

⤜⤛

After Frank left, Giulia drove the four blocks from her apartment to Saint Thomas church. In a car. A clean, dry, warm car. That didn't smell like armpits.

"That's it. I'm buying that used car the Monday after Christmas. This is Heaven on earth. I am not giving this up."

Only three other cars were in the narrow parking lot, and the little Escort maneuvered into a salted space without a hitch. The wind hit her when she stepped onto the asphalt. She wrapped her candy cane–striped scarf around the bottom of her face and headed for the front doors: the church's red-tiled spire was the only roof on either side of the street not decorated with three-foot icicles.

"Gotta love those roof ice-melters. Can't have the faithful entering the church door in fear and trembling of imminent death." She paused at the end of the walkway. "Although that'd make a great sermon illustration."

Giulia was sole occupant of the steps this early on a Wednesday. The lingering blackness of the sky might have had something to do with it. Or the wind that picked up the latest snow crusts and flung them like sharpened fingernails at her face. Or the greedy winter that reminded her too much of the unseasonal cold snap back in October, around Saint Francis Day.

The shivers clawing at her spine as she pushed against the wind weren't just from the weather. The four days she'd spent in her old Motherhouse back in October had rebooted all her convent nightmares.

"Stop griping, Falcone. Taking down Father Ray the scumbag drug dealer and Sister Fabian his accomplice was worth these sleepless nights, and you know it."

Besides, she'd been slacking off ever since she'd jumped the wall. Back in the convent, six hours of sleep was the norm. Some cloistered Orders still kept up the ancient tradition of praying the Canonical Hours, and that included two a.m. Cut the six to five and a quarter.

"I was never cut out for the cloister." She brushed snow off her eyelashes. "Or the convent. That last stint proved it. Time to get over myself."

She climbed the steps to the front doors of Saint Thomas, passing the statue that most of the time was of Saint Thomas kneeling before the resurrected Christ. Under its new load of snow, it looked more like a polar bear in front of a sasquatch.

The wind gave her an unnecessary hand with the double doors, but it failed before the strength gained in her four-days-a-week gym schedule. The *slam* as they closed echoed even through her earmuffs.

She stamped her boots on the runner in the vestibule, then unbuttoned her coat, pulled off her hat, and stuffed it into her coat pocket. As soon as she freed her face from the scarf, she breathed a long, slow, deep, relaxing breath. Incense, lemony wood polish, and candles. The day's knotted muscles and nerves began to unkink.

The holy water in the font was cold enough to raise goosebumps when she touched it to her forehead. Only the two hexagonal ceiling lamps at the front and the ones above her head illuminated the oak pews. The darkness chilled her until she heard the heat kick in and realized the temperature had to be at least sixty. One older woman knelt in the pew across from the Confessional, but the light from the dogwood, blossom-shaped opening in the central door didn't reach farther than the floor in front of it.

When Giulia entered the nave, she heard faint voices from the Confessional. The woman's rosary clacking on the back of the pew made more noise than her rubber soles did on the carpeted central aisle. As she neared the sanctuary, the always-burning candle in its red glass lamp cast an unsettling glow over the tabernacle. Giulia genuflected at the head of the aisle, facing the consecrated Hosts inside their small mother-of-pearl house. A five-tiered bank of tall votive candles stood off-center to the Blessed Virgin statue in its niche on the left. Giulia moved silently to that side of the nave.

She couldn't hear any voices now; good. Privacy for everyone. Her wallet gave up a dollar bill. She folded it into a rectangle narrow enough to fit into the offering slot before lighting a long wick at an existing candle. A puff of smoke mingled with the odor of hot candle wax and the permeating incense. With another deep inhale of the mixture, the last knot in her chest loosened.

As she lit a new candle in the topmost tier, she breathed a prayer to the Virgin for Katie's safe return. Then she knelt. The week had been too long and stressful to try and pray a Rosary on her fingers. *I'd lose my place before the second decade.* She settled for wordless prayer. The Lord knew her intention. Her job was to show up and make herself available to Him.

A kneeler banged behind and to her right. Footsteps headed to the door and vanished. Giulia lost track of time.

"Are you here to pre-Confess again?"

She started, and a large, square hand touched her shoulder.

"It's only me."

Giulia smiled up at Father Carlos, the priest in charge of Saint Thomas Catholic Church and one of the few people she trusted enough to confide in. "Causing parishioner death by heart attack? Are you trying to get on a reality TV show?"

The priest laughed. "It's seven forty-five. Everyone else is gone. I was about to head out for my Wednesday nursing home rounds, but I have some wiggle room. If you need it, there's more than enough time to hear your pre-Confession for sins you might commit in the line of duty."

"It's that late? It's a good thing I have the rental car." She scooped up her purse. "I didn't come in here with that in mind, but I could use a pre-Confession."

Father Carlos's thin black eyebrows disappeared into his wavy salt-and-pepper hair. "I was joking. Come walk back to the vestry with me."

She gave Father Carlos the bones of the story as they walked up the small front aisle and across the sanctuary. "I've got two potential suspect couples and an envelope full of employee information that may give me more. I'll be telling them whatever I think will convince them I'm the best listener in Pennsylvania. Anything to get them to drop their guard."

"I freely grant you permission to deceive evildoers to protect the innocent. He raised his right hand and Giulia inclined her head. He continued, "I absolve you from all sins you may commit in this investigation, in the name of the Father, and of the Son, and of the Holy Spirit. Amen."

When Giulia raised her head, he was smiling. "My own Confessor thinks this is an interesting interpretation of the sacrament. Now, you: how are the nightmares?"

Giulia smiled. He tried to maintain formal speech, but his true self usually kicked that aside within a few minutes, revealing the caring, everyone's-brother he really was.

"I'm dealing. They'll get better soon. It took about six months for them to loosen their grip the first time."

He gave her an admonitory frown. "Take care of yourself so you are better able to help others. Did I hear you say that you have a car?"

"Just a rental for this job. But I'm so happy to be free of the city bus that I'm taking the used-car plunge right after Christmas." She armored herself for the outside again.

"I wish you many years of self-propelled happiness. Drive carefully to work. I'll see you for Midnight Mass."

The wind clawed at her hair the minute she hit the steps and didn't loosen its grip till she shut herself into the Escort. While the heater rattled its way up to a livable temperature, she searched for one of the all-Christmas radio stations.

Oh, I could get used to this.

TWENTY

GIULIA PARKED IN THE alley behind Common Grounds. The coffee shop covered the entire first floor of the skinny brick office building; Driscoll Investigations took up the front half of the second floor. Giulia had never seen the people across the hall. A brass nameplate next to the solid door read *Walters and Griffin, Ltd*. One slow morning she and Sidney had created a two-column list of possible occupations for the mysterious firm.

The 8:20 bus passed without stopping. Giulia mock-saluted it and opened the coffee shop door.

"Hey, you," Mingmei the barista said from behind the glass counter and pastry display. "I haven't seen you in days."

"Saving my pennies to buy that car." Giulia unbuttoned her coat. "However, it's nearly Christmas so I will splurge on a candy-cane cappuccino, please."

"An excellent choice." She measured coffee.

The only other customers were engrossed in each other in the farthest corner, the faux-Tiffany lamp above them shedding the bare minimum of light on their kiss-sip-kiss-sip exercise.

Giulia leaned on the counter, Christmas-party aftermath pushed to the background, Katie's rescue uppermost in her mind again. "I have an ulterior motive for coming in today. I need hair advice."

Mingmei continued the multiple-step brewing process. "You want red and green stripes for Christmas? Please say yes."

"With this mop? Please. I'd look like a candy-factory explosion." Giulia glanced again at the couple in the corner.

"Come around to this side." Mingmei lifted the hinged wooden flap on the wall. "You used to work here. Eleanor won't care."

Giulia scooted through. "Did she marry off her nephews yet? I feel sorry for whoever gets the one who said I had a nun aura."

"Nah. He's gone back to nature—heads a wilderness retreat at the far end of Raccoon Lake. Winter and summer." She shivered hard enough for her short, straight black hair to ruffle.

"That's what I want to talk to you about. Hey—don't be stingy with the whipped cream, please."

"I am a queen among baristas—I memorize all my regular customers' preferences." She mounded whipped cream on top of the cappuccino and sprinkled it with bits of mint-chocolate candy.

Giulia closed her eyes and savored the first swallow. "Dear Lord, that's good. I suppose you deserve a tip for this."

"You suppose right." She executed a precise bow after Giulia paid her. "Tell me what's up before the eight-thirty crowd hits."

"I'm going undercover again."

"Not in another convent!"

"Not in this lifetime." Giulia shuddered and sipped coffee to take away the phantom chill from the thought. "No, at the Wildflower."

"No way. Really? My family went there for years when we were kids. It was a family-type place back then, called Pine Candles. Swimming, archery, canoeing, tennis, campfires, the works. We loved it." Mingmei unwrapped a piece of gingerbread and nibbled it. "What's going on, or can't you tell me?"

"You know I can't. Here's the problem. I need to change the way I look, but not anything drastic. I'm working housekeeping, so it has to be simple." She took a deep breath. "What do you know about chemical hair straightening?"

"Ugh, it smells like that stuff they use for permanents and it doesn't last forever."

"That's great. That's exactly what I was hoping for." She ran her fingers through her curls. "I love my hair. I don't want to change it forever."

Mingmei gave Giulia a calculating look. "Your timing on this is too accurate. I planned to waylay you when you got off the bus today. I need moral support."

Giulia switched into "Sister Regina the counselor" mode automatically. "What's up?"

"I'm getting my navel pierced."

She relaxed, switching back into "Giulia the regular person." "You've got three piercings in each ear. What's so different about your navel?"

"My sister says hers hurt like twenty bee stings. I don't do pain. But my sweetie gave me the most gorgeous lapis lazuli belly button ring for my birthday—look." She took a small jewelry box from her pocket. On a piece of jeweler's cotton lay a gold-veined blue sphere on a curved stainless-steel bar with a smaller sphere at the other end.

Giulia touched the lapis. "It's beautiful."

"I know. I'm dying to wear it, but I'm a big sissy. However, you just gave me the most awesome idea: My best friend for, like, ever works at Glitz, and she does amazing things with hair. If you come hold my hand while their piercing lady punctures my stomach, I'll get Jeanie to work her magic on your hair."

A little of the worry lifted from Giulia's shoulders. "Would she? But I have to be at the Wildflower this afternoon."

Mingmei put the jewelry box back into her pocket. "Piece of cake. My appointment's for eleven forty-five. Glitz is ten minutes on foot if we cut through a bunch of parking lots."

"That's prime time. How will she fit me in?"

Mingmei finished the gingerbread. "That's the thing. She just switched shops and she's rebuilding her client list. She has the time. Here. Wait a minute." She woke up her cell phone and dialed. "Jeanie? Get out of bed, you slug. You got anyone for quarter to twelve today? … Spare me. You know you should've got up half an hour ago … Excellent. You do now." She gave Giulia a thumbs-up. "I'm bringing my friend the ex-nun, and she needs her hair straightened … You can ask her that. How much should she bring? Whoa. Okay, thanks. I'll tell her. See you in a few hours." She put away the phone. "Good news and bad news. Good news is she can do it. Bad news is it's ninety bucks. She's cutting twenty off the price because she wants tons of convent dirt."

Giulia grinned. "I can satisfy her. Honest, I thought it'd cost more than that. There's an ATM for my bank in the convenience store next to the post office." She pointed to the coffee cup. "This is Heaven in a twelve-ounce cup."

"Too sweet for me. I'll take jasmine tea any day."

"If only I were better at forcibly converting people to … anything."

"If you were, we wouldn't be friends."

"Then I'm happy. Here." Giulia reached into her purse and handed Mingmei a square, flat box. "Merry Christmas."

"Ooh, presents. Buddhism's only failing is it doesn't have anything like Christmas." She ripped away the ribbon and paper. "They're perfect! They match the navel ring."

She held the chandelier earrings up to the overhead light. The rows of dark blue crystals glittered against her hair. "I am so wearing these to the All Night Santa Disco."

TWENTY-ONE

"Sidney, could you hand me another piece of tape, please?"

Giulia placed a sheet of the multipage report on the Wildflower employees at the top corner of the collage she'd already created, and taped it down. The connected papers covered half the floor between the window and her desk. Barbara had been more than generous with confidential information. Part of Giulia was appalled at this flagrant breach of confidentiality, even as another part was thrilled at the wealth of knowledge on Katie's behalf.

"How many more?" Giulia said.

"Two." Sidney held one page over Giulia's shoulder, more tape in her other hand.

"Good. This one can go here … and the last … here. Can you help me lift it?"

Together they raised the crazy quilt of information. Several edges flapped, but they walked it over to the bulletin board and pinned it up without incident.

Sidney looked it over. "This is what you call a clue collage?"

"Someday I'll patent the idea." Giulia took six different colored highlighters from the Penguin Santa pen holder on her desk. "Now I'll color-code important points in each employee's information."

"Isn't this against some kind of privacy law?"

"Nope. Captain Reilly had a warrant and the resort owner wants to help." Giulia tapped the pink marker against her bottom lip. The clock was ticking. Katie needed her.

Frank came out of his office. "Nice collage. Where are you going to hide it when clients walk in?"

"The bottom drawer of the file cabinet. Everything else goes in there." She drew pink lines over the housekeeping names.

"Sexist."

Giulia made a face at him. "It was the first color in my hand. Most of the employees are women anyway, so your point is moot."

Sidney squinted at the printouts. "They have male employees at a women-only resort? Oh, wait, they'd have to at least interview them because of equal opportunity and all that."

"Heavy lifting and general maintenance for one. You know, the handyman position. Also cross-country ski instructor." She used green for maintenance and yellow for the chef. "I saw one more male name … nope, two. One of the sous chefs and the head of recreation." Blue for athletics and purple for games.

The phone rang. Frank took Sidney's place over Giulia's shoulder.

"The masseuse—she's married to the ski instructor—gets purple." Giulia highlighted as she spoke. "Back office gets orange. Billing, desk clerks, telephones. Wait staff … yellow like the kitchen. Head chef. Sous chef number two. Table bussers, dishwashers, bartender. Oh, my, one of their chefs specializes in desserts."

"Don't get distracted by the presence of high-class sugar." Frank lowered his voice. "Look ahead to the all-natural desserts at Sidney's wedding."

"There's nothing wrong with expanding your taste horizons," she whispered back.

"I've seen her 'save the planet' menu. I'll be spending my time at the groom's food stations."

Sidney hung up the phone. Giulia returned to her collage.

"Equipment rental, blue. There are only two other housekeepers. You were right, Frank. I'm going to fall asleep on my keyboard tomorrow morning."

"I will tuck a blanket around you and close the blinds."

"What an understanding boss."

Sidney giggled at her monitor. "They have a gift shop. I bet they have X-rated movies for the rooms."

"I've seen it, but I didn't have time to look at the shelves."

Frank came over to her desk. "If it was a guys-only place you know they would. This website looks like a cross between a gardening-club show and a girls' night out."

Giulia came around to Sidney's other side. "The rooms are just as beautiful in person. The bathrooms are to die for. I haven't seen the indoor pool yet. Oh, those menus. If I were gay, I'd go there once a year forever."

Sidney giggled again. "They have in-room massage. I know what that means."

"Maybe not," Giulia said.

Frank and Sidney both stared at her. "Yes, it does," they said.

She held up her hands in surrender. "I'll take your word for it. I shall now retreat to my sheltered corner and learn more about the employees."

She returned all the markers except orange to her penguin holder and took out a skinny black felt-tip pen.

Look at these people from the opposite side. Don't assume they're all basically good. Assume they're all capable of committing kidnapping and murder. She circled the names of the masseuse and the ski instructor and connected them with a thick orange line. With the felt tip, she wrote, "Baby/Fertility/Games." *Their family's nagging them to have a baby. What if they can't? What if there's desperation behind their lovey-dovey act? They knew I was in the break room listening to them.*

"The ski instructor is in charge of games, too."

Frank came over to her and read the profile. "Too bad they don't list religion on these forms anymore."

"Mm." Giulia tapped the black felt tip against her lips. "Nothing is that easy. Here's something. One of the sous chefs has massive college debt." She circled that with the pen. "The daytime desk clerk and the handyman are married, no kids." Another circle. "Here's an interesting one: a waitress sued the resort and lost three years ago because they caught her watering the wine. The judge didn't buy her plea of not responsible because of her addiction to Cabernet."

Sidney laughed.

Giulia took a notepad from her desk and wrote that waitress's information in it. "Captain Reilly will have to check that one."

"Hey," Frank said. "What name are you using?"

"Regina Ryan."

"Regina I get, but Ryan?"

Sidney gasped. "Are you reading that romance, too?"

Giulia smiled. "It's too good to put down, isn't it?"

Frank looked from one to the other. "You're kidding."

Giulia stuck out the tip of her tongue at him. "Says the man who pores over *Sports Illustrated* like a new revelation from God."

"I think I have emails calling me." He retreated into his office.

She returned to the collage. *I can't memorize their names because I have to be convincing when I meet everyone, but I can memorize the job descriptions. Masseuse and games captain. Sous chef. Desk clerk and handyman. Just don't fixate on these five. They could all be perfectly innocent and my real target might be the waitress or the psycho geek or someone else whose profile here doesn't set off any alarm bells.*

Godzilla roared from her computer monitor. She checked her watch. Eleven twenty. She unpinned the clue collage and it flopped over her head like she was folding sheets.

"Sidney?"

A giggle sounded from the other side of Giulia's paper shroud. "You sound like my swim class kids do when their caps get stuck on their heads."

Sidney's hands appeared at the edge of the papers and together they lifted and held it parallel to the floor.

"Come toward me," Giulia said. "Okay, you take the top and I'll crease the bottom. Now I'll take the left side and you take the right." They folded the collage in half and half again, until they'd reduced its original three-by-five-foot dimensions to one-by-three. "That should fit." She squatted by the file cabinet next to the window and opened the bottom drawer. "I swear the junk in this drawer reproduces asexually." She rearranged envelopes and half-filled supply boxes to allow the folded collage to rest on top.

"Sidney, I'm taking a long lunch today. I'll be back by one thirty."

"No problem. I'm having a veggie sub delivered. I have a whole mess of reports to type up before I leave tomorrow."

Giulia knocked on Frank's door frame. "Did you hear all that?"

"Yes. Should I ask why you're doubling your lunch hour?"

"I'll explain when I come back." *Although one look will be explanation enough.*

TWENTY-TWO

GIULIA SAT IN ONE of Glitz's salon chairs and stared at her curls one last time. *Goodbye for now. We'll see each other again soon.*

"Okay, now don't move, okay? This stuff is majorly strong and it can't touch your scalp."

Jeanie, Mingmei's Best Friend Forever, separated Giulia's hair into two-inch sections and poured a thick, vile-smelling liquid onto a glittery red hairbrush.

Mingmei, perched in the next chair, covered her mouth and nose. "Damn, Jeanie, that stinks worse than Crazy Lou in the middle of August."

"Yeah, doesn't it? Is Crazy Lou still making the rounds of all the restaurant dumpsters?"

"Haven't seen him for a few months, but he had a smell you'd never forget."

"Gawd, yes." Jeanie pulled the brush through the first section of Giulia's hair. "You have gorgeous hair, Giulia. So thick. Bet it frizzes up in the summer."

"I have good hair goop with lots of proteins." She grimaced as the brush caught a tangle.

"Mei, what'd you get the boyfriend for Christmas?" Jeanie started on another section.

"A box of reeds for his sax and a gift certificate for new ink. He's been talking about a wolf in dark glasses playing an alto sax since summer."

"Cool. You got a guy, Giulia?"

Mingmei made a coughing noise that sounded like "Boss."

"Don't turn your head!" Jeanie's free hand came down on Giulia's shoulder. "Mei, if you distract my client this stuff'll eat the hair off her scalp. What's Mei being all judgmental about now?"

"I'm sort of dating my boss."

"Oh. Well. Um. I've seen that work out." She paid close attention to the next section of hair.

"Told you," Mingmei kept her hand over her nose. "The convent sucked, so what are you doing jumping into a relationship with major suck potential? That's not the way to rebound."

Jeanie started on the section next to Giulia's ears. "Convent! That's right. Shut up about who she's dating, Mei. Giulia, I've got to brush this through your hair for twenty minutes. Please tell me lots of convent stories. Mei promised you would." She stopped long enough to set a timer and went right back to brushing.

Giulia blinked her eyes several times, but they still watered from the cloud of chemicals enveloping her head. *Oh, well.* She smiled at Jeanie in the mirror. "Where do you want me to start?"

∽◦

Twenty solid minutes of brushing, a seven-minute rinse, and another five minutes of combing neutralizer through Giulia's hair. She'd never spent this much time on her personal appearance in her entire life.

"Rinse time again." Jeanie walked with Giulia to the sinks. Four minutes later, she sat her up. "Sorry about the water down your back. Here, let me wrap your head. Okay, back to the chair for the big unveiling—ha ha ha, that was good. Okay. Three. Two. One."

She whisked away the towel. Giulia's often-wild, curly hair fell to the bottom of her shoulder blades.

"That's me? I had no idea my hair was this long."

"It'll shrink up a bit after it's dry." She picked up a blow dryer and said to the room, "Okay, everyone. The really stinky part's about to begin. Cover your noses and mouths, since it's too cold to open the door."

The receptionist pressed two buttons on the wall thermostat behind her desk. The ceiling fans increased their speed and the airflow from the baseboard vents got stronger.

Jeanie handed Giulia a clean towel and fired up the blow dryer. The odor hit about ten seconds later. Giulia's eyes watered and the back of her throat got scratchy. She clutched the towel to her face. Jeanie said, "Warned you," over the noise.

The torture lasted forever, which by the clock equaled six minutes. Jeanie shut off the dryer and blew her nose. "They couldn't have made that smell nastier if they'd tried. Okay, wipe your eyes and take a look."

"Whoa," Mingmei said. "You look like some relative of yours, but not you. Take off your makeup, and I bet even your boyfriend-boss would have to look twice to make sure it's really you."

"It's so different." Giulia stared at her reflection. "I look like a throwback to the sixties."

"Retro is in." Jeanie ran a wide-toothed comb through Giulia's new look, smoothing it with one hand as she combed. "This is important: don't wash your hair till Saturday. The smell's not that bad, really. If you wash it too soon, you'll stop the chemical reaction from finishing up."

"You're incredible. I wouldn't know myself. It looks great."

"Seriously?"

"Seriously. I'm a whole new me. It feels like … freedom. Like a fresh start."

Mingmei said, "Ever read that *Sylvia* comic strip? She says that a good haircut is better than three months of psychotherapy. Something like that."

Giulia laughed. "I think I agree."

Jeanie gave them both a huge grin in the mirror. "You've gotta come back in a week or so. Do you mind? I want to see how it looks when it settles down."

"No, I don't mind." Giulia swung her hair back and forth. "I feel like a teenager. I should go out and buy new clothes to complete the new look."

"Retail therapy! Let's do it." Mingmei squared her shoulders. "Okay, playtime over. Time to hold my hand for surgery."

"Jeanie, I'll pay you as soon as this one realizes she's going to survive the beautification of her navel."

"No worries. I'm watching the Great Piercing Adventure, too."

Mingmei lay on the sheet-covered table in Glitz's piercing corner, opposite the manicurist's station, kitty corner from the row of hairstyling chairs. The older female technician who performed all piercings laid down her counted cross-stitch and worked a fresh pair of surgical gloves over her fingers. She swabbed a three-inch circle around Mingmei's navel.

"Cold!"

"Yes, dear. This needle is sterilized, and I've sterilized your jewelry while you watched your friend. I'm going to use this little clamp to pinch the fold of your skin right above your belly button and punch the needle through."

Mingmei whimpered a little.

Jeanie gave a loud, theatrical sigh. "Grow a pair, you sissy."

The technician took the clamp in one hand and the piercing needle in the other. "All right, dear. I want you to breathe in for a count of three and breathe out for a count of three."

Mingmei grabbed Giulia's hand.

The technician said, "I'll count for you. In. One … two … three. Out. One … two … three." On *three* she clamped Mingmei's skin and pushed the needle through. Without pausing, she inserted the curved bar so the lapis ball nestled in her navel and attached the smaller ball to the top of the bar. "All done." She released the clamp.

Giulia pried Mingmei's fingers off her hand. "You did fine."

Mingmei inhaled and exhaled several times. "Tell me it looks beautiful."

Janie angled the technician's hand mirror over the piercing. "Hardly any blood. We hire the best. Great job, auntie."

Giulia looked at the technician. "You're related?"

"No, but Shelley's like everyone's favorite aunt. We all love her to bits." She kissed the technician's plump cheek.

"You girls are so sweet." The technician folded a square of gauze over Mingmei's navel and secured it with paper adhesive tape. "This little bit of bleeding will stop soon. Wash it with only antibacterial soap for the next two weeks. The bar needs to stay in twenty-four hours a day, seven days a week for six months. Not a day less. Then you can change your jewelry as long as you use the same gauge bar." She peeled off the surgical gloves. "Don't ignore these instructions or you'll be courting infection."

Mingmei sat up. "Got it. I know the routine from my other piercings." She eased her shirt over her low-rider jeans. "See? I came prepared."

Giulia opened her wallet and handed Jeanie one hundred dollars. "Thank you. You did a great job. Mingmei, are you capable of walking? It's twenty after one."

"Yes, I'll survive. The things I do to look attractive. I bet lover-boy didn't expect that this gift means he can't get near my midsection till next week. Ow." She zipped her quilted jacket. "If he buys me a nipple ring for Christmas, I'll shove it through his big nose."

The technician *tsk*ed. Giulia and Jeanie gasped and then laughed in unison.

"What?" Mingmei looked at them. "The porno magazines he looks at are into models with piercings in all the wrong places." She shuddered. "There's not enough eye bleach in the world to erase some of those images."

"In my wildest dreams I never thought I'd be discussing trashy pictures in a public place." Giulia buttoned her violet coat. *If I had another winter coat, I'd wear it to the resort. I love it, but it's the polar opposite of nondescript.* She grimaced. *I'm really starting to hate that word.*

TWENTY-THREE

"Giulia? Oh my God." Sidney's jaw dropped and stayed dropped.

Frank ran into the main part of the office. "What happened? What's—*cac naofa.*"

Mingmei came out from behind Giulia, laughing so hard she had to lean against the door. "Perfect. Beautiful. I wish my phone took video." She gave Giulia a one-armed squeeze. "Thank you for holding my hand through surgery. I'll see you tomorrow."

Sidney's head swiveled toward Mingmei. "Surgery? Over lunch?"

She pulled up her shirt. "Navel piercing."

Frank said, "Mingmei, nice to see you, but we've got a lot to do on a short timeline here."

"Right. Bye, everyone." Her boots clicked down the stairs.

Sidney came out from behind her desk. "What did you do?"

Frank walked over to them. "Why did you do it?"

"Can I touch it?"

"What were you thinking?"

Giulia tilted her new long hair toward Sidney. "Go ahead." To Frank: "The kidnappers have been monitoring Laurel and Anya for weeks, at the very least. Their schedule. Their movements. That includes who goes to see them. I go to the soup kitchen once a week. I've been to their apartment to see the baby. If the kidnappers are working at the resort, they might recognize me. So I needed an easy change to the way I look."

"That's a helluva change."

Sidney said, "It's soft and it still has waves. I wish I had waves."

"Frank, I'm in a maid's uniform with no makeup. Yesterday Sidney braided it, and today my new straight hair will be tied back in a ponytail. Could it be any more different from curly headed, semi-fashionable me?"

Frank lost his bug-eyed look. "You have a point."

"I brought my oldest jeans and a plain long-sleeved shirt to change into. I can play this part, even though I really belong in the orchestra pit with my flute."

"Smart." He shook his head. "You're too clever sometimes."

"Pfft. I'm just practical."

"Lord knows someone in this business needs to be. Sidney's got wedding on the brain."

"I do not … well, maybe."

Giulia laughed. "Yes, you do. But that'll pass. Until you get baby brain. Then you'll be hopeless for about five months."

The phone rang.

"Since when did we become so popular?" Frank said.

"Should I quote the Bible on blessings abounding to those who do God's work?"

"Are you kidding?"

She hid the laughter behind her hand. "I have to go to my other job now."

⁓

That afternoon, Giulia entered through the employee door armed with a handful of paper clips, prepared to test how well she paid attention to Frank's lock-picking lesson. The presence of two of the waitresses squashed that plan.

She returned their *Hellos* with a smile, thinking, *Hurry up and change, you two. Monica will be in here any minute and I'll be on vacuum duty.*

They took their time, of course, alternately complaining about the extra work the wedding was causing them and rhapsodizing about the novelty of a costume wedding at Christmastime.

Monica walked in just then. "Regina, most of the guests are in their rooms getting dressed for the wedding. Can you do a sweep of the lounge and bar?"

"Sure. Should I use the bags from the cart closet?"

"Yes, and bring wet and dry cloths for the tables. There's a dishwasher rack behind the bar for used glasses." She took one step away and turned back. "Did you do something different to your hair?"

"I had it in a braid yesterday," Giulia said without a qualm.

"Oh. That must be it. Looks nice."

Giulia hit the bar first. Glasses in various states of almost-empty cluttered all the bistro-style tables. The rings they left wiped up without effort. She rubbed her fingers on a tabletop. *Coated. I approve. And whatever malign influence encouraged Monica to appear before I could commit an actual crime, please go torment someone else.*

She dropped more glasses in the sectioned dish rack. One of the sous chefs snatched it out from under her hands.

"Sorry, we need to run these through for the after-party." He ran jangling and clinking into the kitchen.

Giulia wiped another table. *Blond ponytail, missing incisor. He's the one I need to chat up. Need to make an excuse to get into the kitchen. Or catch him on break. Drat.*

He ran past her again, out the front door without a coat.

Maybe tomorrow. Katie's clock is ticking. Come on, Falcone. Think of a reason to "bump into him."

Barbara and Maryjane were setting up folding chairs in the lounge when she entered it. A glass pinecone had fallen off the eight-foot-tall Christmas tree. Giulia set the cloths and trash bags in the corner, retrieved the ornament, and hung it on a free branch. She adjusted the tree skirt and righted one of the empty wrapped boxes.

"Thanks, Regina," Barbara stood by the window and counted chairs. "Six—twelve—eighteen—twenty-four. Okay, Maryjane, we're good."

Someone bumped into Giulia from behind.

"Sorry—sorry—didn't see you." An older woman dressed as Saint Nicholas plopped the box on the nearest chair and took out a red satin pillow with two wedding rings pinned to it.

Right behind her came a horned demon with brown fur and a three-foot long ribbon tongue. Giulia stared. The woman in the costume laughed.

"I'm the Krampus and she's Saint Nicholas. I beat bad children with my birch switch"—she flicked the branches tied to her belt—"while Saint Nick gives the good children treats. We're the perfect pair."

"It's a great costume. I've never heard of that Saint Nicholas story."

"Thanks." The Krampus flipped the tongue over her shoulder and set out a silver tray with a tall white candle and two disposable lighters on it.

Giulia emptied the four wastebaskets in the room, moving them against the far wall. Barbara went out through the door leading to the main lobby. Saint Nick handed Maryjane a wrinkled lump of red plastic. "Blow, please. Thanks. No worries about the old body-fluid exchange risk. Diane and I are proudly disease-free." She tossed a brown plastic lump at Giulia and opened a valve on a similar lump. She took a deep breath and blew air into it.

Giulia caught a momentary look of panic on Maryjane's face before she and the desk clerk found the valves on their plastic bundles. In a few minutes they both held reindeer as Saint Nick finished inflating a sleigh. A few minutes later two more reindeer and a Santa with a sack of toys completed the display.

"Perfect," the Krampus said. "Tessie will cry when she sees them; I know she will." She turned to Giulia and Maryjane. "We dug them out of her attic. She hasn't put them out since her mom died, but she grew up with these and we decided it's time to resurrect the tradition. Good thing we tested them before today. The last thing we need is a reindeer deflating during the ceremony."

"Thanks for helping," Saint Nick said. "Di, do you have the wassail cups?"

Maryjane returned to the main lobby. Two elves and the Ghost of Christmas Past came into the room from the kitchen doorway following the sous chef wheeling a cart. Giulia caught the aroma of hot, fragrant wine as she left with the trash bags. Monica way-laid her at the giant blue garbage tote.

"Regina, can you help me unload some boxes? We want to stock the adult part of the gift shop for the wedding visitors."

Again called away from a potential sous chef encounter. "Sure."

A Virgin Mary with a sleeping, haloed Baby Jesus in a child carrier set down a video camera case. Giulia cooed at the baby before she left. *Katie, Katie, Katie. Don't forget why you're here, Falcone.*

Together they carried three-high stacks of boxes from a basement storage room to the gift shop. Monica inserted a small key into the T-shirt shelf and it swung away to reveal another set of shelves.

Giulia camouflaged her reaction by bending down and cutting open a box. *Oh, my.* Cosmo *never prepared me for this. Drat, I can feel the heat in my cheeks. She's going to think I'm a prude. Then again...*

"I'll take the silk ties first," Monica said. "Ten pairs should do it."

Giulia handed her wide strips of silk in several colors; it only took her half a minute to twig to their use.

"The next box should be vibrators. There's an assortment... let's see. We're missing the ridged ones, the water-filled ones... Here, just hand me the box and I'll fill in the missing spaces on this shelf. Would you hang up some teddies, please? The padded hangers should be with them in the box."

"These are beautiful." It was the only honest remark she could make.

"Aren't they? Barbara has an eye for good lingerie. Fortunately, my husband's never asked to see me in one. I'd look like a sausage tied too tight around the middle."

As Giulia unfolded a shell-pink garment trimmed with white lace, she pictured herself in it for a fleeting instant. Her cheeks flamed up again. She kept her back to Monica and concentrated on the mechanics of hanging the lacy nothings to their best advantage.

"We've got room for more tubes of lotion." Monica opened the last box and set up three rows of five-inch tubes labeled *Ooh-La-la*, *Hot Fantasy*, and *Kiss Me*.

Maryjane poked her head into the gift shop, phone in hand. "Amaryllis 332 needs more towels. Can Regina go?"

Monica nodded. "Sure. I'll take the boxes back into storage."

Giulia had never been so glad to run a tedious errand.

TWENTY-FOUR

GIULIA PEEKED INTO THE lounge half an hour later, hoping to catch the exchange of vows.

A Justice of the Peace dressed like the Ghost of Christmas Present stood in front of the Christmas tree. He looked at least seventy years old, but carried the costume well. The false chestpiece helped. Mrs. Claus on his right held the hands of Cindy-Lou Who on his left. Judging from the backs of guests' heads, representatives from classic Christmas television specials and the works of Dickens, plus various deities and multiple Father Christmases, had accepted invitations to this wedding.

Saint Nicholas detached one of the rings from the satin pillow. Mrs. Claus took it and held it against the tip of Cindy-Lou Who's finger. "The Christmas Waltz" played through the sound system.

Mrs. Claus began, "With this ring, I thee wed …"

A green velvet Father Christmas at the end of the second row leapt out of his chair. He reached Mrs. Claus in one stride and ripped the ring out of her fingers. "Thieving bitch!"

He cold-cocked her. She fell backward onto one of the arm-chairs and slid to the floor.

Someone flipped the world's slow-motion switch.

Giulia ran past the chairs.

Half the guests started to stand. Father Christmas grabbed Cindy-Lou Who.

"Don't do this! Come back to me, please, please come back to me."

Cindy-Lou Who struggled in his grip, trying to get her nails up to claw his face—the only part of his skin visible in the costume. "Let me go, Howard! Let me go! Angie, are you okay?"

His voice clashed with hers like carnival barkers competing for the same audience. "She poisoned you, Tessie! You have to come back to me. We can make it right again!"

Elves and carolers blocked Giulia's path. Three different voices screamed for help. Half the guests tripped over each other to get to Cindy-Lou Who; the other half knocked over chairs to reach Mrs. Claus. Giulia shoved a different Father Christmas out of her way and broke through the pack. Off to her left, someone babbled directions to the Wildflower at a 9-1-1 operator. Two other voices shouted, "Give her some air!" "Lay her on the couch."

"Howard, let me go! Angie and I are getting married!"

"No! Forget that bitch! You belong to me!"

Giulia and the ski instructor reached them at the same moment. The ski instructor's long arms reached around the costume. He clasped his hands at Father Christmas's sternum, planted his feet, and yanked backward. Giulia slipped into the space he created and stomped Father Christmas's felt-covered foot with her sneakered heel.

He howled and tried to bend over in the ski instructor's grip. The ski instructor wrenched Father Christmas around and threw him into the now-empty armchair. Cindy-Lou Who leapt to Mrs. Claus's side.

Barbara and Maryjane waded into the turmoil, pushing the guests back, cajoling them to sit down, straightening chairs. Giulia and the ski instructor hovered over Father Christmas. He tried to strong-arm his way out of the chair toward Cindy-Lou Who, but the ski instructor pinned his costumed arms in place. "Sit, asshole."

Giulia made herself into a wall between them and the couch.

Father Christmas collapsed in the chair, weepy now. Snot ran into his false beard. "Tessie," he kept repeating. Giulia smelled whisky on his breath.

The chaos dwindled enough to let "Holly Jolly Christmas" be heard through the room. Giulia smiled at the ski instructor.

He rolled his eyes. "At least it's not 'The Most Wonderful Time of the Year.'"

Maryjane ran back into the room—Giulia didn't recall seeing her leave—with an ampoule of smelling salts. She broke it and waved it under Mrs. Claus's nose. Three hovering guests stepped backward, blinking. Mrs. Claus gasped and coughed and her eyes opened.

"Angie, are you okay?" Cindy-Lou Who said.

"I hope I broke your jaw, you bitch!" Father Christmas hiccupped.

The ski instructor bent down till they were nose to nose. "Listen, asswipe, shut your drunken trap. Think about Christmas in jail."

Father Christmas glared at him. "Don't matter. I'll make bail. I'll make Tessie see where she belongs."

The ski instructor leaned away, possibly to let the full effect of his skeptical expression sink into his prisoner. "And that'd be with you."

"Damn straight. Taking care of me and having my kids. What real women do."

Giulia laughed. The ski instructor joined in. Behind him, one of the elves relayed Father Christmas's last remark to the Tiny Tim next to her. The game of "telephone" ran the circuit of the room and everyone was laughing, even Mrs. Claus as she held her jaw.

Cindy-Lou Who got up from her knees and stalked over to the armchair. Giulia tried to say something calming, but stepped aside at the look on the other woman's face. The ski instructor stepped back but stayed within arm-clamping distance.

Father Christmas looked up at her, eyes reddened and snot crusting on his face.

"I'm not going to hit you, Howard, because that'd be assault. I will be getting a restraining order against you first thing tomorrow." She smiled. "Maybe not first thing. After all, this is my wedding night."

Father Christmas started up, but the ski instructor slammed him back into the chair, keeping his hands on the costumed shoulders this time.

"I hope you die frustrated and alone," Cindy-Lou Who continued, "because no woman will ever be desperate or lonely enough to come near you again. Now if you'll excuse me, I'd like to finish my wedding ceremony."

She looked at the ski instructor. He nodded, grinning, and caught Maryjane's eye. She ran out and a minute later brought in her husband. The two men wrestled Father Christmas out of the lounge.

"Tessie, you bitch! You—let go of me—that's my fiancée—Tessie—dammit—"

Giulia heard the ski instructor say to the maintenance man as they dragged Father Christmas away, "He's got the right idea, but not the manhood to make it happen."

Cindy-Lou Who and Barbara helped Mrs. Claus off the couch.

"I'm good," she said. "The jaw's going to be multicolored tomorrow, but I'll live." She squinted at the ceiling speaker, which had moved on to "The Little Drummer Boy." "Can we get 'The Christmas Waltz' back again, please?"

"Right on it." Barbara headed to the back office.

Giulia and both waitresses started to replace the chairs in their original rows. The Krampus got on her hands and knees by the tree skirt. Saint Nicholas righted the candle and lighters.

"Only a dent," she said.

"Found the ring," the Krampus said.

The music changed to the requested song.

"All right," the Justice of the Peace said, resuming his position in front of the tree. "Fortunately our gate-crasher didn't spill the wassail, and I for one am in need of spirits. Ladies?"

TWENTY-FIVE

GIULIA AND THE WAITRESSES squeezed into the doorway as the newlyweds lit the white candle together. Everyone applauded when they kissed—gently. Giulia brushed away tears, embarrassed, until one of the waitresses handed her a tissue and they ducked into the bathroom to blow their noses.

Red and blue lights flashed into the lobby when they came out. Barbara led two uniformed policemen into the lounge.

As Giulia ran back and forth, replenishing bathroom supplies, picking up empty wassail cups, wiping spills, she caught bits of the discussion with the police.

"You're welcome to a copy of my recording," the Virgin Mary said. "The camera had the perfect view of it all."

"Ma'am, could you give me your contact information ..."

"About that restraining order ..."

Five minutes later, the policemen followed Barbara across the reception area. Giulia headed for the break room. Three staff members were already there.

"You put him where?" the masseuse said to the ski instructor.

"Face down on the bench for the Universal gym." He swigged most of a bottle of water. "Phineas is sitting on him, figuratively speaking."

"I wish I'd've been there. I wouldn't have just stomped on his foot." She noticed Giulia. "Oh, hi. Why didn't you give that moron a taste of his own medicine?"

"I didn't have enough room for a good swing."

The ski instructor laughed. "Meaning you would've if I'd given you a couple more feet to work with?"

"I was tempted." She found a box of teabags and happily avoided drinking the "coffee."

"You know, honey," the ski instructor said, "the Neanderthal lifestyle appeals to me. Cavewoman in kitchen, roasting a dinosaur leg for supper, cavelings sewing mammoth-skin clothes and trapping lizards for dessert, great male hunter reclining on a nearby rock awaiting service by his fur-clad woman."

The masseuse's smile became brittle. "Cavewoman barefoot and pregnant, of course?"

"Of course." The ski instructor's grin faltered. "All in good fun, right, honey?"

She leaned closer to him, but her whisper carried just like Sidney's.

"Rub it in again, okay? Announce to the world that your wife's had two miscarriages and she's going to clock her mother if the subject of kids comes up again and that she's already wondering if you're looking at other women who might not have fertility problems."

She stalked out of the break room toward the bathrooms, tears welling in her eyes.

The ski instructor shot Giulia an apologetic look and ran after her.

"Well." Maryjane left her spot by the window and sat across from Giulia. "That poor thing."

Giulia sipped her tea. "Holiday stress does things to people. My mother used to nag my younger brother something wicked. She got three years to spoil his kids before she passed."

"I have three sisters and two brothers and my mother expects grandchildren from all of us." Maryjane's smile was less than perky. "As soon as Phineas got out of the Navy we started trying. I except her to corner Phineas soon and demand to know what's wrong with him, since Myers women are always fertile."

Giulia made a pained face. "Ouch."

Maryjane perked up again. "I have faith that I'll hold a baby in my arms one day."

The masseuse came back into the break room, eyes puffy around the edges. "Regina, you're welcome to crush my loving husband's instep anytime." She slammed the phone book onto the table, sloshing Giulia's tea and Maryjane's coffee.

Giulia wiped the spills. "What are you looking up?"

"Reiki practitioners. I saw an ad for one that teaches you how to align your chi. The crystals I bought aren't doing a thing."

"Penny, have you thought about prayer?" Maryjane said.

"I worship different gods. You know that. Aha. Here she is. Lady Morrigan." She opened her cell and dialed.

Giulia stood. "I'd better make another check of the lounge." She detoured into the supply closet for plastic bags first.

The wedding party—minus one Father Christmas—had moved into the private dining room. They'd left minimal debris: mostly

165

wassail cups and monogrammed bubble containers. The handyman was already stacking chairs. Giulia took care of the last few and rolled the folding-chair cart against the far wall. The handyman lugged the armchairs back into place.

"Let me help with the couch," Giulia said.

He appraised her. "Sure you can handle it?"

She gave him her "teacher" look. "I've lugged so much furniture I could open my own moving and storage business. I'll take this end."

They replaced the couch and the end tables. Giulia gathered the trash. The sleigh and reindeer she left for the maids of honor to deflate.

"Phineas?" Maryjane called from the front desk.

"Yeah?"

Maryjane's voice came nearer. "Can you jump-start a car? One of the wedding guests needs to leave."

"Sure. Thanks ... Regina, is it? Nice to work with someone willing to help out"—he lowered his voice—"for a change. I like that in a woman."

Giulia stopped her jaw from dropping, but not by much.

Maryjane came over to her, smiling, after Phineas left. "That's a compliment, you know. Phineas is a little old-fashioned."

That's putting a kind spin on it. You poor thing. She returned the smile. "Hard work builds muscles. Have to keep my girlish figure."

Maryjane's smile broadened. "We need to look our best for our men. That's one of our jobs."

Years of convent-trained politeness kept the smile on Giulia's face till she escaped.

TWENTY-SIX

FOUR HOURS LATER, GIULIA plopped her aching feet on her coffee table and sank into the cushions. Antipasto and garlic pizza sent mouthwatering aromas through her living room; she was almost too tired to open the takeout containers.

"I am such a slug. Six hours of cleaning shouldn't wipe me out like this."

She stared at the Christmas movie on the TV. It took several minutes before she realized it was the movie-zation of that schmaltzy song "The Christmas Shoes." Oh, no. No, no, no. No little kids buying red shoes for their dying mothers. Even in her most naïve early convent days she'd hated such blatant manipulation. She reached for the remote and almost knocked over her glass of Coke.

"All right; sit up. Eat. Write up notes from today's shift."

She speared the antipasto with one hand and clicked through channels with the other. The capicola in the antipasto helped wake her up—this takeout place used the extra-spicy kind. Twelve channels later, she found a Comedy Channel program about surviving the holiday season. She remembered to set down her Coke before every Lewis Black rant. Coke up the nose was a waste of good soda.

She outlined the ski instructor's attitude and the masseuse's conception difficulties. The desk clerk's 1950s-sitcom attitude about marriage. The maintenance man's raging paternalism. The combination almost made Giulia hope that one day a happy Maryjane would be able to show off photos of four or five 1950s-style children. Giulia muttered Italian insults at the blank page for the indebted sous chef.

As famished as she was, she didn't snarf down the garlic pizza—she took the time to savor every bite of cheesy, spicy, yeasty delight. By ten thirty she began to feel human again.

The phone rang. She checked the caller ID, hit the mute button on the TV, and put the phone on speaker.

"Hello, Laurel."

"Giulia, you're awake. Have you found out anything? Did they call you instead of us?"

"No, sweetie, we're still working on it. Of course they didn't call us."

The sound of shoes pacing back and forth on a wooden floor came through the speaker. "Nine hours till they call. They'll call on time, right? Kidnappers always call on time in the movies." The pacing sounded again. "Christ, we're in a movie. A fucking Lifetime Network movie—the ones where horrible things happen to women, and sane people change the channel before the second commercial break." Her voice quivered and broke.

A deeper female voice on the other end said, "You must stop crying. You're going to make yourself sick. How will we help get Katie back if you are huddled in the corner?"

"Hi, Anya." Giulia bolted a forkful of salad.

"Hello, Giulia. What is your opinion about that useless piece of officialdom? Do you think he'll consider the phone call tomorrow morning worth an hour of his valuable time?" A pause. "You are coming too, correct?"

"Of course I'll be there tomorrow for the phone call. I'm sure that tall cop won't show up. Captain Reilly said he was taking charge of this case."

"Good. Laurel, please go wash your face. I'll reheat the soup."

Giulia raised her voice. "Laurel, you have to eat. If you need to do things quickly tomorrow morning, you have to have energy."

"I know." Her voice still trembled. "Giulia, I'll talk to you tomorrow."

The sound of footsteps receding, then Anya's voice, softer. "We are both going to collapse. We spent all day at banks and pawn-shops. We tried to get a home equity loan, but we haven't been in the condo long enough." The deep voice broke once, but she cleared her throat and continued. "We're still twenty-seven thousand dollars short. Who knew that a schoolteacher and a soup kitchen owner wouldn't be able to come up with half a million dollars on short notice? We should have robbed that *yobanyi* bank instead of begging the loan officers to bend the rules." She began to sob in earnest this time.

Giulia said soothing things over the phone until Anya coughed, sniffled, and blew her nose.

"Sorry."

"Stop it," Giulia said. "Don't apologize for anything. Have you eaten anything today, or are you too caught up in trying to coax Laurel to eat something?"

"I am managing. As my grandmother used to say, in Soviet Russia good comrades stay healthy to properly serve the State." She sighed. "On a normal day, I would probably laugh at that."

"You'll be singing lullabies about the glorious Soviet regime to Katie soon."

Anya snorted. "They do exist, did you know that? I found some old music books in my grandparents' attic after they passed. I'll translate the best ones for you sometime."

"Yes, please. I want to sing them to my future children someday."

Anya put on an accent as thick as something from a Cold War propaganda film. "We will find you good Russian farmer with head like barn wall. He will give you many sons to serve the state and not trouble you with much conversation."

"That is priceless." *Keep her talking. She needs distraction.* "Are there strong, virile Russian farmers in Cottonwood?"

"If there are, I can find one for you. I have the radar. Barring that, I could haunt the liquor stores to see who buys the most vodka." She blew her nose again. "I understand that you have your eye on a certain Irish gentleman. The mythical farmer will buy extra vodka to drown his sorrows."

Giulia's Coke went down the wrong pipe. Over the speaker, Anya laughed.

"You used to be a teacher. You should know that nothing escapes us."

Giulia took a deep breath and didn't cough. "At least you're not lecturing me on the perils of an office romance."

"Do you need a lecture? I will be pleased to accommodate you."

"Thank you, no. I've heard it all and knew it before things started. You sound so happy about a potential lecture. Do you use that tone of voice with your student-athletes?"

"They cower in fear when I do. It's a wonderful sight. I understand that when some of their grandparents meet me they are reminded of the old USSR coaches from the Olympics. They tell all the horror stories the newspapers were full of about the training regimens back then, and I am blessed with model students for several weeks afterwards."

"The habit used to trigger an automatic fear response."

"Fear is useful for managing recalcitrant youth." Her voice chilled. "It's wreaking havoc on us, too. Laurel is wandering the rooms now. I will stop her before she starts crying by Katie's crib again."

"Go. I'll see you in a few hours."

Giulia closed the pizza box and finished the antipasto. The former could be reheated.

Her phone rang as she tossed out the salad container.

"Frank, it's nearly eleven."

"Yeah, and you're still up. What did you learn?"

"That housekeepers work harder than most people, that I want to hire the Wildflower's decorator, and that penis-shaped vibrators come in a much wider variety than I expected."

"What?"

Giulia laughed. "Part of my day involved restocking the secret gift shop shelves."

Silence. Then, "Every reply that's coming to mind will get me slapped."

"I'm glad you're learning restraint." She waited for him to splutter. "Calm yourself. When this is over, I'll tell you about today's wedding crasher. There is film and I'm on it. Father Christmas knocked out Mrs. Claus."

"You're serious."

"I am. If I wasn't so tired I'd tell you, but Sidney should hear it too. After her wedding, I think." She stood and walked the living room to keep herself alert. "Here's what I know: The desk clerk and the maintenance man are married. The desk clerk is unbearably sweet and perky. The maintenance man's views of women belong in a fifties sitcom. The masseuse made my back feel like I was a teenager again. She's married to the ski and games instructor and is having pregnancy difficulties. I exchanged two sentences with the sous chef because of the wedding chaos. I'll corner him in the kitchen or break room tomorrow, even if I have to flirt."

Frank laughed. "Speaking as a professional only, your flirting skills need work."

"Thank you. I am aware of my dearth of girlish experience. This will be a good opportunity to practice."

"The interesting stuff always happens when I'm not around. Did you write out your report for today? I'm not near a pen or paper."

"Which begs the question of where you actually are. Sitting in a car in the dark, staking out someone new on the Diocesan assignment list? Perhaps interviewing an unwilling snitch in a shady bar?"

"You've been watching too many old movies."

"You still dress like Nick Charles sometimes. Association of ideas."

"You're punchy. Get some sleep."

"I'll meet you at Laurel's house at seven fifteen tomorrow morning." She yawned like a cave at the thought of her six-thirty alarm.

"Want me to pick you up? Oh, right, you have the rental."

"It's a rust bucket and the heater's spotty, but it's infinitely better than the bus."

"No argument there." Frank yawned this time. "See you tomorrow."

Giulia shut off the television and put the leftover pizza in the fridge, ran hot water into the empty glass, and immersed the silverware in it. Silence filled her apartment. Even the party animals next door were taking the night off.

"Cozy" became "desolate." Christmas did that to her, now that she was on her own. The mini-tree with its generic decorations screamed "lame." The handful of gifts under it broadcast her "outcast from the extended family" status. The single glass and fork in the sink said "alone" with biting eloquence.

She thought of Laurel and Anya, of the newlyweds at the resort, of Sidney and Olivier, of Frank's brothers and their wives and kids.

She turned off the lights and stood in the middle of the short hall, staring. At her neat bed. At her just-cleaned bathroom. At her spotless kitchen. At her sparse living room. At her entire life encompassed by four hundred and fifty square feet of budget apartment space.

"It's still better than the convent and you know it."

TWENTY-SEVEN

LAUREL OPENED THE DOOR the next morning while Giulia's knuckles were still on it.

"Come in, come in, it's only 7:14, but we're terrified they'll call early, do you want some coffee? Holy cats, what did you do to your hair?"

Even though Laurel's long hair was pulled back, it still looked wild. Her flowing clothes, which usually moved like calm waves on a pond, fluttered like bird wings on a windy day. Giulia grabbed her in mid-step and squeezed her until she stood still for a moment.

Laurel broke away. "Don't do that. If I stop to think, I'll lose it. I'll pour your coffee. I've got gingerbread creamer. Your boss isn't here yet. Turn around. I want to see the back." She took Giulia by the shoulders and turned her around herself. "It's so long. And wavy. You look like me—well, you would if you were taller and your hair was darker. I like it. Why the change?"

The doorbell rang on her last word. Laurel dashed to it. "Mr. Driscoll. Come in. I'll pour you some coffee. We're putting coats on the bed. Black or cream or sugar?"

"Black, please. Thank you."

Anya came out of the bedroom and held out her hands for Frank's and Giulia's coats. Giulia squeezed her, too.

"Thank you for coming. Christ, people say that at funerals. I would spike my coffee with Black Velvet if I didn't have to be alert. I would spike Laurel's too. Giulia, your hair is lovely."

"Anya, this is Frank Driscoll. Frank, Anya Sandov."

"Pleased to meet you. Where have the police set up?"

"In the kitchen." Her lip trembled but she controlled it. "I'll put your coats away."

Giulia started to move toward the kitchen, but stopped when Frank didn't follow. His gaze was riveted to the framed print over the couch.

"Why is that tree warped?"

"It's not a tree," Giulia said. "It's placenta art."

"It's what?" His voice rose on the last word.

"Shh. It's an art print made from Katie's placenta."

"You have got to be kidding me."

"Drag yourself into twenty-first century natural art, Frank. Laurel and Anya attended Katie's birth and brought a special container with them for the placenta. I plan to suggest this to Sidney when she gets pregnant."

He looked down at her. "Good God, she'll bring it in to show us."

She smiled. "That's the point. Perhaps I'll take you to The Before and After Shop to buy her an appropriate gift."

"The what?"

"Keep your voice down. It's a new place that Laurel and Anya invested in. Two midwives run it. They sell placenta jewelry, breast-milk soap and lotion, and—my favorite—the hand-knitted anatomically correct pregnancy doll, complete with baby and birth canal."

"Good God."

She patted his hand. "Clear your mind. It's twenty-five after."

Jimmy and an officer Giulia didn't know sat at the green-glass kitchen table. Jimmy was talking about triangulation and cell phone towers on his phone. Laurel's phone sat on the edge of the table, next to a mini tape recorder with an earbud attached. Anya stirred creamer into a cup of coffee; Laurel handed Frank a Santa Claus mug.

Jimmy nodded at Frank and Giulia, listening to a nasal-sounding voice on his cell phone.

Anya handed an elf-eared mug of gingerbread-flavored coffee to Giulia.

Everyone waited. Laurel put the earbud in her left ear and hovered over the phone.

The snowman clock said seven thirty. The second hand ticked around the dial. Fifteen. Twenty. Twenty-five. Thirty. Thirty-five.

The phone lit up. Laurel, Anya, and Giulia jumped. The ringtone started an instant later.

Jimmy signaled to Laurel. She pressed the *Record* button on the tape recorder and the green *Receive* button on the phone. Her knuckles gripped the phone till they were as white as its case.

"Hello?"

The sound of a male voice reached Giulia, but not the words.

Anya clutched Laurel's right hand.

"Yes," Laurel said. "Yes, we have it … yes … yes, I understand … Can we hear Katie's voice? Is she all right? Please. Please!" Tears ran down her face. She lowered the phone and turned off the tape recorder. "He wouldn't let me hear Katie."

From the opposite side of the table, Jimmy said, "Dammit."

Frank said, "You couldn't trace that call?"

Jimmy waved "shut up" at him. "How close is the car? Damn. Try anyway. Call me back."

He ended the call and slugged half his coffee in one gulp. "Carnegie Mellon."

Frank shook his head. "If he's smart enough to call from a place like that, then he's smart enough to have used another burn phone."

"Which he did. Dammit." He swiveled his chair to face Laurel and Anya. "Your cell phone company triangulated the call to the campus of Carnegie Mellon. The problem is, of course, that your kidnapper went to any one of a hundred places and bought a disposable phone. With cash, no doubt, and loaded it with the smallest possible amount of minutes. So all your carrier can do is triangulate the call to a narrow area, in this case, Carnegie Mellon. Which has several thousand cell phone users. An unmarked car was only a few minutes away from there, so it's driving around, but don't expect too much."

"What does that mean?" Anya said, her hands still clenched around Laurel's.

"It means we figure the kidnapper will have blended into the student body or driven away by now. Hell, he could've called from an idling car. Did you hear any noises like that?"

"I—I don't know."

Giulia said to Frank, "A burn phone?"

"A disposable one. He'll have tossed it into a trash can or dumped it in the lap of the nearest homeless guy as soon as he finished the call."

"Then we have nothing." Anya pried Laurel's fingers off the phone. Laurel sat down hard on the floor, Anya sinking down with her.

"Not true," Jimmy said. "We have the recording." He rewound the tape.

The little recorder's speaker hissed and then half of a ringtone blasted out. Jimmy decreased the volume.

Laurel's voice: "Hello?"

A man's voice: "Are you ready to receive my instructions?"

Laurel: "Yes."

The man: "Do you have all the money?"

Laurel: "Yes, we have it."

The man: "Place the money in a cardboard box and write on the sides and top in large black letters the words 'Spare lights.' Go to the used bookstore on 42 Welkin Street and place the box on the ground next to the side entrance steps. Do you understand?"

Laurel: "Yes."

The man: "You may have someone drive you, but do not bring the police."

Laurel: "Yes, I understand."

The man: "Bring the box at eight thirty precisely. That is all."

Laurel: "Can we hear Katie's voice? Is she all right? Please. Please!"

Four beeps, then nothing. Then a click and tape hiss.

Jimmy stopped playback.

Giulia said, "Play it again, please. I want to see if I recognize his voice." She set down her coffee and leaned her elbows on the table.

"I heard shoes on a hard floor," Jimmy said. "Tile or slate. He muffled his voice."

When the recording started, Giulia closed her eyes. The voice gave its instructions. She leaned so far over the table the edge bit into her stomach. When it finished, she walked around right next to the tape recorder and said, "Once more, please."

Jimmy's phone rang. He pushed away from the table and took it in the other room.

This time Giulia heard the rhythm of the kidnapper's boots on flooring. Of course he was inside; the wind and snow would make it difficult to hear and respond. She pictured work boots on a tiled bathroom floor. She pictured ski boots in the break room. If only she'd looked at the sous chef's feet when he picked up that tray of used glasses.

She shook her head when the recording ended. "I can't narrow it down yet."

"Damn," Frank said. "I suppose it was too much to hope for after only two days."

Jimmy returned. "No luck at the university. Too many footprints in the snow, and we don't have a warrant to check all the trash bins in every building."

"Giulia says she's not sure which guy at the Wildflower the voice belongs to, if it even belongs to any of them."

She dragged a hand through her new hair and said to Laurel and Anya, "It's either the maintenance man, the ski instructor, or the sous chef." She tugged through a knot. "I need more time."

Anya said before Jimmy replied, "We never saw any of the kitchen staff. I remember the games instructor a little. He was happy and full of energy when we participated in one of the activities, but other than that … Did we even see a handyman while we were there, Laurel?"

Laurel wiped her eyes on a napkin. "Maybe. I don't remember. We were too busy telling everyone about Katie and having a last pre-parenthood fling."

Anya's and Giulia's eyes met.

"Staff are invisible," Giulia said. "They're trained that way. Even at the Wildflower, where guests and staff are semi-friendly, who really thinks about the guy fixing the electrical outlet in the corner when you're having a heart-to-heart or telling everyone about the greatest thing that just happened?"

Laurel said, "Or while you're in the hall, reading the TV screen of what's happening that day at the resort. Nobody thinks about the housekeeper dusting the furniture two feet to your left. Oh my God."

Jimmy said to the officer still seated, "Call the resort and ask the owner for any records she hasn't given to us already on the head of maintenance and the ski instructor. Giulia, what's the name of the sous chef?"

Giulia drew a blank. "I don't remember."

"Doesn't matter." He wrote on a fresh piece of paper and handed it to the policeman. "Here's the owner's private number. Have her courier the records to Frank's using his name, not the business title. We don't want to alert the desk clerk, just in case her husband's the kidnapper." He looked at the clock. "We've got forty minutes to get to the drop address."

Anya ran into the laundry room. "I'll get a box."

"Giulia, will you drive me?" Laurel said.

"Of course."

"Wait a minute," Frank said.

"Ms. Drury—" Jimmy said.

Laurel placed her hands flat on the table. "Anya's as ragged as I am. I wouldn't trust either of us to drive. Giulia stays calm no matter what, and she's seen this bastard. She can—how do they say it on cop shows—make a positive ID. Right?"

"I'll try."

Anya came back with the box taped on the bottom and took a Sharpie from a drawer. While she wrote "Spare lights" according to instructions, Laurel opened the cupboard under the sink and brought out a yellow box of garbage bags. Giulia was about to ask what she was doing when she opened the box's perforated top.

"You hid the money under the sink?"

She shrugged, a banded packet of bills in each hand. "On the off-chance we were robbed, we figured this was the safest place for it."

"Smart," Jimmy said.

Laurel handed Anya packet after packet, Anya setting them in the cardboard box in rows and layers.

Frank pulled Giulia aside. "What are you thinking?"

"I'm thinking that we're going to get Katie back."

"Jimmy will drive her, not you."

"No he won't," Laurel said, handing money to Anya without pause. "He said no police. I'm not going to jeopardize Katie's return."

Jimmy looked as long-suffering as any martyred saint. "Ms. Drury, Ms. Sandov, I won't try to force you into using myself or Detective Kane as your driver."

"Good," Laurel muttered.

"However, we have a great deal of experience in these situations. Here's what I propose: Frank and I will park a block away in his car. I'll have two men stationed nearby, watching for the ransom pickup. They'll let us know what he's wearing, what car he's driving, and which way he's headed. Then we'll follow him."

Anya stopped packing. "No. If you stop him, there is no guarantee they will return Katie to us."

Jimmy and Frank exchanged looks. "That's not the plan. We'll follow him to discover where he lives, and stake that place out. He'll likely make a move with the baby today or tomorrow."

"That's right," Frank said. "The ransom money from the other kidnappings turned up in places far away from here. He'll bolt with his wife—if it's one of the two married guys—to spend it like drunk sailors on leave."

"No he won't, he has a job …" Giulia trailed off. "It could work. The resort closes on Christmas Eve and reopens on January third. Monica told me."

The second officer came back into the kitchen. "When I got the resort owner to understand that she needed to handle this as low-key as possible, she woke right up. Said the courier will be at Driscoll's in an hour and a half."

Frank leaned into the archway between the kitchen and living room to look out the window. "Longer. The snow's not letting up."

Giulia imitated him. "Laurel, we have to leave. Is the box ready?"

"Ready," Anya said.

"I'll get my coat and boots." Laurel ran into the abbreviated foyer.

Frank buttonholed Giulia. "Be careful. We'll be right around the corner. Don't do anything stupid."

"Don't worry." She broke away from him to put on her own boots.

Anya came over with their coats and the box. "Your gloves are in the pockets." She handed Giulia a black knit hat and an over-sized pair of sunglasses. "Here. A disguise. Drive safely. Don't get pulled over."

Giulia kissed her. "Not a chance."

Laurel took the box. "Let's go. My car's in our garage."

TWENTY-EIGHT

GIULIA TRIED DRIVING TWENTY-FIVE miles per hour in Laurel's Honda crossover. The road disagreed. She lowered her speed to twenty.

"We'll get there in time. Don't worry."

"Why aren't the plows working? School might be out for the week but people still have to get to work. Shit!" She clutched the Jesus Bar above her head as a taxi ran a yellow light less than two feet in front of them.

"It snows every year, people," Giulia said at the taxi's disappearing taillights. "Learn how to drive in it."

The light changed. They fishtailed, but the tires caught pavement the moment after. The windshield wipers kept ahead of the storm as long as she kept warm air blasting at it. The back window heater was the only reason the mini-wiper had any effect on it at all.

"Three blocks. It's only eight twenty. We'll make it." Giulia took one hand off the steering wheel to pat Laurel's hands, but a patch of ice changed her plan.

"Stupid street signs are covered," Laurel said. "I hate winter. I hate these roads. We have to get there. We have to."

"We will. Stop that. Here's the street. I've bought books at this bookstore a few times." She scanned both sides of the street. "No parking spaces. All right, there it is. I'll double park while you set the box in place."

They were the only traffic at the moment. Giulia thanked God for small favors like this. Laurel jumped out, slipped, caught herself, and ran onto the unshoveled sidewalk. Fresh snow covered her boots and the bottom of her coat before she reached the side entrance. She kicked a spot clear and tucked the box as safely out of the wind and snow as she could. Turning right around, she skidded across the street—not checking for traffic—and jumped into the passenger seat.

"Let's go." She slammed the door. "Come on! I don't want them to think we're watching." She jammed her fingers in the seat belt mechanism. "Ow!" The seat belt caught as the car spun its wheels. "Come on, Giulia!"

"I'm trying." Giulia gritted her teeth and backed up a foot. She put it in drive and gave it a little gas … a little more … one more spin … and the tires caught. She pulled into the street. Still no traffic.

"Take my cell," Giulia said. "Frank will call when they catch up to him."

"They can't risk Katie. They know that, right? She's all that matters."

"They know." She swerved to avoid a car with a snow-covered back window backing out of a driveway. "Clean it off!" The tires spun again but Giulia found traction right away.

Laurel shook the phone. "Ring, damn you, ring."

"Don't break my phone." The brake lights of the row of cars in front of them all lit at once. Giulia pumped the brakes and stopped less than a foot behind the last car. "Is the whole world trying to get to work at the same time?"

"He's not calling. Why isn't he calling?"

"Sweetie, please stop talking. I have to concentrate on the roads."

"Sorry. Sorry, Giulia. I'm so scared. We've got to get her back. We've got to."

Giulia infused "angry teacher" into her voice. "Laurel, please."

The rest of the drive was a horns-blaring, tires-skidding, profanity-laden glimpse of Purgatory. Giulia muttered the old guardian angel prayer because she needed a supernatural jump-start for her driving skills. Two years of riding the bus five days a week had coated them in rust. She muttered it so often she could've been beta-testing a new version of the Rosary.

Her shoulder muscles introduced her to a whole new level of clenched when she finally pulled, without incident, into Laurel's garage. *Thank you, Lord.*

Laurel stared at the dark phone. "He didn't call." The frantic energy in her voice drained out.

"He will. Let's go inside. He may have called the policeman there so he wouldn't distract me in that hellbound traffic."

They slogged through more unshoveled walks and stomped most of the snow off themselves and onto the porch.

"For what we pay in fees, each row of condos should have a dedicated cleaning minion," Laurel muttered.

Anya flung open the door and wrapped her arms around Laurel. "I was so worried. Come in. I made tea. Giulia, thank you for driving her. Close the door. No, I'll close it. You two get your coats off." This time she draped their snow-clumped coats over the nearest chairs.

"No one called," Laurel said.

"He hasn't picked up the box yet."

"What?" Giulia and Laurel said.

"How do you know?" Laurel clutched at Anya.

"Mr. Driscoll is on the phone with Detective Kane. He's relaying word from the two planted officers as they report to Captain Reilly."

Laurel tripped over herself running into the kitchen, Anya at her heels, Giulia right behind them. Kane's phone lay on the table. The screen brightened as the three of them entered.

"Nothing yet."

"Your partner's back, Driscoll."

"Good. Great roads, aren't they, Giulia? Having second thoughts about the reliable, heated, comfortable bus?"

"Not on your life. Stick to the topic at hand, please."

Jimmy's voice said something Giulia didn't catch.

"Guy approaching wearing gray parka … Nope. He walked past."

Laurel sipped hot tea too fast and hissed.

Jimmy's voice again. Frank talked over it. "Another man. Dark ski-type jacket. Dark hat with earflaps … Stopping … Come on, asshole, take the bait …"

Laurel's mug crashed onto the counter.

"He's bending over the stairs … he's screening the box from the street."

Anya and Laurel clutched each other.

Frank continued with more undertones from Jimmy. "He's moving. He's got the box. Come to Frankie, scumbag."

Jimmy's voice: "Shut up, Driscoll."

Kane struggled to hide a smile.

Frank's voice: "We're following him. He headed east on Muegel." A curse interrupted him. "Use the turn signal, moron!"

Giulia leaned over the phone. "Focus, Frank."

"Yes, ma'am. He's turning onto Lake. Bastard's making better time on foot than we are on these roads. Shit, Jimmy, don't brake so hard."

"You want me to plow into that pickup?"

"Just don't lose him."

"I know my job." Silence. "I'm going to retire to Texas and raise longhorns. As far south as I can get and still be in the States."

"You're years from retirement. Somehow I don't picture Eileen telling the family that they're having Crown Roast of Bessie for Christmas dinner." Frank's voice got louder. "He's getting into a car. License plate … Echo Zulu … uh … no, zero … uh … eight … no … shit, he pulled into traffic."

"Turn up the defroster while I navigate." Jimmy's voice sounded distant.

Giulia heard the louder hiss.

"That pickup's seen better days. It's snowing harder. Giulia, talk to God, will you? We can follow criminals better if the weather cooperates."

"Been doing that all day."

"Damn this weather. Shut up, Driscoll. I have to concentrate."

Giulia leaned closer, but all she heard was creaks and breathing. She glanced at Anya and Laurel; they were still imitating a piece of sculpture.

"Dammit, where are the salt trucks?" Jimmy's voice. "My tires aren't exactly new—shit!"

Giulia stared at the phone as though by force of will she could change the audio to a video feed. Only silence came from the speaker. She touched it to revive the screen and confirm that the connection was still open.

Jimmy's voice came through at last. "We lost him. That idiot in the pickup must've hit black ice. We're staring at a three-car crash in the intersection fifty feet from us."

"Please tell me the kidnapper's in that pile-up," Giulia said.

"No. He got through the intersection before it happened."

"Shi—" Giulia stopped herself.

"We're coming back. Kane, give what Frank caught of the license plate to the geeks and have them run a search. Be there as soon as we can."

TWENTY-NINE

ANYA HURLED HER MUG to the floor.

Blue ceramic shrapnel flew across the room. Giulia dodged it; some bounced off Kane's trousers. Laurel stared at the shards scattered across the pale yellow linoleum.

No one spoke for a long minute.

Laurel pushed herself off the counter. "I'll get the broom."

The Valkyrie in rumpled clothes was gone. An old woman in Laurel's flowing sleeves and skirt shuffled to the laundry room. Giulia picked up the bigger pieces. Anya appeared to be looking at the mess, but when Giulia reached the still-intact mug handle at her feet, Anya was standing there crying silently, eyes not focused on anything.

Giulia took the broom and dustpan from Laurel and nudged her toward Anya. The two women held each other, Laurel stroking Anya's hair, murmuring to her. Giulia swept slivers and chunks of mug from under the table, the refrigerator, and as far as the archway to the living room. The other officer held the dustpan for her.

After dumping everything in the kitchen trash, she hung the broom and dustpan on hooks in the laundry room. She closed her eyes to collect herself, but hate blasted through her instead. It roared in her ears and flushed her skin, louder and hotter than an incinerator. She rubbed the heels of her hands against her temples, taking slow, measured breaths.

The doorbell rang.

"I'll get it," said Kane.

Freezing wind rushed into the condo. Two sets of boots stamped on the outside mat. The edge of the wind tickled the back of Giulia's neck, raising brief goosebumps. The hate fizzled and curled into a ball in her gut.

"Giulia?" Frank called from the living room.

"In here." She walked back into the kitchen as Frank and Jimmy entered it.

Anya had soaked a dishcloth and was holding it to her face.

Laurel's hand rested on the teapot. "Can I make anyone some more tea?"

Her phone rang. Everyone jumped this time.

Jimmy yanked out his and hit redial. "Quick, use the earphone and record it. You never know."

Laurel fumbled the earbud into her left ear and pushed the buttons on the tape recorder. "Hello?"

The same voice, angry this time. It shouted for more than a minute without pausing to let Laurel answer. Giulia doubted Laurel could've answered. Her face grew paler and paler as the voice berated her; her hand shook. Frank rolled a chair behind her, but she kept her feet until the voice stopped.

Jimmy said into his phone, "Figures. Someone's got to be near there. Have them look anyway. Call me back." He said to the room, "Duquesne this time. I'm amazed he got there in one piece. He'll be long gone before a car gets through this weather to look for him."

Anya pushed Laurel down into the chair and took the phone out of her hand. Laurel removed the earpiece and Giulia unplugged the tape recorder.

"Let's hear it," Frank said.

Giulia fast-forwarded through the first phone call, making Laurel and the kidnapper sound like cartoon mice. When she reached an instant of silence, she released the button.

"Hello?" Laurel's voice said.

"Did you think we wouldn't count the money you agreed to give us? You didn't cheat us, silly women laden with sins. You cheated the work of the Lord. What pride you have, thinking you could be faithful with a human made in his image. You can't even be faithful with money that buys only the fleeting pleasures of sin. You are proof that the ways of the Lord are righteous and only those who serve him in faithfulness are worthy of his highest blessing. Repent before death takes you and you may yet escape the pits of Hell."

Tape hiss. Giulia stopped the playback.

"He didn't say when he'd call back." Laurel grabbed at Anya's hands. "He has to tell us what we have to do next."

Frank glanced at Jimmy, who nodded.

"Ms. Drury," Frank began.

"He's not going to call back," Giulia said.

Laurel and Anya turned into deer in the headlights.

Giulia took a step toward them. "That was his way of saying he's keeping Katie because you gypped him. To hell with him."

Frank stared.

"Don't worry." Giulia put a hand on each of their shoulders. "I'll get her back for you."

"Giulia—"

She didn't even bother to look at Frank. "He disguised his voice, but I'm due at the resort in a few hours. I'll talk to all of them on today's shift, somehow. I'll pick up their speech patterns. He talks like you and me but he slips into King James Version speech patterns. I can hear it. I'll find a way to weasel into their confidence." The hate in her gut blossomed into energy; Frank's eternal Red Bulls had nothing on it.

She kissed both of them on the cheek and headed for the front door. "I'll call you. Tomorrow at the latest. I know the rules have changed. I'll work fast." She yanked on her boots and grabbed her coat.

"Giulia—"

She ignored Frank again and went back out into the weather. The condo's maintenance staff was at last making a dent in the still-drifting snow. She waved at the angry man running the miniature Bobcat along the sidewalk.

Her hapless Ford resembled a giant collapsed snow sculpture. Even though the rental place included a newer snow brush for the price, it took her a good ten minutes to brush off the accumulation and scrape the frost from all the windows.

A layer of salt crunched under her tires as she drove the still-treacherous streets. Halfway to the office a combination plow and salt truck pulled in front of her. She made decent time in its wake, only fishtailing at one-third of the red lights.

She glanced in the rear-view mirror several times, but no Frank. In between fighting the roads she decided he was butting heads with Jimmy. Fine.

It seemed that most workers had taken a snow day. The parking lot behind their building had plenty of empty spaces. Giulia parked in the space farthest from the door and closest to the street entrance. The plowing service still needed to arrive, but she kicked her way through the snow-covered asphalt to the door to the back stairs. Melting slush slopped over the edges of the mat at the foot. She stepped around it and ran upstairs, stamping her boots on the mat outside Driscoll Investigations' door. Icy clumps hung from her jeans from mid-thigh to mid-calf. She brushed it off and let herself in.

Plans blossomed and withered in her mind like a time-lapse nature movie. She couldn't pretend to be a die-hard Evangelical. None of the potential suspects screamed "Westboro Baptist Church Wacko." She didn't possess enough medical knowledge to somehow make conversation with the masseuse about fertility. Too awkward anyway.

She fired up her computer and started on the ridiculous accumulation of emails.

But … she knew just enough about Pagan religions to talk comparative religion with the masseuse. Christmas vs. Yule, Holly and Oak Kings, No Room at the Inn.

In a perfect world, maybe she could get a three-way discussion going with the desk clerk.

Frank stomped his boots on the mat a few minutes later.

"I'm so glad the plowing service fee in my rent is being put to good use. Giulia, what the hell are you planning to do?"

"I'm working on it. I'm going to play up to the desk clerk and the masseuse so they trust me. I'm going to figure out some way to talk with the sous chef. I will channel my inner Saint Paul." She looked up at him. "I know that expression. You'll have to look this one up for yourself. I'm buried in emails."

He opened the blinds. "And this will accomplish what, exactly?"

She inhaled slowly. "I will keep it up, with subtlety, until one of them lets something slip."

"Not in time to accomplish anything useful."

"You're wrong. Have you forgotten that people talk to me? You said it yourself when you asked me to help with the Bible-quoting stalker suspects." She grimaced. "I'm going to gain the trust of all of them and betray it. You can start calling me Judas Iscariot."

Sidney opened the door on Giulia's last sentence. "It's Christmas, not Easter. Hey, Giulia. Good morning, Mr. D. Theologically speaking, Jesus's life hadn't yet gone into the compost pile."

Giulia laughed out loud. "Sidney, if I'd been drinking anything, you would owe me a keyboard. Where did you come up with that?"

Sidney shrugged. "It sorta hit me after the last RCIA class. The guest priest had a zillion degrees in theology and psychology and he was wicked old. He went on and on about the deep spiritual meaning of everything Jesus did and said. One of those people who love the sound of their own voice, you know? When he finished talking about how everything in the Christmas story points like a laser pointer to the Crucifixion, I had to sit on my hands so I wouldn't say something snarky."

Giulia managed, "Why?"

"Come on. No way do I believe that Mary made swaddling cloths with cross patterns. Oh, and get this: He drew a flow chart on the whiteboard using the Cross to show the important points in the life of Jesus and which Church doctrines line up with them. Then he drew another one to show how the amount of money we put in the envelopes each week is connected with these doctrines and that knowing this and tying it into our weekly offerings proves how good a Catholic we are." She banged her purse into the bottom drawer of her desk.

"No, it doesn't," Giulia said.

"Yeah? Then tell him. I almost had a fight with Olivier over this. Two days before our wedding, and we're arguing about nutso theology." She pounded her password into the keyboard.

"Listen, I've dealt with some of those antiquated priests and nuns. You're not saying Olivier agreed with that drivel?"

Sidney un-ruffled. "No, he doesn't. He said I should just let it wash off my back and concentrate on the important things."

"He's right. When I was a Novice, one of the retired Sisters gave all of us a little ceramic baby Jesus, adorable and curly headed and smiling—and he was sleeping on a cross."

"Ew." Sidney shivered.

"Exactly. There's an old school of thought that won't let these macabre ideas go, and you should take Olivier's advice. Ask Father Pat. Right, Frank? He'll set you straight."

"Yeah. Pat's all common sense. He'll love the compost line. Might use it in a sermon."

Sidney's one-hundred-watt smile came out. "Really? That would be totally cool. Father Pat's the best." She did a double-take at Giulia's plain-as-possible clothes. "That's right! You're working at the resort. How'd it go? What's it like?"

"Wait a second, Sidney. Giulia, your plan needs some definite steps. This is a partnership, remember?"

"I am quite aware of that." She lifted her fingers from her keyboard. "Sorry. That came out wrong. I'm not trying to frost you. It's more like improv in my head than a scripted piece."

"You've been playing in the orchestra pit too long. It's giving you dangerous ideas."

"On the contrary, it's giving me useful ideas. Costuming, for instance." She plucked at her drab beige sleeve.

"I wondered why you were wearing that," Sidney said.

Giulia laughed. "Because it's frumpy and bland? Perfect. You'll notice I'm not wearing makeup and have done nothing fancy to my new hair. It's all camouflage."

"What's wrong with the regular you?" Frank said.

"I'm reimagining myself as a female Uriah Heep." She looked from Sidney to Frank. "You don't recognize the reference? If you'd been my students you'd know the classics." Her hand felt in her central desk drawer and emerged with a ruler. "Listen up. In Dickens's *David Copperfield*, Uriah Heep is the epitome of false modesty. He is forever saying how humble he is and sucking up to his employers, when he's really scheming to defraud them."

Sidney's mouth hung open. "You're going to pretend to steal from the resort?"

Giulia whapped the ruler against the palm of her hand. "Pay attention or I'll have you take a test after this. Of course I'm not going to pretend to steal from the resort. The character's complete humility gave me the idea. I'm going to play up to the three people I've pegged as possible kidnappers until I get what I need."

Frank took the ruler from her hand. "I'm not happy with this non-plan."

"If you can come up with a better one by two o'clock, I'm willing to listen."

THIRTY

GIULIA WALKED THROUGH THE employee door at two thirty and Monica pounced.

"You're early. Wonderful. Ellen called in sick and I'm losing my mind. Can you clean Snapdragon 105 and 107? The guests are being patient but we don't want to push it."

She dashed away while Giulia was saying, "Yes, of course."

The plumbing worked in both rooms, and no guests appeared while her hands were in the toilet. Monica pounced again while Giulia rolled the last room's sheets into neat cylinders.

"Trade you." She took the sheets and handed Giulia a Post-it note. "Two rooms in Amaryllis need the full treatment. We've got late arrivals tonight for tomorrow's Christmas party. Thanks. You're a peach."

It was nearly five thirty before Giulia collapsed into a plastic chair in the break room.

A portable radio played "Sleigh Ride." She rubbed her eyes and kept her hands over them. The darkness was restful.

A cup of black sludge slid under her nose. "Here."

She raised her head and smiled at the masseuse. "Thanks, Penny." She sipped it without grimacing. *I'll be an actress yet.*

"I see you passed the unofficial initiation."

"Initiation?"

"Restocking the hidden shelves in the gift shop without over-reacting." Her warm smile took in Giulia's blush and flicked to the cup of coffee.

"I admit I was startled, but it's all part of the job."

"Where on earth did they find you? You talk like my college ethics teacher."

Giulia gave her a lopsided grin. "I get that a lot."

"You're a helluvan actor, too. That coffee should have a warning label, and you're not batting an eye. Did Barbara hit you up about starring in a skit yet?"

"No. I'm not an actress, really."

"Heh. That won't stop Barbara. Besides, you've got balls. That's pretty much all you need to get on our stage." She opened a bottle of water on the table and drank.

Giulia coughed and set down the coffee. "I'm sorry?"

Penny laughed. "Yep. Ethics teacher. I meant the way you dive-bombed the jilted Father Christmas yesterday." She slugged more water.

"Watch where you're going, jock-boy." An irritated baritone voice from the hallway.

"Least I can get it—" The ski instructor and both sous chefs entered the break room at the same time.

"Matt!" The masseuse scowled at her husband.

"Yeah, yeah, sorry. Want me to get the boss?"

"Yeah, thanks. She wanted everyone to test this."

Giulia stared at the tray in the first sous chef's hands. It held a dozen dessert plates.

"Is that cheesecake?" she said.

The second sous chef—the one she'd been trying to corner—said, "This is my first solo dessert. I need to convince the dessert chef to take me as an apprentice. So you're all forcibly volunteered as guinea pigs."

Maryjane came in from the front counter. Giulia and Penny looked at each other.

"You think you have to convince us to try cheesecake?" Giulia said.

"You aren't married or dating, are you?" Penny said.

"Am too. Who do you think cooks at home?" He handed everyone napkins and forks. "Where's the boss?"

"Here! Cheesecake ahoy!" Barbara hurried to the end of the table and held out both hands. "Gimme, please."

"Okay. Crust is gingersnaps, macadamia nuts, sugar, butter. Filling is the usual, plus sour cream and lime juice. On top is sliced kiwi and pineapple, with a mango coulis artistically drizzled over all."

Maryjane stabbed a forkful. Giulia and Penny put the first bite into their mouths at the same instant. Penny moaned. Maryjane's wide smile stayed on her face even as she popped more cheesecake into her mouth. Giulia made a show of being too overcome to stand. Barbara ate one bite, then a second, set down her fork, stood, and beckoned the sous chef over. He came, color draining from his winter-pale face.

Barbara put her hands on his shoulders and kissed both his cheeks. "I'm going to talk to Tim about adding this to the dessert rotation."

The sous chef inhaled like he'd forgotten how for a moment. The other chef removed the rest of the plates from the tray and went back toward the kitchen.

Barbara sat back down and ate another bite. "Could someone pour me half a cup of coffee?"

Giulia stood. "Anyone else?"

"Sit down, please," the sous chef said. "I'll get it."

"I'll take a half," Maryjane said.

"Me, too," Penny said. Her husband entered, tucking in his thermal undershirt. "Honey, want some cheesecake? It's heavenly."

The ski instructor glanced at Barbara, whose eyes were on a glazed kiwi slice, and sneered. "Nope."

The sous chef followed his glance and gave him the Italian hand gesture for "Kiss my ass."

Giulia coughed and swallowed coffee to cover it.

Penny stabbed her fork into the dessert. Giulia expected flames to shoot out of her eyes. After a moment, the masseuse stood and beckoned her husband into the hall.

Barbara stood and picked up her half-finished portion. "I'm working on payroll, and this will definitely help. Gordon, I'll recommend that Tim add this to the Sunday-night dessert choices. This is as good as his tiramisu, and you know how much I adore tiramisu."

Gordon passed out coffee cups and sat next to Maryjane to sample his own cooking. Giulia, under pretense of fetching a napkin, eased over to the doorway. Penny and Matt hadn't moved far enough away from the door, for which Giulia was thankful.

"...don't give me that," Penny hissed. "I hacked your email yesterday."

"You underhanded bitch," Matt hissed back.

"And what are you? Telling your sister that you think I miscarried because I screwed Gordon and got an STD." Giulia heard tears in her voice.

"I've seen the way you look at him. I've also seen those mailings from the adoption agencies. What aren't you telling me?"

"Nothing! I'm tired of your games. I want a baby with a husband who loves me. Is that so hard to understand?"

Giulia returned to the table before someone noticed her hovering too close to the doorway. Penny and Matt didn't return to the break room. Giulia finished her dessert. The other housekeepers and the wait staff came in a few minutes later. Gordon looked like an actor taking a center-stage bow.

Giulia poured the rest of her coffee into the sink and rinsed the mug. No one paid any attention to her while they had gourmet cheesecake in front of them. She walked through the door into the break room. The bank of four lockers facing the doorway screened the opposite bank that held Gordon's. No one followed her in. She slipped the paper clip out of her pocket, scowling at her hands, which had decided to tremble.

Wuss.

And the lock wasn't engaged.

Thank you, patron saint of breaking-and-entering.

She eased the shank out of the body. Gordon must have been in a hurry. Or angry. *Hmm.*

The Wildflower kept the lockers oiled. The door didn't make a single squeak when she eased it open.

Coat, boots, hat. Scattered papers on the top shelf. She picked them up, careful not to disarrange them. Rent bill. Department store credit card bill. RSVP card for a New Year's party. Nothing that pointed to the kidnappers. She listened for a moment. The noise from the break room continued. She stood on tiptoe and felt farther back on the top shelf. Something heavy and flat. She pulled it out. An iPad.

Bingo.

She paused to listen again. No change. No footsteps coming her way. She booted the iPad and the screen came to life right away. *The hibernation button is a wonderful thing. All right, who's emailing you?*

A woman with the same last name. Giulia opened that one.

> **Gordie, my Gyno called back. She says the Pill's still in my system. I told her that it's been six freakin' months but she says we just have to relax and keep trying. I'm opening a bottle of wine and we're going to role-play, if you get my drift. Brew some espresso before you leave, because it's baby-makin' time!**

The pitch of the voices in the break room changed. Giulia closed the email and hibernated the iPad. Making sure to slide everything back in as near as possible to their original positions, she closed the locker door. She caught herself just before she clicked the shank all the way into the lock.

She was inside the supply closet before the waitresses reached the hall. Her hands still shook.

"Calm down. Slow your breathing. Anyone would think you're new at this."

To cover it, she checked the supplies on the cart, restocking the lotion and toilet paper. When she opened the door, hands steady again, Monica was leaning in the break room doorway finishing a cup of coffee.

"You had some of the cheesecake, right?"

"I'd like to kidnap him and chain him in my kitchen forever," Giulia said, pitching her voice just a little too loud.

Penny's laughter came from the break room. "I just said the same thing."

Giulia and Monica joined Penny and Maryjane. The busboys and dishwasher walked past them all, plates in hands. The radio gave them "Christmastime Is Here."

Maryjane shook a finger at Giulia and Penny. "That is not the way good women talk. What will your husbands say?"

Giulia held up her naked left hand. "I'm single. Although I hope to get a husband without having to kidnap one."

Penny said, "Want to borrow mine? He might cure you." She glanced at Maryjane. "Don't say it. Just because you have the perfect *Ozzie and Harriet* marriage …"

Maryjane gave Penny a maternal type of hug, which looked awkward with Penny's six-inch height advantage.

"I'll add you to the prayers at tonight's service. It's a special one for children and parents."

Penny disengaged herself. "I know you mean well. Thanks. I'm about to dedicate a shrine to Brigid, which will cover the Druids and the Catholics. Regina, do you know any more bases I could cover?"

"Sorry, no. I'm not familiar with religions that have multiple deities."

"Oh, well. I'm off to surf the Web in the game room before my next appointment." She paused in the gift shop to finger the lingerie.

Maryjane's gaze followed her. "Some days I have a very naughty desire to buy one of those teddies."

Giulia smiled. "I had the same idea when I was hanging them up yesterday."

The desk clerk lowered her voice. "I've been hoping for years for him to surprise me with one for Christmas."

"Would you like me to drop a hint?"

Maryjane gasped and looked around, something like fright twisting her face.

THIRTY-ONE

Giulia pounced—in her head. Out of her mouth came friendly, calming words.

"Is he old-fashioned about what 'good girls' should wear?"

Maryjane gave her a weak smile. "He's my husband, but he's also our church's pastor. We have to set an example for his flock, in public and private."

How to say it... But before Giulia could frame the question without sounding offensive, Maryjane came to her rescue.

"You're thinking that good Evangelicals wouldn't be working here."

Giulia called up a blush and Maryjane mirrored it.

"It's the job market. Phineas and I had been here for six years when the original owner retired. Barbara begged us to stay." She lowered her voice. "I do like her, even if she's not exactly what our church elders would approve of. We brought it to God in prayer. After consulting with our church elders, we realized that God works in mysterious ways. We chose to be open to the possibilities he presented to us in this setting."

Good Heavens, I've landed in a syrupy Christian novel. Giulia managed, "I see."

Maryjane's smile changed. "We've had some interesting opportunities here." She straightened. "You, for example."

Giulia didn't have to pretend to be startled. "Me?"

"I've seen you listening to Penny's marriage woes. I've seen the look on your face." She used a one-armed maternal hug on Giulia. "You're searching for answers."

This time, the plan sprang into her head fully formed. All she needed to do was play on Maryjane's combined sweetness and role as a pastor's wife. She called on a little-used, mostly useless skill: she started to cry.

Maryjane's embrace tightened. "What's wrong?"

"I thought I had found a good man, I really did, but last night…" She snatched a scratchy napkin from the holder on the counter and wiped her eyes. *This will make them redder and more pathetic. Perfect.* "Last night … he said such terrible things to me."

"I was sure you weren't married."

Giulia let more tears flow. "I'm not. He said I was the perfect woman for him and he loved me. He's so skinny. I'm a good cook and he always compliments my cooking and he never seems to gain a pound. He's so charming."

Maryjane waited, the hug taking on extra reassurance.

"I always made sure not to get pregnant, you know? Because we weren't married." Giulia rubbed her arms. "He's not the father type, but he took good care of me."

The radio gave her Faith Hill singing "O Come, All Ye Faithful."

Thank you, radio. "But last night he showed me who he really was."

Maryjane handed her another napkin.

"I gave him his Christmas present early, you know, so he could wear it to church. I never really talked to him about church before. I knitted him a sweater. He—he threw it on the floor and stepped on it."

"Why?" Maryjane's voice was all soothing honey and warmth.

"I told him about this Lessons and Carols evening I wanted to go to. It would've been so great—early music singers, candlelight, and a Lord's Supper afterwards." *Don't overdo it. Remember to sound sincere.* "He told me that church was a crutch for the weak and that Jesus was a fairy tale like Santa Claus and the Easter Bunny."

Maryjane grasped Giulia's hand.

"I should've asked him if he was a Christian before I moved in with him, I know. I assumed he was because he hung out with friends of mine." She tried for a dramatic pause. "When I tried to ask him about that, he grabbed my arm and yanked me right up against him and told me that the only time he wanted to hear me shouting God's name was when … well … I won't repeat it."

Maryjane *tsk*ed. "You poor thing. You poor dear."

Giulia let the tears run another fifteen seconds by the clock above the refrigerator. Then she blew her nose and went to the sink. Grabbing two paper towels with one hand, she ran cold water with the other, soaked the towels, and pressed them against her face.

"I know what you need."

Giulia lowered the wet towels. She hoped she looked miserable. "What?"

"An evening in our church." When Giulia shifted her weight onto her right elbow and twisted around to look at her, Maryjane's smile tripled in wattage. "I mean it. Our church is just like coming home. It's all about family and love. Oh, Regina, say you'll come tonight. We're having an extra-special pre-Christmas service. It's just what you need. I'm sure of it."

The radio began a seven-o'clock news break. *Escape route open.*

"I've been on break way too long. I have to vacuum the eating area now that dinner's over." She squeezed Maryjane's hands. "I'll think about it, I promise."

She straightened her hair and uniform skirt before walking out of the room. The utility hall was empty and the supply-room door was the kind that closed on its own if not propped. She let it hiss and click shut, then propped herself against it.

Dear Lord, I'm going to need a marathon Confession after this. I must be more hardened than I thought, because I was more worried about saying the right words to her than I was about the tower of lies I built.

The vacuum needed a new bag, which gave her a few more minutes to compose herself. When she opened the door, she was Regina the invisible housekeeper again. Her face and eyes had regressed from "hot and swollen" to "tepid."

Forty-five minutes later, she was the last one eating dinner left-overs in the break room. The maintenance man entered, a dusting of snow on his parka, and walked straight up to her.

"Regina, my wife told me your story."

Giulia looked startled and embarrassed.

"You come to our church tonight. You will be very welcome at the Valley of the Redeemed."

"I'm sorry; I haven't heard of this church." In her head she paged through the "Churches" section of the phone book. Nothing.

"We raised the money to buy our own building two years ago. Before that, we met for worship in each other's homes. At the moment the Valley consists of our extended family members only." He patted her back in an awkward, fatherly way. "Maryjane will write out directions for you. Our church is located halfway between here and Cottonwood. The area is quite rural and without street-lights, so familiarize yourself with the directions before you start out." He looked at the clock. "What time is your shift over?"

"Nine o'clock."

"Good. The service is a late one because Maryjane is filling in for the night clerk until eight thirty. If you leave here by nine fif-teen and the weather holds, you should reach us well before nine forty-five."

"Sounds good."

The phone on his belt *ding*ed. "Phineas, can you come jump a battery? White Land Rover, third row under the light."

He unhooked it and pressed a button. "I'll be right out." He sighed. "Someday I will invent a car battery that never dies, sum-mer or winter. And then I'll retire. See you at quarter to ten."

Giulia put her hands to the small of her back and stretched. *I'll need to practice happy-happy-joy-joy. Phineas's paternal attitude ticks me off, but at least he doesn't seem to be the fire-and-brimstone type. It could be an act, though. Act. Games. God, I hate this duplici-tous garbage. Myself included. This Christmas Week service might not be a bad way to end the day—after all, church is church.*

THIRTY-TWO

A PSYCHIC EMAIL APPARENTLY went out at eight o'clock, because fifteen couples all decided to use the pool and spa at once. Giulia ran back and forth with fresh towels twice. It being three days before Christmas, the chef wheeled a chocolate fountain and piles of cut fruit on a decorated trolley into the lounge at eight thirty. The newlyweds and their friends who'd stayed at the Wildflower converged for that; the pool and spa people joined them, and that meant more towels and a run for extra dishes.

Caroling began at nine. Giulia deposited a full tray of dessert dishes onto the dishwasher cart and escaped.

After she scraped her car, she dialed Frank with freezing fingers. "Hello. Distract me while this zombie car warms up, please."

She heard a smile in his voice. "Better make sure that Saturn you have your eye on has a working heater."

"Darn right I will. Wait a sec, I have to put down the phone to get my other glove on." She jammed the warm wool onto her hand

212

and snugged it into the webbing between her fingers. "Okay, I'll still be able to play the flute for Midnight Mass."

"I'm expected to be a good Catholic and come hear you, aren't I?"

"You're expected to be a good Catholic and attend Mass on Christmas. If you want to come with me to Saint Thomas's, that would be acceptable." She held out her right hand to the air vent. Not quite as cold as air-conditioning. "This isn't the distraction I meant. I've done some snooping. The sous chef looks like a bust. He's got a boatload of debt and a wife who's recently off the Pill, but according to the email I read—"

"You read a potential suspect's email? I'm proud of you."

"I'm not." She inhaled, held it, and exhaled. "Don't give me the speech about this being what I signed on for when I agreed to be your partner."

"Fine. What'd the email say?"

"That her body chemistry is retaining the Pill hormones longer than expected."

"Uh, can we skip the intimate female plumbing details?"

"Can you tell me why men are supposed to be tougher than women?"

"Muscle structure. Skull density." He paused. "I didn't mean to feed you a straight line. What else?"

"They're planning a baby-making session for tonight."

"Heh. All right, here's what I've got: He and his wife are not quite drowning in debt, but they're close. Her call-center job is base salary plus commission, and chef school is more expensive than I thought."

"But?" She held her wool-covered hands over the vents. Lukewarm.

"But they don't appear to be much different than thousands of other couples working off student loans. They call their parents and friends. They order pizza. They don't go to any church. The worst thing Jimmy found against them is a few speeding tickets."

"Blast. I refuse to cross them off. They could be flying way under the radar."

"Stubborn woman. If I were still Detective Driscoll, they'd be dropped to page three of my suspect list."

"I'll take it under advisement. What else do you have?"

"The mother from hell."

"Whose?"

"Masseuse's. Her Twitter feed is two kinds of vents. The first about her mother nagging her to spawn. The second about fertility goddesses and clinics."

She nodded. "I know this. It's all she talks about."

"Here's what you might not know. Her husband tweets to a dozen different adoption clinics and support groups."

Giulia sat up. "What's the general tone of his tweets?"

"What, are you looking for increased frustration?" She heard the smile in his voice. "I should win a prize for hiring the right people for the right job."

She heard an answering smile in her own voice. "Stop preening or I'll call your mother."

"I should never have taken you to the Christmas party. All right. Your instinct is correct, but the evidence is iffy. He's frustrated, but it seems to be focused on the mother-in-law and the wife's goddess-hopping."

"He's made comments that imply he likes a traditional, submissive wife."

"A man after my own heart."

"Frank, I hope your wife, whoever she will be, makes twice as much money as you and relegates you to househusband status." Giulia cringed. Banter was all well and good, but she was hitting a little close to home.

"Christ on a crutch, you're an evil woman sometimes."

"Frank."

"Yes, yes, sorry. Their phone records show calls to Erie, but he has college friends there. No calls to Akron."

"That doesn't mean anything and you know it," Giulia said.

"I know. Burn phones. Technology makes our job that much harder."

"I get frustration from both of them, but not desperation. Not yet, at least." She stretched her booted toes toward the bottom vents. "Heat at last. Frank, I've got to get moving. I'm going to put you on speaker."

"Where do you have to be that's so important?" Frank's voice echoed now that it wasn't against her ear.

"Maryjane—she's the desk clerk—invited me to their church tonight."

"What?"

"I am a fast mover."

He spluttered. "You are a hardened little liar. How did you finagle this invite?"

She headed down the long entrance driveway. "I have a hidden talent."

"Which is?"

215

"I can cry on cue. I wove Maryjane a saga of The Wrong Man, The Wrong Choices, and The Need for Change, making my tear ducts gush at the most heart-wrenching point."

The night was utterly dark; only her headlights hitting the mounds of snow gave her any hint of the winding road's boundaries. At least it wasn't snowing.

Frank's voice echoing from the other seat distracted her. "I'll remember this ability the next time I see you cry."

"Since you've seen me cry exactly once, I'll make sure to let you know if you've stomped on my heart or if I'm playing you."

"I have no plans to stomp on you. I presume you'll cry at Sidney's wedding like every other female there?"

"Of course. It's a girl thing. Don't try to understand." She reached the end of the Wildflower's driveway, put the Escort into park, and turned on the overhead light. "I want to pay attention to the road and not to you, no offense intended. What else do you have for me?"

"A cautionary tale of the hazards of working with radioactive materials back in the day."

"What? Wait. Penny and Matt or Maryjane and Phineas?"

"The latter. Phineas McFarland ran away after high school to have a good time. Volunteered for some under-the-table science experiments for the cash, and his little swimmers paid the price."

"Little—oh." She raised her eyes to Heaven.

"He and Maryjane met when she started at the resort as night desk clerk back when it was a standard family-vacation place. Their marriage was fine till the fertility issues started. You know, it's the duty of all good Christians to pop out lots of little Christians."

"'Little swimmer' issues could also be the problem of Matt, the ski instructor."

"With the added difficulty of a wife who's into a different religion."

"True." She backed the heat down a smidgen. "It hinges, I'm pretty sure, on who's the biggest closet super-Christian. Maryjane came out to me, but I haven't talked to Matt enough. I've hardly said ten words to the sous chef."

"Super-deluded enough to convince themselves that taking babies away from one adoptive couple and giving them to another is what God wants them to do."

"If they're having trouble conceiving, then it could be a warped attempt to even the playing field."

"Sports metaphors are my territory." The sound of his voice changed. She thought he was pacing. "So why are you putting yourself in the hands of one potential set of kidnappers? I don't like it."

"You know why: to learn Katie's whereabouts. We're running out of time. I'll use my hardened liar's talents"—she paused while he cleared his throat—"to make them believe their church is what I've been looking for all my life. That should be the quickest way to get them to open up to me."

"If that happens, you're going to call me and I'll call Jimmy, right?"

"If there was a way to ingratiate myself with the ski instructor tonight, I'd do that too. I suppose it's too much to hope that he'll go to the same church." She replayed that last sentence. "If he went to the same church … that would make a whole lot of sense …"

Frank's voice sharpened. "You didn't answer my question."

"I need to move if I'm going to find this place in time. We can discuss things tomorrow to prevent me from falling asleep on my keyboard."

"Giulia—"

"'Night."

She hit the *End* button and turned on the overhead light. "Take Route 30, merge right onto 376, right onto Cliff Mine Road ... Good Heavens, how many little streets? All right. Here goes."

She merged into light traffic. For the Thursday before Christmas, it wasn't too bad. Even as she got closer to Cottonwood it stayed sparse, and when she hit Cliff Mine, she owned the road.

"My kingdom for a streetlight." The houses had plenty of room to breathe and all were set deep into their extensive lots. She flicked on her brights. She turned left, left again, right, followed a narrow road across a wooden bridge and into a copse of naked hemlocks and chestnuts. "It should be right around here ..."

A ten-foot privacy fence loomed up on her right. Pickup trucks, a minivan, and several cars parked in semi-regular order on the near side of the fence. She aimed for the most driven-over part of the snow and parked close to the road. The Escort needed all the help it could get.

The gate had created a half-circle in the snow. She expected her movement to trip security floodlights, but the darkness remained. She flicked the mini-flashlight on her keychain.

Good thing I checked these batteries last week.

A narrow, shoveled path began at the gate and led straight to the Amityville Horror house.

"Good Heavens."

She looked again. Her first impression had been almost right: the third-floor windows were octagonal, not quarter-circles. Instead of an enclosed porch, an open deck circled the front and around both sides. A pair of rocking chairs and a lump that might be a small table rose out of the snowdrifts on the left side of the door. Two windows took up the wall on the other side of the door: one shuttered, one missing a shutter.

The third-floor octagonal windows were dark. *Good. No Satanic silhouettes. Um … you might want to ease up on the horror movies, Falcone.*

Her mini-light illuminated only a small circle of snow. She swung it left to right a few feet in front of her. The snow had been trampled by many human feet and at least one dog. A big dog— she stopped to compare a paw print with one of her own feet.

Rock salt had eaten holes into the packed slush on the wide front steps. It crunched under her boots. Still no lights, not even an old-fashioned porch lamp. No noises from inside, either. She shined the flashlight on her watch: ten minutes to spare. There should be people moving around inside, talking, warming up their voices, something.

An engraved sign above a circular brass knocker read, *Valley of the Redeemed. Ps. 104:8.* It wasn't a verse she knew. She raised the circular brass knocker and let it fall. The sharp sound bounced through the empty house. But it couldn't be empty. The cars outside, the fresh rock salt, the shoveled path. She banged the knocker again and again till paint flaked off the door.

The knocker pulled out of her hand.

"What do you want?"

THIRTY-THREE

A MAN IN A dark suit blinded her with a ginormous flashlight beam.

She blocked some of the glare with one arm. "Mr. McFarland invited me."

"Pastor McFarland. He didn't tell me. Come in then." He lowered the light and opened the door wide enough for her to enter.

When her eyes adjusted, she saw he was wearing a dark-gray business suit and navy tie. A large pin on his lapel gleamed in the reflected light: an American flag with a gold-colored cross on top of it.

He moved deeper into the house. "How do you know the pastor?"

She followed, noting the shabby wallpaper in the entrance hall. To her right, more reflected glow showed her multi-paned glass doors and a hexagon-shaped dining room. The light from a large fireplace to her left was what stretched into the hall and touched the glass doors.

"I'm a housekeeper at the resort."

"Okay. I'll set out a chair for you. It's a busy night to be inviting strangers, but the pastor knows what he's doing."

Five rows of six folding chairs filled the center of the room. Floor-to-ceiling drapes on the far left wall covered what must have been windows. She walked past the fireplace, unzipping her coat, to finger the drapes. Stiff, heavy velveteen—she'd been right. Combined with the folding chairs, they made the room look like a school auditorium.

Floor lamps, the kind stores called "torchière," were the room's other illumination. Two flanked the curtains, two more hugged the wall behind a tall coffee table at the opposite end from the fireplace, and a last pair lit the chairs on the wall that backed up to the hallway.

An artificial tree at least nine feet tall commanded the front corner of the room, next to the drapes. Some colored glass balls hung from the inner branches, but the rest of the decorations looked handmade. Tiny white lights sparkled all through it. But the real centerpiece was the Nativity set in front of the tree. Even kneeling, Mary and Joseph were four feet tall, and no human womb could've held that three-foot-long baby. Two shepherds and three kings flanked the Holy Family; sheep, a donkey, and a camel lurked behind them. Everyone in the tableau had pinked cheeks, blue eyes, and pale white skin.

If Frank had been there, Giulia would have said a few uncomplimentary words for this abomination from the days of *Ozzie and Harriet*. But that would sabotage her real purpose, to win these peoples' trust.

221

Two grade-school girls knelt next to the sheep and camel, singing "We Three Kings." They ignored Giulia. Three boys—one high-school age, one middle-school age, and one perhaps in kindergarten—had draped sheets around their shoulders and set paper crowns on their heads as they whispered lines to each other. Next to the tree, Maryjane spread a hand-embroidered cloth over a tall coffee table. Angels in many-colored gowns played various musical instruments all along the border. Giulia went up to her.

"Did you do the embroidery? It's beautiful."

Maryjane smiled. "You made it. I'm so glad. Yes, thank you. I let my nieces help. Some of the angels have interesting wings."

"Kids love Christmas."

"As do we all. There is no better celebration than the birth of Our Lord and Savior."

"Yes, indeed."

Maryjane looked around. "I don't see my sister. She may be changing the baby's diaper. Could I ask you to help me with the Lord's Supper supplies?"

"Of course." Giulia followed her through the hall and back into a big, square kitchen.

Maryjane took a gallon jug of grape juice out of a refrigerator. "The tray is in the pantry behind you."

The pantry was a cook's dream. Five cupboards with leaded-glass panes and deep shelves. Matching, solid-door cupboards below them. The paint was peeling, but that seemed to be the condition of the whole house. She wondered if the church members had pooled their savings to buy this place and were going to repair it when the weather got better. The stainless-steel tray and a bag of three-ounce paper cups had sole possession of the cupboard nearest the door.

"Found it. Do you need the cups, too?"

"Yes, please."

"That pantry is a little slice of Heaven." Giulia set the tray on the counter and began setting out cups.

"I agree with you. If only this place was in better repair. But all in good time. We'll need thirty-three cups, please." She began filling them halfway with grape juice. "We have a baptism tonight in addition to the Lord's Supper."

Giulia kept setting out cups. *No wonder she called it a special service.*

The man who'd opened the door wheeled in a cart with a plastic laundry tub on it. "Pastor says fill it with hot water and it'll be lukewarm when it's time for the baptism."

"Thank you, big brother. I remember." She finished pouring the grape juice.

Giulia ran hot water into the sink.

"Thank you." The woman squatted and took out two half-gallon water pitchers from a bottom cupboard. She and Giulia took turns filling the tub with steaming water.

"I'll let Pastor know you're making yourself useful," he said to Giulia as he wheeled it out. "That is a good beginning if you seek to join the Valley."

Giulia resisted her evil imp's the temptation to curtsy. *What is it with overbearing, paternal males here? Thank Heaven Frank's only overprotective.*

The opening chords of "Blessed Assurance" played on an electric keyboard sounded from the meeting room. The man pushed the cart with care and the water still sloshed. Maryjane carried the tray and Giulia followed, resisting an even stronger temptation to cast down her eyes and clasp her hands in front of her. Maryjane's bright perkiness was considerably subdued now.

Twenty-eight chairs were filled. Giulia wondered where everyone had been hiding. The house must be bigger than it looked. She slipped into the last seat in the back row, the only one not in neat alignment. Maryjane set the tray on one side of the coffee table, next to a loaf of round, flat bread on its own tray. The cart-pusher flipped down a braking mechanism on the cart's back wheels and sat down next to her in the first row.

Giulia glanced at the congregation. She wasn't the only female in slacks, but she was the only one dressed way too down for church. The kids were unnaturally quiet: no fidgeting, no surreptitious poking of younger siblings. A keyboard had been set up next to the Christmas tree, and a white-haired man played it, with a teenage girl turning pages.

The chords increased in volume, and the keyboardist dipped his head in an ostentatious nod. Everyone stood and began the first verse. Giulia was glad she'd gone to several nondenominational church services over the years. Ecumenism. She'd always pushed for it.

The Wildflower's maintenance man entered on the last verse, severe in a black suit and white shirt, relieved by a dark green tie. He took a position in front of the table.

"Blessings of the Savior, Maryjane. Blessings, Peter and Jane. Blessings, Herbert, Marcia, Mary, Luke, and John."

He blessed every single person by name, his naturally deep voice resonating in the high-ceilinged room. Giulia steeled herself for unwanted attention as he began the back row.

"Blessings to our guest, Regina. May the light of our Savior guide her."

Every head swiveled in her direction. She didn't have to try and fake a blush; all those strangers eyeing her stressed her out on its own. Only on the first day of school, when she was in charge of two- to three-dozen new teenage lumps of attitude, did that many stares give her energy.

McFarland started preaching. Giulia schooled her face into neutral. She was glad it didn't seem that this was a church where people shouted "Amen!" and "Hallelujah!" because she wasn't sure how sincere she could make herself sound.

His voice could be the one on Laurel's phone. Trouble was, the ski instructor's voice had the same timbre. McFarland in preacher mode took on a resonance that did not sound like the phone caller … sort of. Sixty percent. *If only I had a tape recorder. I can't bring out my cell. Everyone would notice. Drat.*

He nodded to the man nearest the door, who went out. His footsteps faded upstairs as McFarland compared the Nativity to being born-again, and that to the standard Gospel passage "Except ye be converted, and become as little children, ye shall not enter into the kingdom of heaven."

Giulia stopped listening to his words; all her attention was focused on the footsteps she could still hear echoes of. So the new church member lived here? Not a hospitable place. The footsteps stopped. Another set of footsteps joined them, and both pairs walked a short distance down a hall and then descended the stairs.

That's the sound of two pairs of adult feet. They practice adult baptism then. I need to get baptized here. That would make them open up. Just do it, Falcone. Do whatever it takes to find Katie. If I have to tell Penny I saw a vision of her goddess of fertility, I'll do that, too.

A woman entered carrying a baby. The man who'd left a few minutes earlier was at her side like a bodyguard.

Giulia's dual-religion plans screeched to a halt.

It was them? So much for innocent-seeming sweetness. Everyone turned to see, so Giulia would've looked out of place if she didn't stare. *They've been keeping Katie in this rat trap?* She didn't dare crane her neck to see if it really and truly was Katie. *It has to be. It has to be. I should've focused my exclusive attention on Maryjane. I might have charmed her into revealing something yesterday. Thank Heaven I came up with that sob story today.*

The woman handed the baby to McFarland. He unwrapped the fluffy towel from around it, and the woman removed its diaper. It was a girl. Giulia forced her hands and feet not to twitch, schooled her face to match the generic eagerness on every other face.

Maryjane unlocked the cart and wheeled it in front of the coffee table. The baby lay limp in McFarland's arms. So limp, Giulia wondered if they'd drugged her. *Would they have drugged Katie to keep her mind confused because this isn't home? Babies are smart. They know where they belong, right?* She tried to see the baby's hands. *What if I'm nuts and it's not Katie? What if it's that woman's baby? What if that woman lives here even though it's a church?* She sought that quiet place in herself that she could find kneeling in an empty church. *Please be Katie. Please.*

"Come, Brethren, and speak for this infant." He held up the baby. "What do you ask of this Church of God?"

Everyone answered, "Life everlasting."

"Hear our prayers, O Lord; and by Thy perpetual assistance keep this Thine elect, so that, preserving this first experience of the greatness of Thy glory, she may deserve, by keeping Thy commandments, to attain to the glory of regeneration."

He nodded at the congregation, and everyone joined in. So did Giulia. McFarland had simply altered the old Catholic rite of Baptism.

"Break all the toils of Satan wherewith she was held: open to her the gate of Thy loving kindness, that she may be free from the foulness of all wicked desires, and may joyfully serve Thee in Thy Church, in the name of Jesus our Lord and Redeemer." He paused and everyone said, "Amen."

The baby hadn't moved through any of this, not even a shiver. Giulia ran through infant CPR in her head, in case she had to make a last-minute rescue. No one else seemed to notice the baby's unnatural stillness. Just because the baby looked like she was sleeping…

McFarland spoke to the baby now.

"Do you renounce Satan?"

Everyone responded, "I do renounce him."

"And all of his works?"

"I do renounce them."

"Will you be baptized?"

"I will."

The unknown woman slid the towel out from under the baby, and McFarland stood at the long end of the laundry tub. The water had stopped steaming. The keyboardist started playing "Just As I Am." McFarland put his hand over the baby's face and submerged her completely.

Giulia clutched her hands together to keep herself in place. Her mouth sang the lugubrious hymn, but all of her real attention was focused on the baby. *Wake up. Cry. Don't be dead. Wake up, little one.*

He dunked her again. Nothing … nothing … he lifted her out … and she squalled. Giulia breathed again. McFarland submerged her a third time, still squalling. When he pulled her out, she coughed in that tiny baby voice, vomited water, and squalled louder than any tiny baby voice should be able to. It was beautiful.

The woman wrapped the dripping baby in the towel and McFarland held it against his chest. The baby stopped yelling and snuggled against him.

Everyone shouted, "Hallelujah! She is saved!"

McFarland said, "Her silence was evidence of Satan's tight grip on her, the curse of Original Sin. When she cried, I knew that she was fighting Satan for her soul. When she coughed up the water, it was a sign that the power of Jesus had expelled the evil."

The keyboard player segued into "All Hail the Power of Jesus' Name." The back rows began to clap and sway. McFarland brought the baby over by the keyboard, and row by row the congregation came up to kiss her. Giulia's ten years of convent training to appear calm and serene as all nuns should saved her—if she'd given in to her desires, she would've bounced in place or pushed through the others to get to the baby first.

When her row's turn came, she went first. *It's like a reception line at a wedding.* The baby was still awake and staring at everyone.

Giulia reached her at last. She bent down to kiss her forehead. The baby's arms came out of the blanket and patted Giulia's cheeks.

"Hello, sweetie," Giulia said.

The baby cooed.

Giulia put her hands over the baby's and played pat-a-cake. The baby cooed again. Giulia smiled at McFarland and made way for the woman behind her. She walked around to her seat, returning smiles and saying "Amen" when anyone said "Praise Jesus."

She resumed her seat, looking at the tree, the table, the other people, anything at all to hide her elation. Because when she'd held the baby's hands, she'd felt the skin tag on each one from the botched surgery to remove the extra pinky finger.

THIRTY-FOUR

When everyone had welcomed Katie into the church family, the woman took her from McFarland and walked out. Katie fussed as soon as she left the pastor's arms. The woman shushed and rocked her. There was too much noise for Giulia to hear their footsteps, but she heard Katie's cries fade upstairs to—she calculated—a second-floor room on the left.

McFarland said a blessing over the bread and grape juice before tearing the bread into thirty-two chunks. He kept a chunk and a cup for himself, and two men approached the table to take the serving trays.

Giulia had a wicked desire to debate McFarland about the use of real wine in biblical times, with relevant passages from several places in the Old Testament. *Get your head straight, dummy. Katie's important, not your snarky desire to smack down this kidnapper.*

Everyone ate their morsels and drank their juice in silence. In this only was Giulia reminded of an actual church service. At the same time, she admitted her bias. Even though she'd been to many

Masses and other church services in nontraditional venues, the Cradle Catholic in her still thought of "church" as a stone building with high windows, a Tabernacle, and an altar.

She handed her empty cup to the woman next to her, who passed them down the row to the man with the serving tray. The keyboard player began "What a Friend We Have in Jesus."

The hard part started after the song. Several men surrounded McFarland to congratulate him on his successful expulsion of Satan from Katie. Giulia knew what was expected of her, so she hung on the outskirts of a group of women, smiling at anyone who looked her way.

Maryjane came over to the group, in hostess mode. "Ladies, this is Regina. She's new at the resort and needs a spiritual home."

"Welcome, Regina."

"You'll be spoiled for any other church now."

"Are you in a Godly relationship? My nephew is traveling today, but he'll be here for Christmas."

"It's refreshing to see a young woman who lets the face God gave her shine through."

Giulia thought, *Cat,* at that last one, since every woman in the circle was wearing makeup. She had no illusions about her own looks—she considered herself attractive but not beautiful—but subtle digs weren't the Christian thing to do. And that was another comment she knew better than to make.

Instead, she gave polite, neutral responses to everyone, glancing at Maryjane and then lowering her eyes after the older woman's "Godly relationship" comment. That's what the Regina who made up the Wrong Man story would have done.

The woman who made the makeup comment put out a hand to touch Giulia's hair.

"This will sound strange, but you look familiar to me. Do you work in downtown Cottonwood?"

Giulia tamped down panic. *She can't recognize me like this. Can't.* "I work the early shift at a coffee shop."

"No, I don't think that was it. Is the coffee shop near the theater district?"

Dear Lord, cloud her memory. "No, I'm sorry."

"Hmm. I must be thinking of someone else. Someone with very curly hair." She fingered a piece of Giulia's new, straight hair. "I blame all memory loss on my kids. They drive me to distraction."

No one laughed. Maryjane's smile froze into something decidedly less than companionable. The woman with the eligible nephew stepped into the breach.

"We're all praying that Maryjane and Pastor's next adoption petition is approved, aren't we, Yolanda?"

Yolanda, blushing, nodded with vigor. Maryjane returned the nod and went over to a group of older women sitting near the fireplace.

Yolanda groaned. "I should duct-tape my mouth before I go out in public."

Giulia didn't have to pretend to be puzzled. "Is something wrong?"

The woman with the nephew said, "Maryjane and Pastor have been trying for years to have a baby." She leaned closer to Giulia. "They even snuck over the border to Canada to try some risky procedures, even though Pastor's father says anything like that is telling God you don't trust his will. Nothing worked, and they've been turned down twice for adoptions."

Yolanda said, "There's a prejudice against true believers, you know. We're not politically correct."

Giulia dug her fingernails into both palms. *Don't say a word, Falcone. Not one word.*

"So we try not to brag about our kids too much around Pastor and Maryjane," Yolanda said. "It doesn't build up the believers to foster jealousy."

"That's very kind of you," Giulia said.

"God takes care of his own," Yolanda said. "God will make sure there's a baby in Pastor's home soon. Look at the good work he's doing."

Someone unplugged the Christmas tree. Someone else started turning off the lamps. Two people took the trays and the laundry tub to the kitchen. The kids trooped behind their parents to get coats and boots. Giulia started singing "Let It Snow" in her head—the first song that popped into her mind—to force out the phrase "Stepford wives and kids." Coming out with random secular Christmas lyrics would earn her less censure, if distraction brought her thoughts out of her mouth.

Maryjane fell into step with her. "What do you think of Valley?"

Giulia sat on her conscience and smiled. "After everything that's happened, it's like coming into a warm home after being trapped outside in the snow."

"That is very sweet. Will you be able to join us on Christmas morning?"

"May I? I'll be finding another place to stay between now and then, because I can't stay with … him. It would be so comforting to be among friends on Christmas."

"Of course you may." She turned her head and called into the auditorium room, "Phineas? May I invite Regina to Christmas services?"

McFarland came into the hall. "Of course."

Maryjane tucked her arm through Giulia's. "Can you follow us to our house? I have printouts of the schedule of services there."

Giulia's new talent for easy lies took over. "I really have to get home. It's after eleven, and I have a part-time day job in addition to working second shift at the Wildflower."

McFarland actually patted her shoulder. "Then get home before you're too sleepy to drive. These unlit roads cause too many accidents." He looked around the hall. "Is everyone out?"

"Just banking the fire, Pastor. Be right there." The keyboard player ran into the hall, followed by the makeup-comment woman. "We're the last ones."

McFarland followed them out and locked the front door. "You four go ahead. Maryjane, let me know when you're at the gate."

The keyboard player lit the path with one of those huge camping spotlights. The other woman took Maryjane's arm and walked ahead with her, their voices too low for Giulia to hear. Giulia wanted to ask what McFarland was doing, but chose the smarter option and walked to the gate in silence. When they all were on the outside of the privacy fence, Maryjane called, "Okay!" She inserted the padlock in its hook and let it dangle.

Giulia heard a chain rattle, then a series of deep barks. McFarland's voice said something Giulia couldn't catch. His feet crunched through the snow a moment later and squeezed through the open gate. He said, "Go!" in a sharp, commanding voice. Maryjane slammed the gate and hit the padlock closed. A second later something large galloped along the inside of the fence, barking.

"He protects us," Maryjane said.

"I see." *Should I say anything else? Play dumb? Keep with the wide-eyed act?*

The keyboard player took the choices out of her hand. "I'm on the early shift this week. I'll see you all Saturday night."

"Certainly." McFarland led the way to the parking area. "Regina, I'll see you tomorrow."

Giulia shook hands with him and ran to her rented Escort. All the heat had evaporated while she was in the house church. Of course.

Freezing or not, she followed their cars for several blocks. The two cars continued straight onto Cliff Mine Road; she turned left onto a street that led in a more roundabout way to Interstate 376. She pulled into the parking lot of a closed mom-and-pop convenience store and turned off the lights but left the engine running.

She had to do it and it had to be tonight. The church wouldn't have another service till Saturday—Christmas Eve. The keyboard player said so. Maryjane had said tonight was a special service. Sure, special to celebrate that they were keeping Katie's ransom and keeping Katie. Bastards. *Sorry, Lord.*

If she went back tonight, she'd only have to fight that babysitter for Katie. What if the babysitter was armed? It was possible. Whatever rationalization the McFarlands were using to justify the kidnappings, the fact that they were keeping the children behind a padlocked security fence said it all. She'd bet that the McFarlands, if pressed, could corkscrew a Bible verse to justify their crimes.

She should call Frank and Captain Teddy Bear for help.

No. She could hear them now. Katie wasn't the only infant with botched extra-finger removal surgery. That wasn't enough evidence for a warrant. It'd be safer to wait and gather more. Even Katie's recognition of Giulia wouldn't be enough. Babies aren't reliable, they'd say.

Frank probably would believe her. Captain Jimmy might not, but they'd both remind her that she was so determined to get Katie back and shove it in their faces that she wasn't thinking like a detective. She was thinking like a friend helping a friend.

Tough turkey, Frank. Besides—the new thought surprised her—what if they planned to give Katie as a Christmas present to some couple approved by their insular little church? There was no guarantee that couple lived around here. The kidnappings in Erie and Akron could prove that. They might be planning to drive Katie somewhere first thing in the morning.

Now. No hesitation. She wasn't Wonder Woman, but she wasn't a helpless, obedient drone, either. She was Giulia Falcone, P. I. in training, and she would do this.

She turned on the headlights and drove back to the Amityville Church of Perfect Happiness. It wasn't till she parked next to the fence, facing out for a quick getaway, that she remembered the guard dog.

THIRTY-FIVE

Giulia wanted to kick herself. Where was her brain? Easy: deep in superhero-land. They were using a guard dog and a padlock. Blast.

She used the flashlight on her keychain to look into the glove compartment. Bungee cord. Owner's manual. Service history log. Spare fuses for the parking lights. Nothing that remotely resembled a cutting tool. Why would there be? Rental-car places don't want to give means and opportunity to a disgruntled driver with road rage.

The biggest weapon in her purse was a nail clipper. Even if she owned a Swiss Army knife, she wouldn't know how to pick a lock with it.

Pick a lock.

Her hand dived into the inner pocket of her purse. Gum. Life Savers. Pen.

Paper clip.

How long was it—just two days?—since Sidney had pushed in the file-cabinet lock and Frank had shown them the paper clip method to open it? He'd mentioned that padlocks and bike locks were the same type of lock. She clutched the paper clip in her fist. She had been prepared to pick the padlock on the sous chef's locker. She could pick this lock.

Next problem: the guard dog. She always had mace in her purse. If it worked on humans, it would work on a dog. Wrong of her to mace an animal that was just doing its job, but she'd do it anyway. She took out her miniature spray can and shook it. Full. Enough to spray the dog going in and coming back out. It had to be enough, because she couldn't protect Katie and dodge an attack dog.

Do it now, Falcone. No hesitation.

She unhitched the flashlight from her keychain and removed the mace from her purse, leaving the purse in the glove compartment and the keys in the ignition. Fast getaways were just as important as well-planned heists. The absurdity of this plan sent a fit of giggles through her. An often-clueless, repressed, former English teacher and nun was about to MacGyver a padlock with nothing but a large-sized paper clip. She squashed the giggles before opening and closing the car door as quietly as possible. If luck was with her, when the dog barked—because it was going to bark before she could mace it—Katie's guard would have to leave the room and come to a window in the front of the house to see what was going on. That should be time enough for Giulia to run to the porch and get inside the house.

The babysitter. Giulia was in decent shape, but she wasn't a fighter. The woman who'd brought Katie in to be baptized was taller than Giulia by three or four inches. Enough to give her an advantage in a hand-to-hand fight. Mace worked on humans and dogs. She could mace her and tie her with the bungee cord. A quick knot, long enough to keep her out of the way while Giulia rescued Katie.

So go. Of course you're scared. Channel that fear into action.

No cars were within sight or hearing on this out-of-the-way street. Chosen on purpose, no doubt. They didn't have to worry about the neighbors hearing kidnapped babies crying, because the nearest neighbors were wide patches of trees.

She had to use the flashlight or risk slipping on ice and blowing this whole rescue operation. The tops of the house's second-floor windows were visible over the fence from this angle; that meant she should assume Katie's babysitter could look out and see Giulia. She hugged the fence.

Nothing worse than snow tipping into her boots happened between the car and the gate. The easily distracted part of her brain made a mental note to up her vitamin C and zinc intake. She shined the light on the padlock. Basic knockoff Yale model, no bells or whistles. Her teeth took over flashlight duty while she broke the paper clip the way Frank had showed her and Sidney.

Okay. The first piece goes under the wafers. No, pins, I think. Whatever. Which way is up on this thing? She picked up the lock and aimed the beam of light at its bottom. *There. It goes underneath the pins, L-shape facing up.* She clamped her mouth around the flashlight first. When both hands were free, she inserted the straight piece above the L-shaped piece and maneuvered it in and out. The pins moved just a little, like they were supposed to. Her bare hands protested touching metal in this weather. She ignored them.

Slow. Steady.

She pushed her left index finger on the bottom half to get … torque, that was it. It slipped out but she grabbed it before it got lost in the snow. *Frank was right. I should've practiced this.* Her fingers manipulated that piece back into position under the still-caught top half.

Before she put her fingers on the top half, she blew on the tips to get a better grasp of the round end. *It's too cold out for anyone but Santa and his reindeer.* Next, she was supposed to jog the top part up and down. In theory, that would make the pins move like she was putting in an actual key.

She tried it. Nothing. She slowed herself down and tried again. There. Something moved. The next step was … Right. Push and turn the bottom piece like opening one of those childproof aspirin bottles. Smooth but don't hurry it.

The pins adjusted to her pressure. *Come on.* She finagled the paper clips another millimeter. *Come on, come on.* More pins adjusted. She expected a click. Nothing. *One … more … tweak …*

Click. Pop. The shank released from the body.

"Yes." She whispered around the flashlight in her teeth. The pieces of paper clip went into her coat pocket and the mace came out. She unhooked the lock from the gate and flipped open the panel that held the gate to the wall. The mace went into her right hand, the flashlight into her left.

Now.

She rattled the gate. An immediate growl rewarded her. Her index finger slid into position on the spray button. She raised the flashlight in an overhand grab to the level of a large dog's head. Another gate rattle. Another growl, nearer this time.

She took a quick breath, said a prayer to Saint George, and shouldered open the gate.

Rapid, loud, deep barks came toward her along with heavy legs galloping. Her head snapped to the left. German shepherd. She adjusted the flashlight, saw the glint from the dog's eyes, and sprayed. The dog yelped and checked its run, skidding on the snow. Giulia found its eyes and sprayed again. The dog hit the ground whimpering, rolling in the snow and rubbing its face with its paws.

Giulia ran up the shoveled path and onto the porch. The old, peeling door was fitted with a shiny new deadbolt. She bit off another curse. Behind her, the dog still whimpered and thrashed, but she had no idea how long the spray's effect would last.

She leaped to the first window and shined the light on the catch. Just as she hoped: old house, old single-pane window, old-fastened catch. Before she thought about it too long, she took a page from TV detective shows and smashed the pane nearest the catch with her elbow. Glass tinkled to the wooden floor inside. She reached in with her bare hand and opened the catch without cutting herself. Her luck was in: no glass cut her as she pulled out her hand, either. She pushed up the bottom half of the window and climbed inside. Her feet hit the floor with tiny thumps and she turned right away to close the window.

Only then did she notice her heart was beating on triple fast-forward. Her breath came in rapid pants and the flashlight jerked like a strobe.

She flicked it off and sat on the window ledge till her body returned to near-normal. When the blood stopped pounding in her ears, she listened for footsteps. Nothing. The only sound was the fainter whining of the guard dog coming through the hole in the window.

She pushed off the ledge. The mini-flashlight jerked only a little this time when she turned it on.

The stairs would be on her left once she got out of this room. She aimed the flashlight in front of her feet again. A good thing, too, because she was about to trip over a tangle of chair and table legs. She veered left and stopped at the door.

Dear patron saint of silence, whoever you are, please muffle this door.

The latch picked up to let the pocket door slide on its track. She moved it an inch. Silence. Six inches. Still silence. Twelve inches and she wormed through the opening, angling her breasts through one at a time and clenching her butt cheeks so they wouldn't bang the frame.

She left it open as a secondary escape route, but went straight to the front door and pushed back the deadbolt. The new hardware was well-oiled. As she suspected, the original keyhole had no key—the church relied on the deadbolt in here and the padlock out there. And the poor dog.

Stairs now. They were wide and swept clean. She wondered if Katie's babysitter was forced to clean the house they were both locked into.

She turned off her flashlight. *Yes.* Light shone low upstairs, near the floor. Another quick on and off. Fifteen steps to the second floor. She trailed one hand on the banister and stepped up.

No creaks. Another. Good. A third. *Cree—* She stopped. When the second-floor doors stayed closed, she raised her right foot and set it on the next step. Silence. She raised her left foot. *Creak.* Much quieter the second time.

Another creak on step nine, but that was all until she stood on the second floor. Halfway down on the left, warm yellow light fanned out from underneath a closed door. She walked to the door with soft steps. This floor didn't creak. Her right hand felt in her coat pocket for the mace, her left hand in that pocket for the bungee cord. The plan was simple. Throw open the door, pinpoint the babysitter, aim and shoot. Like the guard dog, she'd be incapacitated long enough for Giulia to bungee her legs. Her hands would be occupied with scrubbing the mace deeper into her eyes, as she thought she was wiping them clean.

Big risk: walking past the door so she could turn the doorknob with her left hand. If she jumped to the other side, the noise would give her away. If she walked past, the babysitter might see her boots break the light. She weighed her agility against the potential noise and opted for two quick, light steps to the other side of the door.

Mace ready. Assume she heard the steps or saw the boots. Open the door.

She turned the handle.

BANG.

THIRTY-SIX

GIULIA FLATTENED HERSELF AGAINST the wall. So much for calm—her heart beat so hard the material of her coat trembled.

Move fast!

Light shone through a bullet hole in the door a few inches off of center at about stomach level.

She wrenched open the door, spraying the mace as she leaped in at an angle. The rifle cracked—she saw the woman's face behind it and sprayed the mace again. A streak of fire ripped into her leg. Katie screamed. The rifle hit the floor.

"Shit! You thieving—ow—bitch! What did you—owww—shit—"

The woman stumbled out of a rocking chair, a quilting frame, needle, thread, and material tangling around her feet. She dropped her hands from her eyes and lunged at Giulia. Katie kept screaming. Shoulder down, Giulia tackled the woman. The breath *oof*ed out of her. One of her hands ground into her red, dripping eyes. She clawed out with the other one. Giulia kicked the rifle to the other side of the room, knocked the woman's clawing hand away, and shoved. The woman's feet caught the mess of quilt, frame, and rocker. She fell sideways, her head cracking against the crib corner.

The woman slipped to the floor, head under the crib, and lay still. Katie screamed louder. Giulia fell to her knees and dragged the woman out. Tears still leaked from her closed eyes. Giulia pressed three fingers against her carotid artery, too panicked even to pray. The woman's pulse came strong and steady. Giulia released a breath she hadn't realized she was holding. She explored the woman's head with her fingertips and found a bump, not large and thankfully not on her temple. She pressed on the skull around it: everything good and solid.

Katie was still displaying some impressive lung power.

"Katie, I'll pick you up in a minute, just a minute. I have to tie her up so she can't chase us." Giulia yanked the woman's ankles free of the quilting paraphernalia. She knotted the bungee cord around the crib leg, then around the woman's ankles.

"Katie, please. I'll be right there. Right there, sweetie."

She looked around for another length of string or rope—anything. Finally she lifted red-faced, squalling Katie out of the crib and set her on her blanket on the floor. The pink sheet came free of the thin crib mattress and Giulia whipped it into a narrow roll. It would have to do. She tied a square knot around the woman's wrists, bent her like a boomerang, and tied the ends of the sheets to the other leg of the crib.

Last, she retrieved the rifle and tossed it out into the snow.

As she closed and locked the window, she looked down at her left leg. Her pant leg and boot were soaked with blood. Now that she noticed the blood, she also realized her leg was throbbing like a bass drum. *Huh. The stories about adrenaline are true.*

"Katie, shush. We'll leave in a minute."

Giulia looked around the room again, but no rope or string magically appeared. Katie's incessant wailing was addling her brain. She was about to just pick up Katie and leave, risking bloodstains on the rented car, when she tripped over the unfinished quilt. She dived for it and tried to rip a strip off the long side. The cloth was too strong. She upended the overturned workbasket and a pair of long sewing scissors fell out.

"Thirty seconds, Katie, promise."

She cut a six-inch slash and ripped an equally wide strip down the side. Dropping the rest of the quilt, she wound the strip around her calf at the top of the bloodstain. It burned her leg like fire the instant she put pressure on it. Bingo. The right spot. She tied the ends with another square knot.

"Okay, Katie. Let's get out of Dodge."

Giulia folded the blanket around Katie and scooped the baby into her arms. Katie deafened Giulia's left ear for a few seconds, then sniffled, hiccupped several times, and rested her head against Giulia's shoulder.

In the midst of the chaos and blood, with her ears still humming a little from the gunshot and Katie's imitation of a loudspeaker, Giulia experienced a fierce moment of *want*. The earth paused for her to catch her breath and get her head back in the game.

The next moment she was halfway across the room. She ran down the stairs with great care, veering into the dining room rather than straight for the front door. Katie snorked and hiccupped in Giulia's ear, but Giulia heard no dog noises from outside louder than that.

"All right, sweetie, here we go."

Giulia tucked Katie into the crook of her left arm and folded that arm up to put a secure hand behind Katie's head. She readied the mace into spraying position in her right hand, leaving her last two fingers free. Those fingers wrapped around the icy doorknob. *One…two…three…*

She turned the doorknob with a combined wrist-finger-action and opened the door six inches. The doorknob wrenched itself out of her hand, and a force from the other side slammed the heavy wooden door into her shoulder. Thrown off-balance, Giulia twisted to the side, keeping Katie uppermost, and crashed onto the floor, right knee and shoulder taking the impact instead of Katie's head.

Katie screeched.

"Liar!" Maryjane's voice.

Two hands yanked Giulia's head up by her new long hair.

"That entire story you told me today was a lie."

Giulia covered Katie with her body as she pulled against Maryjane's hands.

"You won't steal my baby!"

Giulia slid her hand out from under Katie's head, then freed the rest of her arm. Easing into Maryjane's grip before she pulled out two handfuls of hair, Giulia balanced on her left wrist and her right hand that still gripped the mace canister.

"No one will take my baby away from me!" Maryjane kicked Giulia in the ribs.

Stars flared behind Giulia's eyes and her body bent sideways. Maryjane kicked again, but Giulia rolled out of her reach, exposing a still-squalling Katie.

Maryjane fell on her. "My baby. My precious baby." She'd ripped away the mask of a sweet woman who loved gourmet cheesecake and dreamed of wearing lacy lingerie. A desperate, obsessed Fury crouched over a terrified Katie.

Giulia clenched her teeth against the fire in her ribs. In one compact movement she slammed her hand into Maryjane's cheekbone and emptied the rest of the mace into her eyes and nose.

Maryjane screamed, choked, and clawed at her eyes. Giulia shoved her aside and snatched up Katie.

"No"—cough, wheeze—"My baby! Give me"—wheeze—"my baby!" Maryjane writhed on the floor, one hand reaching for Katie, the other knuckling her eyes.

Giulia ran around her and got a grip on the doorknob. "She's not yours."

She slammed the door on Maryjane wailing, "Mine!"

One arm around a still-howling Katie and the other hand clamped to the back of the baby's head, Giulia ran.

No sign of the dog. Maybe Maryjane had chained it up again.

Only a few more feet to the gate. Two steps One. She slammed the gate closed. Slapped the lock plate into place. Finagled the padlock shank into the hook. Slapped the shank into place.

A half-hearted bark came from far away on the other side.

Giulia ran to the car. The Katie bundle—silent at last—she tucked more or less securely under the dashboard on the passenger side. She turned the ignition key and the engine came to rough life. One thing about the outdated hatchback, it started every time.

She hit the gas and spun her wheels. Panic clawed at her. She eased off of the gas pedal and the tires caught. The Escort screeched onto the road as she turned east toward Cottonwood.

Don't speed. If you speed, a cop will stop you and how will you explain the baby on the floor of the passenger seat?

The car hit forty-five miles per hour. She eased up on the gas again and reached over to the glove compartment. Her purse fell open when she opened the compartment door. She groped for her cell, swerving onto the shoulder and jerking back into the lane. At the first stop sign, she dialed Frank.

"H'lo?"

"Frank, it's me. Wake up. I've got Katie. Call Captain Jimmy and meet me at Vandermark Memorial ER."

Hers was the only car on these rural winding roads at this hour on a weeknight. Which was a good thing, since this was possibly the worst driving she'd ever committed. She turned left on the way to I-376. Katie started to fuss again.

Frank's voice snapped awake. "Is that a baby?"

"Yes, Frank. Wake up. I snatched Katie out of their church and I'm headed to the ER. Maryjane attacked me and her guard shot me in the leg, so I could use a little help."

"What?"

She signaled to no one to merge onto 376. "I have to hang up. I'm hitting the freeway. I should be at the ER in twenty minutes." The phone hit the passenger seat. "Katie," she cooed, "we're almost there, sweetie. The doctors will check you out and then guess what? You get to see your mommies again."

Katie kept fussing. Giulia reached the speed limit but made sure not to exceed it. Traffic was light on 376 as well. Fine with her, because she was still driving like a teenager putting on makeup while changing the radio station. The throbbing pain in her leg increased at every mile marker.

In seventeen minutes she pulled into the emergency room parking lot. The closest space after the handicapped-reserved section was still a good two hundred feet away. Katie's wails were loud enough to make Giulia consider opening a window.

"You're probably starving, sweetie, and Lord knows what's in your diaper. I'd fuss too." She didn't trust her leg on the tarred parking lot. It could be covered in black ice. She took out her purse, shoved in her phone and the car keys, and pulled out Katie within her blanket cocoon. "We're here. Time for both of us to get warm and taken care of. Up we go." Her ribs and leg throbbed and burned, but she hefted Katie into a safe position anyway.

She stepped with care onto the tar and felt salt crunch under her boots. Excellent. Katie snuggled against her shoulder again, fussy noises quieting.

The salt helped her footing, but her leg demanded attention like a spoiled two-year-old. She gritted her teeth and put as little pressure on it as possible with each step. Trouble was, that jogged Katie like she was riding a pony named Giulia.

At last the automatic doors hissed open. Light and warmth enveloped them.

Safe.

THIRTY-SEVEN

THE WARM AIR REINVIGORATED the blood flowing from her leg. Fresh rivulets dripped over her boot; she took another step and slipped in it.

Without conscious thought, she curled herself around Katie, letting her right hip and shoulder hit the floor. Her teeth rattled. *Déjà vu. God, that hurts.*

"Are you all right?"

"No, don't move. Let us help you." Two nurses appeared at her sides. They each put an arm under hers and walked her straight back into a room.

She didn't want to let Katie go—she had a confused idea that the nurses would call the McFarlands and she'd disappear forever.

"Honey! What on earth are you doing back here?" Fuchsia nails on dark brown hands touched hers.

Giulia looked up and blinked a few times. "Aida?"

"Lord, honey, you get into more trouble ... is this your little one?"

"No." She shook her head and the room tilted. "It's Laurel and Anya's. I think she's hungry."

"You just give her to me. We'll take care of her. Is she hurt?"

"I don't think so. The kidnappers were taking care of her."

A doctor came into the room just then. "What did you say, miss?"

For a moment Giulia felt like the room had morphed into a sailboat in heavy seas. The hard emergency-room cot seemed like the perfect place to counteract this. She relinquished Katie to her friend the nurse. She could trust Aida.

Aida opened the blanket. "Hello, little bundle. What have you been up to, out in the cold? I'm gonna nom your fingers, yes I am, nom nom—" She stopped. "It's the baby born with two extra pinkies. Doctor, you remember her."

The doctor stopped cutting the unsoaked side of Giulia's pants up to her knee. "Indeed. Yes, I was the one who reported that useless intern for botching the child's finger ligation. I'm glad to see she is otherwise thriving."

"Honey, I'm going to take her into another room to get her checked out. Don't you worry."

"I won't if you have her." Giulia lay back on the pillows. "Sorry, doctor. I'm a little dizzy."

"Blood loss does that. This looks like a gunshot wound." He took water from the cart and soaked her stiffened quilt bandage.

"It is. Katie's guard shot at me. Is the bullet in there?"

He cracked opened the layers of cloth. "It carved a ridge in your calf, but no. There is no bullet. I will report this gunshot wound to the police after I've treated you."

She closed her eyes. "I called them from the car. Captain Reilly should be here any minute now."

The double doors banged open. "Giulia! Where are you?"

She smiled. "And there they are."

A nurse's voice reached her, shooing Frank out into the waiting room.

"All right then," the doctor said. "Let me get this treated."

Giulia lay there, trying not to jerk too much at the sting of the liquid he used to disinfect her leg. More footsteps came into the room.

"Nurse, I need gauze and Steri-strips, please."

More pressure on her leg, this time soothing and cool. "That's good."

"Merely a topical antibiotic. You've stopped bleeding, but don't remove the Steri-strips for at least three days. I'll tape gauze over the wound to prevent your clothes from irritating it. The nurse will give you bandages and more ointment. The wound is clean and should heal with minimal scarring."

She heard him stand up before he opened her eyelids and shined a light into each pupil. The nurse checked her pulse and blood pressure, entering the numbers into a compact laptop.

He tucked the light into his shirt pocket. "Apple juice, please, nurse. Two boxes, and something sweet. Are there any gingerbread cookies left at the reception desk?"

"We just refilled the plate. I'll be right back."

Giulia ordered her eyes to stay open. "Could you check my ribs down here?" She touched her last three right-hand ones. "Maryjane kicked me. I think she had hard-soled boots on."

He raised his eyebrows. "I'll just lift your shirt."

"Not a problem. Ow."

He palpated her ribs one after the other.

"They won't play a tune. Sorry."

The doctor didn't smile. "The bottom two ribs are bruised, but not broken. You will be sore for several days, but that will pass. Take ibuprofen regularly. I'll write you a prescription for eight-hundred milligram tablets."

"Thank you. My insurance information is in my purse."

His smile was tight but genuine. "We always like to get paid. I'll have the intake nurse come in here while you eat. We're slow tonight."

He left the room as far as the hall doors. "Is there a police officer here? Ah, good. You may talk to the patient now. Room one."

Frank and Jimmy appeared like a pair of Jack-in-the-boxes.

"What the hell is going on?"

Giulia smiled, a wan effort. "Frank, I can always count on you for a kind word."

"If you got a phone call like that you'd be less than polite, too. Holy shit, that's a lot of blood."

"Giulia, I'm glad you're all right. I'm prepared for an interesting story." Captain Reilly's warm, furry voice soothed her.

"First, you have to send someone to untie the babysitter. Mary-jane is probably gone. I maced her but didn't tie her up or anything. I was too focused on getting Katie out of there. Oh, and see if the guard dog is okay. I had to mace him first to get inside the house." She gave them the address.

Jimmy took out his phone. "Before I call this in, a few words of explanation, please?"

"The desk clerk and the maintenance man at the Wildflower hid Katie in a room on the second floor of their church, which is in a decrepit version of the Amityville Horror House. They had a woman guarding her. She shot at me but I maced her at the same time, so she didn't do much damage. She hit her head on the crib but she was only knocked out, so I tied her to the crib legs with a bungee cord and the crib sheet." She smiled at their beached-fish expressions. "So, you probably want to get out there in case she figured out how to untie herself. It's been at least half an hour."

Jimmy said, "Maryjane is the desk clerk, right? And the dog?"

"They have a huge privacy fence around the property, with a German shepherd inside. I had to mace the poor thing so I could break in and get Katie. One of the church women recognized me in spite of my new hair and must've outed me to Maryjane. When I snuck back after church to get Katie, Maryjane followed me and tried to stop me."

A pause. "Okay." He walked into the hall to make the phone call.

Frank loomed over her. "She shot you."

Giulia gave him a one-shoulder shrug. "She shot through the door first. The bullet hole gave me a good idea of where to aim the mace."

"You are going to drive me to an early grave."

This roused her from her adrenaline crash. "Why do you keep acting as though private investigation will involve danger for you but not for me?"

"It's not that—"

"It's completely 'that.' When something's important, you take risks for it. So do I. Not fake risks, like pretending to be a housekeeper, but real ones, to rescue the innocent." She huffed at herself. "Now I'm preaching. It's your fault. Seriously, Frank, for the umpteenth time, I'm a grown woman. I don't need a big, strong man to take care of me."

"The hell you don't." He bent down and kissed her.

Above them, the nurse cleared her throat. "I brought your juice and cookies."

Giulia laughed. "It sounds like kindergarten."

The nurse poked the straw into the first juice box. "Think of it more as renewing your strength after giving blood."

"I like that." She sipped the juice. That first taste woke up her taste buds and she inhaled the rest of the box, alternating the next one with bites of gingerbread cookie. "These are delicious."

The nurse smiled and inserted the straw into the second box. "I'll tell the day shift. They baked them."

Aida returned with Katie in a new blanket. "I have a happy little girl for you, honey."

Giulia set the cookies and empty juice boxes on the table next to the cot. "Is she okay? They didn't hurt her, did they?"

"They dosed her with Benadryl, probably to keep her quiet, but she's in perfect shape. Want to feed her the rest of this bottle?"

Giulia held out her arms. "You bet." She snuggled the baby in her left arm and popped the bottle in with her right hand. The WANT returned, less powerful because she was crashing again. She smiled down at Katie, who opened her eyes and grinned, dribbling formula onto her onesie.

Jimmy came back into the room. "I sent two cars to the church and two more to McFarland's house. Animal control's meeting them at the church." He opened a laptop and shivered. "I had to bring this from the car. Can you start from the top, please, Giulia?"

Giulia told them about the church service and the triple-immersion baptism. About seeing Katie's telltale extra-finger leftovers. About returning after everyone left and picking the padlock.

"You did?" Frank looked impressed. "I'm a good teacher."

"Hah. I'm a quick learner." She continued with spraying mace in the guard dog's eyes to disable him, breaking the window, sneaking upstairs. The gunshots, the fight, Maryjane's attack, the escape, the drive to the emergency room.

Katie finished the four-ounce bottle. Giulia plucked several tissues from the box on the table and draped them over her left shoulder. While she burped Katie, she said, "You'll both forgive me for saying this, but I told you so."

THIRTY-EIGHT

JIMMY HEAVED A THEATRICAL sigh. "You were right. We were wrong. You win this round. Of course, if you worked for me, we could have many more of these competitions. Safer ones."

Frank said. "Shut up, Jimmy." He gave Giulia a long-suffering look. "You're going to lord it over me now, aren't you?"

Giulia patted Katie and smiled. "Maybe a little. Could someone get my phone out of my purse? I want to call Laurel and Anya."

Jimmy forestalled Frank. "Already done. I told them not to speed, but I don't think they were listening by then."

Giulia craned her neck to see Katie's face. "She's asleep. Frank, can you give me a hand up? I have an idea."

He took her arm and she leveraged herself off the cot. He kept her arm on his and she leaned on him for support out into the waiting room. The intake desk, the sparse potted ficus trees, and the framed posters about giving blood and flu prevention all had large bows or garland, with plastic ornaments hanging from them.

Giulia went up to the desk. "May I ask a huge favor? Katie here"—she patted the sleeping baby's back—"had been kidnapped, and her parents are coming to get her. They thought they'd never see her again." She gave the nurses her most winning smile. "May I have one of the bows to wrap around her?"

"Aww," the nurses said in unison.

"Of course you may," the nurse at the computer said.

"I'll come around and fix one up for you," the other nurse said.

Frank leaned on the counter. "Let me give you Giulia's insurance information. Katie's parents will be able to give you hers."

The nurse walked along the walls, Giulia watching from the desk. When she reached the decorated ficus tucked behind the pop machine, Giulia said, "Would that one be okay to take?"

"Absolutely." The nurse unhooked a bright red bow from a branch, tugging on the attached ribbons. "Lay her down on the desk and we'll turn her into a Christmas present."

Giulia eased Katie off her shoulder onto the wide reception desk. Katie didn't flicker an eyelid. The nurse cooed at her as she attached the bow's plastic hook to a fold of the blanket. Giulia held up the baby, and the nurse tied a loose knot of the trailing ribbons around the back.

"Perfect," they said together.

"My leg is telling me to sit down now," Giulia said.

Frank left his position near the computer and helped her into an understuffed vinyl loveseat out of the draft from the doors.

"You look haggard."

"I disagree. I look like the conquering hero returning victorious from battle."

"Fine, rub it in. I know you're not supposed to argue with success, but I still think you pulled a boneheaded stunt. You should've called me, and we could've come up with a plan together."

She adjusted the blanket. "I considered it, honest. But it was a situation where we had to act now or the chance would be lost."

The outside doors whooshed open. Laurel and Anya dashed into the emergency room.

"Giulia? Giulia! Where are you?" Laurel's unbuttoned coat flapped against her arms.

Anya had neither coat nor hat. "There she is. Giulia, you have Katie? You found Katie?"

Both of them skidded to a halt, cartoon-character style, in front of Giulia, their untied sneakers squeaking on the linoleum.

Giulia held her up, still cradled in her arms. "We have a present for you."

Frank moved away as they squeezed on either side of Giulia. For a very long moment, no one said anything. Then Katie yawned and stretched and they each took one of her hands.

"Hey, baby, Mommy's here," Laurel said.

Katie's eyes opened, staring right into Laurel's face. Her tiny pink lips curved up and her mouth opened into a toothless smile. Laurel's eyes welled up. Katie's hand gripped her index finger and Laurel started sobbing.

Anya's eyes were red as well. "We missed you, *malyshka*."

Katie turned her head at Anya's voice and cooed. Anya lost it. She snatched Katie off of Giulia's lap and crushed her to her chest, destroying the bow. Laurel wrapped her arms around them both and they stood there rocking back and forth, the women crying and Katie cooing.

Frank slid next to Giulia. "You're crying too, you know."

"I know. Isn't it beautiful?"

"Actually, your nose is getting red, just in time for Christmas Eve."

She pretended to slug him. "You know what I mean. This makes it all worthwhile."

"Even getting shot?"

"*Pfft*. Nothing a few Steri-strips and some painkillers can't cure."

Laurel looked down at them. "Shot? You got shot?"

"What?" Anya stopped kissing Katie's cheeks.

"I had a little tussle with the woman guarding Katie. She only grazed my leg. I got her in the eyes with two direct sprays of my trusty jogger's mace."

Laurel untangled herself from their squish-Katie reunion. "What happened?"

Giulia gave her a condensed version of the church service and its aftermath. When she was done, Laurel squeezed her till she gasped for breath.

"You did that for us? You are amazing. You saved our family."

"What else could I do? Besides, it wasn't just me."

Anya shifted the baby onto her shoulder and hugged Giulia, then Frank, then Jimmy. "We owe you everything."

Frank said, "We'll work up a bill."

Giulia said, "What?"

"It's a joke. I'd prefer it if everyone stopped crying."

"You're such a male," Giulia said. "Anya, the nurse at the desk needs your insurance information for Katie's exam."

Anya handed the baby to Laurel and ran over.

Jimmy's phone rang. "Yeah … you do? What? … Hold on." He gestured to Giulia and Frank. They followed him into the first treatment room. "I'm putting you on speaker."

He pressed a button and a male voice from the phone said, "Cap, can you hear this broad? She's worse than one of those TV preachers."

As though the policeman on the other end had put his phone up to the woman's lips, a strident female voice said, "… Know ye not, that to whom ye yield yourselves servants to obey, his servants ye are to whom ye obey; whether of sin unto death, or of obedience unto righteousness? He told us that and we believed him."

Frank mouthed at Giulia, *What?*

The policeman's voice interrupted the tirade. "She's been talking Bible-type talk since we showed up, all about obeying. The dog was chained up in its doghouse, so it wasn't a problem. When we got into the house this woman was sitting on the floor next to an empty crib, and she was talking real fast on her cell phone."

Behind his voice, the woman switched to something from the Old Testament, judging by the complex names.

"Before she started preaching at us, she said that she'd been deceived and that our presence in the house opened her eyes."

The woman's voice again: "The pride of my heart hath deceived me."

The policeman made a frustrated noise. "Cap, we got the hang of it after a while. What she seems to be saying is that her brother-in-law, the pastor of whatever church this is supposed to be, convinced them that they were doing God's work by kidnapping babies. When we showed up, this proved to her that God … wait a minute, it's complicated. Hey, what did you say about higher authority?"

"He taught us that he was the righteous in authority and we rejoiced, but your presence in our sanctuary proves that his pride led us into sin."

The policeman, sounding weary, said, "We're bringing her in. The other team's probably going to get an earful of the same."

"Excuse me," Giulia said. "The woman on the second floor was the only person in the house?"

"Yes, ma'am."

Jimmy ended the call. "I wish them luck. Giulia, you deserve a medal. Can you make it into the station later today so I can get this all written up for you to sign?"

"Of course. I'll keep the rental for an extra day." She put too much pressure on her injured leg and winced.

"Come on," Frank said. "I'll take you home."

"No, you won't. I can't leave the car in an emergency-room space overnight." She leaned on his arm again. "But I won't say no to a hand with the ice in the parking lot."

They returned to the waiting room, where all three nurses were talking nonsense to Katie and laughing when she laughed. Aida came over to Giulia with a plastic bag.

"Gauze, tape, antibiotic ointment, and ibuprofen, honey. I don't want to see you in here again."

Giulia grinned. "I'll do my best. Merry Christmas."

Laurel and Anya enveloped Giulia and Frank in another hug. "We're going to get her home where she belongs. We can never thank you enough."

"Just doin' our job, ma'am," Frank said in a bad John Wayne imitation.

They went out first, Giulia leaning harder than she wanted to on Frank.

"You can quit the tough-broad act. I know how gunshot injuries take it out of you."

"Just help me to the car so the Stone Age heater can begin its epic journey toward the light."

The parking-lot lights reflected off the snow and threw lumpy shadows onto the plowed sections. Giulia slipped on an uneven mess of slush and ice.

"Will you please—"

Giulia held up a warning hand to Frank before he finished the sentence.

"Fine." He put an arm around her waist. "For steadiness, okay?"

An older station wagon ran the light at the entrance and screeched into the parking lot.

"Why didn't they just call an ambulance?" Giulia said.

The wagon cut across several empty rows, heading right toward them.

"Come on, we're in the way of the ER turnaround." Frank eased Giulia toward a minivan parked next to a Hummer.

The station wagon jumped a low barrier of ice and snow and aimed itself at Giulia.

THIRTY-NINE

GIULIA SLIPPED AND FELL, taking Frank with her. The car braked, slid, reversed, and launched itself at them again.

Frank shoved Giulia under the Hummer. He reached for his gun, but patted an empty coat.

"Shit." He jumped to the other side of the minivan just as the wagon slammed into the Hummer's grill.

"You okay?" he called.

"Fine." Giulia pulled herself up using the oversized hubcaps.

Steam billowed from the wagon's radiator. The driver tried to reverse again. The bumper caught under the Hummer's bumper and the station wagon's wheels spun, but didn't move the car.

Jimmy ran out of the emergency room entrance, followed by the doctor and Aida.

The driver's door opened. Maryjane jumped out and ran toward Giulia. "Give me my baby!"

Giulia tried to back away using the Hummer's mirror and door handle for support. Maryjane screamed something wordless, her hands clawing, her hair wild, her eyes still red and swollen.

Frank tackled Maryjane. They crashed to the ground. Maryjane's shoulder bounced off the asphalt. She hit at Frank, trying to get leverage with her sneakers.

Anya and Laurel came out, carrying Katie. Maryjane battered Frank's head so hard that his hold on her loosened.

"That's my baby! She's my reward! Give her back to me!"

Frank got a grip on Maryjane's arm and bent it up behind her back until she yelped and tried to wrench around in his grip rather than going for Katie. Jimmy reached them and pulled out his handcuffs. He read her her rights as she shouted biblical curses at him, Frank, Giulia, Laurel, and Anya.

A well-worn pickup truck careened into the parking lot, following the same path as the station wagon. It stopped a foot from Jimmy, and McFarland hit the ground running.

"Maryjane! Shut up, woman!"

A police car, lights and sirens at full force, drove way too fast up the aisle between the rows for cars. McFarland glanced at it and ran up to Maryjane, who kept ranting, globs of spit flying from her mouth. He slapped her hard enough to knock her chin against her shoulder.

"I said *silence*, woman, and be subject to your husband!"

The front doors of the police car opened simultaneously. Two uniformed officers came out and ran toward the struggling tableau.

Maryjane transferred her wrath to her husband. "This is your fault! You said God gave you this mission! You told us to use modern technology to rescue these babies. My daddy warned us against the Internet—why didn't you listen to him? Now those women have my baby!"

McFarland slapped her again. Her lip split and dripped blood. The police officers each grabbed one of his arms and cuffed him. One of them read him his rights. A second car running lights and sirens at full power drove into the parking lot.

Maryjane ranted on at her husband, blood mixing with flying spittle. "Did you listen in on my call from my sister? She told me she'd shot that lying bitch over there. I knew she'd come to the hospital. I knew what I had to do." She struggled in Jimmy's hold, handcuffs rattling. "You people are supposed to mete out justice—where is my justice? A woman is charged with bearing children unto the Lord, but he shackled me to a man whose sins are visited upon me!"

She kneed her husband square in the groin. McFarland squeaked and bent double. The policemen yanked him upright and wrestled him to the car. Two policemen from the second car ran to Jimmy.

"You need us to take this one, Cap?"

"Please. Can you put her in the back and give the other guys a hand with these cars?"

"Right away. Come on, ma'am."

Maryjane fought them all the way and when the officer put his hand on her head to push her into the back seat, she tried to bite it.

Frank skidded around the minivan to Giulia. "Are you all right?"

She pressed the gauze over her leg injury, grimacing at each touch. "I don't think it's bleeding."

He squatted next to her. "Let me see." His hands ran up and down her calf. "It's dry. Jesus, Giulia, what a couple of freaks."

"Don't blaspheme." Her pulse was returning to normal, and her leg pounded in rhythm. "I'd really like to go home."

Jimmy walked over to them. "Is everyone okay?"

"Fine," Frank said. "We'll see you tomorrow. I'm going to escort Wonder Woman home."

"I was technically off-duty at midnight, so I'm headed home to my blessedly sweet and normal wife. Are any of the cars blocking you?"

Giulia and Frank looked around. "No."

Frank walked her to the Escort and inserted himself into the passenger seat while the heater groaned and hissed.

Giulia rested her head against the back of the driver's seat. "I'll trade you tonight's overtime for a late arrival tomorrow morning."

"Your work ethic is slipping. I have a more pressing question: how are you going to dance with me at Sidney's wedding?"

She laughed, a tired sound. "I didn't think of that when I was dodging an angry quilter's shotgun. Oh, look: the air is slightly less cold."

"Please tell me she was smoking a corncob pipe and complete the stereotype."

"Sorry. Do you know how to find out if the guard dog is okay? I hated to mace it."

"Will you stop worrying about the damned dog?" He leaned over the gearshift, a few inches from her face. "You have got to learn to think before you act. You're reckless. Reckless can get you killed."

"Yes, sir."

"Cut it out." He held a hand up to the windshield vents. "It's warm. I'm following you to make sure you get home safe. Don't argue, because I'm not changing my mind."

"Yes, sir."

"I said, cut it out." He looked out the back window. "The cops are gone. Just give me a minute to start my car."

Giulia forced herself upright and belted herself in. *He didn't kiss me. That's not like him.* She backed out, grateful that her left leg was the injured one. Frank's Camry swung in behind her. His new overprotective streak gave her the warm fuzzies, but it also made her think.

There was no risk of her falling asleep at the wheel; the renewed pain in her leg and ribs made sure of that. She drove along the deserted streets, the Camry's lights always in her rear-view mirror.

Her luck was in when she reached her apartment building's parking lot. The SUV that treated the space facing the front door as its personal property wasn't there. Frank idled behind her. She limped to the glass door and waved at him after she locked it behind her.

He didn't walk me in. Every time I think I understand that man, he throws me a curve ball.

She used the wall for support down the long, silent hall to her apartment. The only good thing about being up this late was that everyone else in her hall wasn't.

How am *I going to dance at Sidney's wedding?*

FORTY

Sidney and Olivier's reception line stretched around the koi pond, under the palm trees, and down the little hall to the bathrooms.

Every time Giulia said the name of the reception hall—The Best-Kept Wedding Secret—she wanted to add the words "and Barbecue Joint." Then she'd have to stop herself from snickering.

The hall was light years away from being a dive restaurant. Multi-patterned carpets, the hotel type designed to hide dirt, covered the floors of the meet-and-greet room and the main dining room. Gauze curtains covered floor-to-ceiling windows in both rooms, with red velvet drapes for Christmas. Swaths of white miniature lights hung from the ten-foot-tall palm trees in each corner of the huge room. More lights festooned the ceiling, looping around and over themselves, drooping here and there like a shining version of the small fountain in the koi pond.

One of Sidney's small cousins had already splashed into the pond, calling, "Fishie!" One of her older cousins had improvised a fishing pole from a fork and her hair ribbons, baiting it with a piece of cheese from an hors d'oeuvre tray. She cast from the apex of the footbridge that spanned the wide, shallow pond. One of the orange-splotched white fish opened its mouth for the bait while the other cousins whooped and cheered her on. Parental wrath descended like the Sword of Damocles, the fish lost its meal, and the hair ribbons were rebraided into a much tighter 'do.

Giulia balanced on Frank's arm as they waited in the reception line, holding herself as upright as possible. The leg injury only throbbed if she kept weight on it for several minutes at a time.

"Sidney's extended family is as enormous as mine—or yours," she whispered. "Do you know anyone here besides the bride and groom?"

"Nope. We're stuck making polite conversation with a boatload of strangers for the next four hours."

"Since when are you a curmudgeon?"

"Since I have a backlog of paying work because I didn't realize I'd hired Wonder Woman under her new secret identity."

Giulia stroked her chin. "Hmm. I like it. I expect my skintight sexy crimefighting outfit to arrive any day now."

They reached the first of the bridesmaids and introduced themselves six times before they finally stood in front of Sidney and Olivier.

"Sidney, you are one of the most beautiful brides I've ever seen," Giulia said.

"Thank you," she squeezed Giulia and Frank. "I was so nervous. Thank God we didn't write our vows or anything like that, because I would've forgotten everything the minute I got up in front of Father Pat. He looked so official!"

Giulia kissed Olivier. "You look like James Bond."

"Thank you. I'll remind Sidney of that the next time she ogles Daniel Craig." He kissed his bride's cheek.

"What, honey?"

"Nothing." He winked at Giulia. "I've merely been informed that I am channeling my inner Bond today."

Sidney took a step back and looked him over. "Ooh, you kinda do look like James Bond. I like it."

The older couple behind Giulia cleared their throats.

Sidney looked guilty. "Sorry, Aunt Louise." She stage-whispered to Giulia, "I'll come by your table later. I want to know what happened to your leg and where's the baby? It's safe, right? Otherwise you'd still be looking all stressed out. Okay, later."

Frank took Giulia's arm and steered her to their table at the corner near the parquet dance floor.

"Drink?"

"Yes, please. White wine." She reread the eco-lecture card on her plate.

Frank returned with two wineglasses while they were still the only ones at their table.

"Thank you. Did you know that we're drinking low-sulfite wine from local, naturally processed fresh grapes?"

"Don't tell me everything at this wedding comes with proselytization." He sipped from his own glass. "It's pretty good."

"Did you see this?" She held up a tent card placed in front of the holly-and-mistletoe centerpiece. "Our favors will be on a table near the coat room, because it's unsanitary to have alpaca fertilizer near the food."

Frank's wineglass hit the table. "She went through with it? Only Sidney would give all-natural, odor-free," he lowered his voice, "excrement as a wedding favor."

Giulia bit down on a laugh. "Perhaps you should stake out the non-organic food stations early."

"Already have my game plan worked out. I notice they also have two cakes. Oh, forgot to tell you. When Jimmy's guys searched the McFarland's house they found all the ransom money still in the box. Your friends will get it back soon."

"That's what their message meant."

"Huh?"

"Yesterday afternoon, after you left, the phone rang and I couldn't get to it in time. It was Laurel calling to say that they're broke right now, but as soon as their bank account gets back to normal they'll send us a check."

The recorded music—a mixture of Christmas carols and mellow pieces by classical composers—began an instrumental version of one of the arias from Handel's *Messiah*. Two couples came to the table and Giulia concentrated on making small talk. Olivier's brother introduced the wedding party, and the wait staff initiated the march to the food stations.

"Sit," Frank said to Giulia. "You can't carry a plate if you're limping. You want whole-earth, right?"

"Yes, please. I'm adventurous."

He returned with chicken dumplings, mushroom pâté on bruschetta rounds, and a bowl of corn-and-pumpkin stew. "I'll grab you some cornbread on my way back. Red meat, here I come."

They stood together on the footbridge after the traditional bride plus groom plus mother and father dances.

"The fish must think we're a new kind of two-headed, three-legged human." Giulia leaned on her elbows, looking down into the clear water at the bubbling fountain.

"I wonder if they'd be good fried in butter and garlic."

She laughed. "Haven't you had enough carnivore victuals to satisfy you?"

"Oh, yeah. Food was great. But I've always got room for fresh-caught fish." He reached for her hand. "I've been thinking. It's time we stopped playing around."

Her chest clenched. *He's going to dump me at a wedding reception?*

"Don't look like that. What, did you think I was pulling a 'We have to talk' on you?"

"Well…"

Two of the cousins raced over the bridge behind them, followed by the would-be swimmer from earlier. The deejay put on the "Cha Cha Slide" to much laughter and calls for everyone to get on the dance floor or be dragged there.

Frank scowled at the speakers. "At least we'll have privacy. Look, we both know what the elephant in the room is: office romance. We've survived it so far, right?"

She nodded.

"We're adults. We know where to draw the line. Usually. You're my conscience."

She looked at him. "That's not what I intended to be."

"Exactly what I wanted to talk about." His hand kneaded hers. "I'm pigheaded and overprotective and I swear too much and I have a short temper. Marry me anyway."

Zzzt. Giulia's brain blanked.

Frank continued to hold her hand. After a moment, he said, "I was hoping for maidenly swoons and a fluttering acceptance."

"I ... um ..."

"Don't tell me you're surprised. Sean and Pat told me that I was practically telegraphing it at the house party." He pulled her arm around so she had to look at him. "Do you need me to say it?"

"No. No, I don't need you to say it." Her fingers trembled in his.

"Well, then?"

Her voice got very small. "No."

The look on his face said *zzzt.*

"I think you're caught up in the baby-wedding-Christmas thing, Frank. I've caught you looking at me when I was holding your niece or Katie, or when we were dancing at your parents' house." When he didn't say anything, she continued, "I'm getting the warm fuzzies too. When I picked up Katie in that horror-house church, every maternal hormone in me snapped to attention."

"I'm not asking you to marry me just to knock you up." Irritation crept into his voice.

A small smile touched her lips. "I didn't think you were. I just think we shouldn't make life-changing decisions while we're both on a combined high from rescuing Katie and Sidney's wedding."

"Fine." He released her hand.

The noise and laughter from the dance floor covered the sound of his shoes walking away. Giulia stared at a black-and-orange koi swimming in lazy circles around the bubbling fountain below her.

Have I just made the stupidest decision of my entire life?

The dance finished. Applause drowned out the deejay's voice. When most of the dancers headed for the bar or their tables, he said, "We're going to take it down a notch and play something just right for a romantic Christmas wedding."

He started "The Christmas Waltz."

"May you get a zit on your nose the day before an important date," she muttered at the deejay. Tears pricked her eyes. *Falcone, you're an idiot.*

Fast, firm steps climbed the bridge toward her. "Hey. This is our song. You're dancing with me if I have to hold you up for half of it." Frank took her arm and helped her down the side of the bridge toward the dance floor.

When they were waltzing with care at the edge of the parquet, he said into her ear, "I don't give up that easy."

His voice challenged her: she'd heard that tone in it when he coached his recreational basketball team. She looked up. He was smiling. "You haven't heard the last of this subject."

She smiled, hoping the earlier tears didn't show. "I'm open to discussion."

"How businesslike of you. To hell with business." He kissed her as they swayed in time to the music.

Sidney and Olivier danced over to them. "Get married in the summer, you two, when all the flowers in our fields will be blooming. No—in my family's fields." She giggled. "I've got a new home now." Sidney kissed Olivier and they waltzed away.

Frank gave Giulia a wicked grin. "You can explain it to her when she comes back from her honeymoon. You're the one who said no."

"A choice which has received instant punishment."

"You're a good Catholic. You know about owning the consequences of your sins."

She smiled. "You're lecturing me on dogma?"

"I'm giving you a taste of the next several weeks. You think you're stubborn? Lady, you're about to meet your match."

A weight lifted off her heart. "I accept your challenge."

THE END

ACKNOWLEDGMENTS

Every book has an amazing team behind it. Many thanks go to my editors, Terri Bischoff and Brett Fechheimer, who make me look good; Kent D. Wolf, my Awesome Agent and indefatigable supporter; Christopher Johnson, M.D., Joe Richardson, Dona Grzybek, and Amy Bai, who kept my facts straight; Alex Harrow, my invaluable beta reader; my husband and sons, who never doubt that I'll get everything done correctly and on time. And, always and forever, Purgatory and Absolute Write. These books would not have happened without you.

© D. Steven Hodge

ABOUT THE AUTHOR

Alice Loweecey is a former nun who went from the convent to playing prostitutes on stage to accepting her husband's marriage proposal on the second date. A contributor to BuddyHollywood .com, she is a member of Mystery Writers of America and Sisters in Crime. She lives with her family in Western New York. *Force of Habit* was her first novel, followed by *Back in the Habit*.

Please visit Alice's website, at www.aliceloweecey.net.